The Searing Stone

Book I

The Children of Erym Saga

R.D. Neal

The Searing Stone

Book I – The Children of Erym Saga

Copyright © 2021 by R.D. Neal.

All rights reserved. Printed in the United States of America. No part of this book may be used or reproduced in any manner whatsoever without written permission except in the case of brief quotations em-bodied in critical articles or reviews.

This book is a work of fiction. Names, characters, businesses, organizations, places, events, and incidents either are the product of the author's imagination or are used fictitiously. Any resemblance to actual persons, living or dead, events, or locales is entirely coincidental.

For information visit www.rdneal.com

Cover art designed by: Kory Miller

First Edition: 2021

Dedicated to my wife and my children, born and unborn.
May you forever be in the arms of Grace and Truth.

CONTENTS

PROLOGUE – O'Varth's Fall ... 2

CHAPTER 1 – The Drudge ... 14

CHAPTER 2 – The Devastation Ruins ... 28

CHAPTER 3 – Levithe's Alarm ... 63

CHAPTER 4 – Out of Levitheton ... 83

CHAPTER 5 – The Tombs of the Seared ... 102

CHAPTER 6 – The Traveler ... 122

CHAPTER 7 – The River ... 138

CHAPTER 8 – The Bridge ... 157

CHAPTER 9 – The Barren Plains ... 175

CHAPTER 10 – Tuskoth Caves ... 196

CHAPTER 11 – The Remnant ... 209

CHAPTER 12 – The Weapon ... 236

CHAPTER 13 – The Searing ... 261

EPILOGUE ... 293

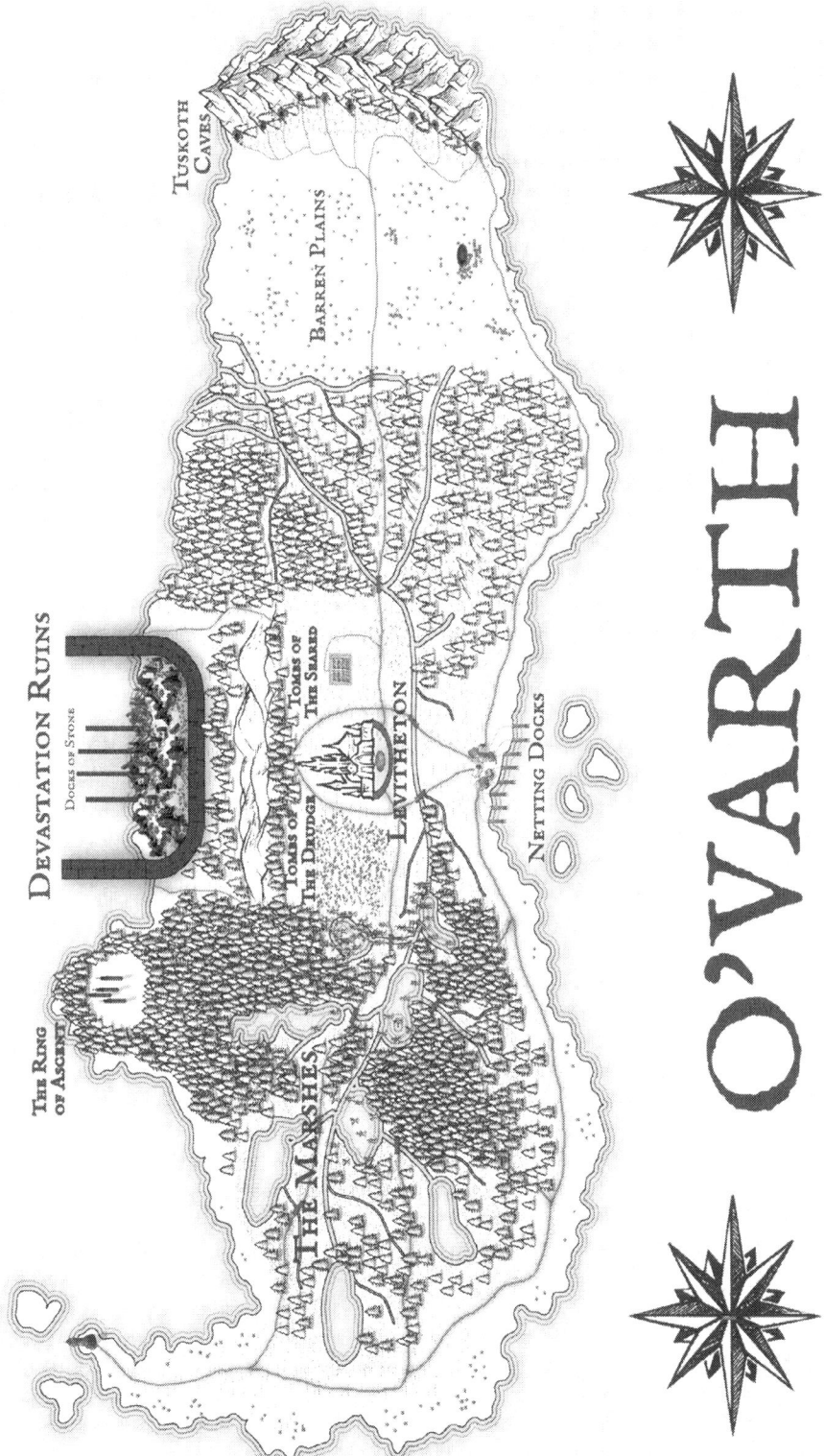

Prologue

O'Varth's Fall

COLOSSAL PLUMES OF BLACK SMOKE filled the sky above the great city of Hai'sedon as tempests of fire and cracks of lightning shattered the pristine stone buildings to pieces. Aven gasped for air as she fled in terror, unable to comprehend what was happening. The destruction wasn't caused by a storm but a slaughter; somehow, she had escaped the city walls just before the devastation ensued.

As she glanced back towards the city, vigorous nausea rose in her throat, causing her to choke on her breath. She clutched her stomach with both hands as sharp pain seared through her abdomen. *Not the baby,* she thought, mortified. Inhaling through her nose, she recognized the terrible smell of smoldering timber and burning flesh, causing her insides to churn. Her perfect city, destroyed by the most unexpected event: an ambush from her *own* people. *How could this happen?* Aven's mind raced. Hai'sedon had been unified, and in harmony since before she was born. Now, it stood in utter ruin. Delirium struck as the sights before fleeing the destruction flashed through her mind.

Swarms of people stampeding each other as they rushed to the Docks of Stone to flee the island by ship.

Friends and family, too many to count, slaughtered before her eyes.

Hundreds of women and children, young children, being bound, blindfolded, and led out of the city toward the south.

Still clasping her stomach, Aven gulped for air as her legs began to burn, desperately trying to distance herself from the city's collapse. The towering pines closed in around her, and the thick brush slowed her escape. Suddenly, she saw a small opening ahead. Lowering her shoulder, she burst through the undergrowth. Her eyes squinted as she raised her forearm to block the beaming rays of sunlight. She stumbled and fell to her knees, crashing onto the velvety smooth ground, causing no disruption to the soil. Aven inhaled through her nose, holding her breath at the cusp, and placed her palms on the bloody cuts from the briars. Her wounds healed instantly, along with the nausea and tearing pain in her stomach. Aven's body warmed every time she used her gifting, *keha*.

Her eyes blinked rapidly as she gazed in wonder at the anomaly before her. A massive portion of forest had been carved out of the landscape. Within this perfect circle, far out of human reach, four metallic pillars hovered. Their width was that of ten men, but their height far surpassed that of the surrounding trees. Three of the pillars formed a triangle, with the fourth in the center. *The Ring of Ascent*, Aven thought, staring upward. The pillars weren't what captivated her but what they held. Suspended above them was a gigantic ancient disc-shaped stone emanating a faint glow of blue flame. The island's crown jewel. The reason *keha* and the other giftings existed.

There must be something helpful here, Aven thought, wiping the sweat from her forehead. She crept towards the center of the Ring, staring up at the glowing Stone. Reaching her hand towards the center pillar, the hair on her neck suddenly stood. The loud rumble of men's voices boomed just outside the tree line. Aven's heart skipped a beat as she dashed behind the thickest tree in the area. She slowed her breath and listened. The voices entered the clearing, and she peaked around the edge of the tree. A young man in white approached the pillars, followed by a dozen guards dressed in armor. His rich golden hair was tied back into a perfect knot, and his smooth skin gleamed in the sunlight.

A Servant, Aven thought as her eyebrows descended in confusion. The Servants were the city and the island's helpers and respected by all. Their height was unmatched, as even the female *Servants* towered over the tallest of men. With soft golden yellow eyes and ageless white skin, their bodies seemed to glow like water struck by sunlight. The Servants arrived by ship many years ago with a gift for the island. The Stone. These seemingly divine men and women placed the gift above the pillars where Aven currently knelt. Every time she had encountered the Servants, their graceful beauty and immense willingness to obey always left her feeling peaceful. However, as she perceived the hateful resentment in the Servant's eyes before her, the opposite feeling ensued. Dread consumed her body.

"Lord Levithe, what do you mean to do?" asked one of the twelve. Aven's head tilted at the formal title. *Lord?*

The Servant responded with a smooth yet vile voice, "With your help and the help of many others, the city has fallen to rubble and ash, just as I'd hoped." He paused and looked up. "I intend to take sole possession of the Stone. Then I will finally be able to escape this cursed rock and destroy the *Ones Beyond*. The ones who sent *us*."

"How are we going to take the Stone?" another shaky voice asked.

"With your giftings, of course. Your *eshe* will work perfectly," he commanded. "I need all twelve of you to torch the points where the Stone meets the metal. Once the Stone loosens, we should be able to pry it from the Ring."

The young man in the white robe, the leader of the city's ruin, stood upright with a wide grin. Reaching in his cloak, he removed a long iron rod with a small metallic symbol fastened to its end. Aven's mind trembled, recognizing at once what Levithe was holding. A *Tri-Symbol*. One of the three on display at the city hall. Aven focused on releasing her breath as slowly as possible. Every tiny movement she made resounded through her ears. Even her heart beat seemed loud enough to draw the Guard's attention. *I saw the Servants take these symbols before fleeing by ship. How does he have one?!* Aven thought. No one understood much about the *Tri-Symbols,* other than their assumed immense power. However, since she was born, the island had an unwritten command concerning them. They were never to be used.

She watched in horror as the young man gave the order to fire. All at once, beams of flame propelled from the guards' chests. Aven raised her forearm to block the blinding glow from the *eshe*. As the fire collided into the Stone, the earth below her trembled, and an ear-piercing sound of metal on metal caused her jaw to clench as she covered her ears.

"Don't let up," the Servant shouted, staring at the scene. "More!" His gaze made it appear as if he were almost salivating as his piercing yellow eyes fixated on the flames.

The earth quaked, causing Aven to stumble. The screeching sound of metal grew almost deafening. Aven's stomach seemed to grind into a thousand pieces as she stared. The heart of the island was being shredded and ripped from its body. The pillars shimmered and vibrated as if they were gripping the Stone tighter. As the flames grew brighter, the young man continued shouting his orders.

All at once, the flames, screeches, vibrations, and quaking culminated into a deafening explosion, knocking everyone on their backs, including Aven. She stared in horror as the giant Stone released from the pillars, splitting into three fragments. One crashed downward with immense force, crushing a few guards in its path, painting the smooth dirt red. The other two catapulted upward and soared out of sight in opposite directions. As she stared in terror at the blood-soaked Stone fragment, everything around her seemed to dim. It became harder to take a full breath, and the sky above changed from a perfect sapphire to a greying blue. Despite the terrible destruction, the Stone fragment still glowed a fiery blue.

The man in white struggled to stand, screaming with horrifying rage. Aven sensed from the scream the Servant's plan did not go as he'd hoped. Because of the destruction, the other fragments might never be found. He took the rod and aggressively pressed it to an unrecognized symbol on the upper portion of the Stone. The metal hissed as the Stone seemed to cry out in agony. Then, with a glare, he branded his flesh just below his hairline, on the back of his neck.

Energy seemed to flood his face as he glared at his other guards and let out a horrid roar. Flames burst from his chest as he screamed. Aven tilted her head as she realized the flames weren't as bright as before. Nor as powerful.

As Levithe released the flames, he approached the guards. One by one, he placed his hands on their injuries. Instead of the typical relief brought by *keha*, the guards let out tormented screams. Aven's eyes squinted as she saw their wounds slowly close up and heal.

Levithe, still frowning, approached the Stone once more, eyeing the three remaining symbols carved into its bottom portion. Aven gazed as Levithe reached for each carving, removing a small matching metallic symbol from their center. He examined each one and placed them in a pouch tied to his belt.

"Find a way to transport this fragment," he commanded with a booming voice. "It's time I deal with the rest." The guards leaped to their feet in a hurry to follow his command. Levithe, wearing a face of both rage and victory, marched back towards the city with the rod in hand.

Aven's chin trembled as she sat behind the tree in shock, focusing on her breath, regaining her composure. Nausea once again crept toward her throat as she placed both hands on her lower stomach. *The baby is okay,* she thought as she kept her eyes closed, struggling to keep the queasiness at bay. Her mouth hung open as panic flooded her mind. *Where can I go? Who can I tell? This island was a paradise. What will become of it now?* She inhaled, rose to her feet, and headed south toward the ridges, away from Levithe and the devastated city.

A soft breeze struck her face as she approached the peak of the first ridge. She looked out towards the horizon and detected a never-before-seen shimmer. Multi-colored and almost transparent, it lingered a few leagues offshore and seemed to stretch around the entire island, causing some sort of ethereal barrier. Her eyes shot open as the pores on her skin pointed to the sky like spears. *The ships. There were dozens of them. Where did they go?* She thought in shock as she stared at the empty waters surrounding the island. Aven realized from that moment on Levithe's destruction had not only shattered the Stone, but the island's entire existence.

Ŏ

Levithe's mind raced as he marched back towards Hai'sedon. A city now destroyed by *his* deceit. By *his* beautiful plan. The power from his new giftings flowed copiously through every fiber of his being. *Keha, eshe,* and *kasa.* The surge was euphoric, but not enough. The gifts were something he had desired since his existence began. However, only a portion of his plan had succeeded. The rest was a miserable failure. Shock and rage filled his heart as images of the perfect Stone releasing from the pillars flashed through his mind. He needed all the fragments to escape and all the gifts to destroy the *Ones Beyond.* After years of planning his rebellion, he went from Servant to Savior. But in that instant, from Savior to Devastator.

As he continued treading forward, Levithe noticed the sound of metallic symbols chiming against each other within his pouch. He grabbed all three of them and examined their elegance. Each symbol was a perfect circle with a unique shape in its center, small enough to fit in the palm of his hand. The first, the shape of a three-tongued flame. The second, a simple face with a line down its center where half was smiling and the other half frowning. The third, a four-petal flower in mid-bloom. Glancing down at his rod, he examined the *Tri-Symbol.* He couldn't explain it, but the symbol was a perfect combination of the other three. Forged together, harmonizing each shape. *No one will ever use this one again*, he thought, removing the *Tri-Symbol* from the rod and placing it in his pouch along with the other three.

An awful scream from a hundred paces east caused Levithe to stand tall for a closer look. *The women and children*, he grinned viciously, as he spotted the long line of blindfolded prisoners.

THE SEARING STONE

Levithe's plan for them was excruciatingly intentional. Since coming to the island, he had mastered the art of deceit and control. Children were his favorite because they were the most exploitable. As for the women captives, all of them were pregnant. Still alive, only to complete their last service to Levithe. To care for their infants until weaned, then slaughtered and forgotten. For the unborn would become the purest of his followers. The most ignorant to the past and the easiest to mold for the future. Levithe almost salivated as he watched them stumble forward in line.

As he got closer, he detected the screaming woman lying on the ground with a few of his faithful guards kneeling at her feet. He sprinted towards them with menacing excitement, distracted from the failure of his plan. His new kingdom was about to begin. The first birth of a pure follower under his new reign was occurring before his eyes.

The woman let out a blood-curdling scream that seemed to echo off the ridges. She then threw her head back to catch her breath. The infant's screams replaced her own, and one of the guards cut the cord and stood holding the blood-soaked baby. The mother's hands were still bound, and her blindfold remained.

"My baby," she yelled through tears. "Let me hold my baby!"

"The infant must meet his new master first," said the guard, releasing a muffled laugh through his nose.

Levithe peered into the baby's eyes as it wailed. Waiting.

"Just tell me," she shouted once more. "*Keba? Epha? Azaq?* Which one?"

Nothing came. As Levithe stared, something diabolical in his mind clicked. Ever since the Stone was placed on the pillars when he arrived at O'Varth, all people were *born* with a unique gift. Each gift displayed itself in one form or another, immediately after the child released its first wail. *But not this child,* he thought. He reached up and touched the branded flesh at the base of his neck as a dreadful, ingenious idea surfaced in his mind. *I control the gifts now. Even more control than I could have imagined,* he grimaced, twisting the symbols in his pouch between his thumb and forefinger.

Levithe handed the baby back to the mother and said, "Your child has none of them. From this moment on, all newborns on O'Varth will grow up to drudge the earth. To help build our new city."

The woman's screams increased as Levithe turned and walked away. He knew his vision of complete control would require patience. It would take years to populate O'Varth. However, those years would allow him time to prepare and find the remaining fragments. *There is only one Stone fragment and only three gifts,* he thought as his eyes nearly clamped shut.

To move forward, a great sacrifice needed to be made. Levithe's faithful had gotten him to this point, but there remained a great inconsistency. Some of them had gifts that were unlike his own. To gain true control of both the island's history and people, all followers not sharing one of his three gifts would need to be erased. *Including the captive children,* he thought with a terrible grin.

As he continued towards the ruined Hai'sedon, Levithe pictured the gathering in his mind, and his heart raced with eagerness. He would assemble his faithful for a special ceremony and divide them by rank and gifts. Then, without warning, he would incinerate the skin from their bones and erase them from history. A perfect sacrifice for unabridged control — of the gifts, people, history, and the island. Ultimately, time didn't matter when it came to finding the two fragments and building a kingdom powerful enough to defeat his true enemies. Levithe's hatred had fueled him all his life. Now, finally, his true road to his victory had begun.

300 Years Later

Chapter 1

The Drudge

THE TOMBS OF THE DRUDGE, read the splintered sign barely clinging to its post. Zayn and his two younger siblings, Tanyel and Lyu, treaded in silence along the desolate path outside Levitheton's western walls. Zayn gazed at the vast dirt field beyond the broken sign. Thousands of graves, marked by broken stones and shards of bark, littered the barren ground. His eyes stretched beyond the field, noticing thousands of dead grey trees covered in moss. The Marshes. An unending maze of a knee-deep swamp that covered most of the Western part of the island. Focusing back on the dirt, his eyes squinted as he saw a few Drudge walking through the graveyard, paying their respects. As he blinked, a thick knot formed in his stomach, realizing what each of them held. Rusted shovels with wooden handles wrapped in stained cloth. His eyes bounced to a few of the poorly dug mounds nearby. Because of the heavy downpour from the night before, a combination of decomposing limbs and bones jutted out of the mud. Staring further off, the knot tightened as he noticed the same effect across the entire field. The Drudge holding shovels weren't paying respects; they were re-burying the dead.

Zayn's eyes glossed over as he continued forward in silence. The knot turned to stone and buried itself deep within his stomach. The sight of the Tombs no longer caused sadness or fear, like when they were younger. He and his siblings had taken this crumbled path countless times before. Half of him was numb to it, and the other half hated this place. Not because of the horror, but because it reminded him of who he was and where he would eventually end up. Even worse, because he never had a choice in the matter. *Born Drudge, to be buried Drudge,* he thought.

They were heading north, keeping to themselves, both out of respect and exhaustion. Grime and sweat still painted their grey cloaks, and the stench of fish clung to their hands. The morning after a storm was the ripest time for Fishers. The more successful the catch, the harder the cleaning. Every morning, since Zayn could remember, they had used a dull knife and splintered board to slice, gut, and scale thousands of fish at the Netting Docks. Drudge work, at its lowest.

The thudding sound of shovels striking mud faded as they approached the northern end of the Tombs. Despite the long day, a soft smile drew across Zayn's as he admired his siblings a few steps ahead. They were more than family. Lyu and Tanyel were his best friends.

Lyu, olive-skinned and short in stature, was the spitting image of their mother. Her dark brown hair, with a slight wave, hung past her shoulder blades. Her eyes, so brown they were nearly black, held a slight squint in the corner, like her mother's. The way her ears twitched as she raised her eyebrows resembled their father's. Two small dimples appeared on the upper part of her cheeks directly below her eyes when she smiled. Even though she was approaching her sixteenth year, Zayn always viewed her as more mature than Tanyel and him combined. He smiled, pondering her strength and boldness, and even though she was the youngest, she was the one to calm, direct, and lead them.

Tanyel had incredibly fair skin compared to the rest of their family and always wore an excited grin on his face. Towering above the siblings, he was even taller than their father. With light golden hair and blue eyes, he stood out amongst them in both appearance and personality. Tanyel's optimism and sense of humor always impressed Zayn. He always brought smiles to their faces, even in uncomfortable situations. Zayn couldn't believe his little brother was entering his eighteenth year.

The mid-afternoon breeze struck Zayn's face as he looked down and observed his olive-skinned, calloused hands. Whether staring at the dreadful Tombs or his worn hands, he couldn't escape the constant reminders of his life as a Drudge. For his siblings, though, the Drudge life didn't seem to bother them. Lyu, in particular, was even proud of it. What good could come of a life without giftings? He still held an unspoken resentment towards his parents for the life they had chosen for them. Even towards his mother. *I wish you were here,* he thought. It had been ten years since she died, and the pain still remained. As the oldest, his mother's death affected him much more than his siblings. Some memories of her were as clear as the water on the coast. At the same time, others had been completely forgotten.

As Zayn's bitterness rose, he attempted to shake the thoughts away. His siblings were supposed to look up to him, but even though he was two years older than Tanyel, they were the ones leading him.

"Storm uncovered more than usual," Tanyel said, looking back at Zayn with a smirk. "Weird to think that will be you someday."

"I was just thinking the same thing," Zayn said, laughing through his nostrils.

"Always making everything so morbid," said Lyu, shoving Tanyel's shoulder, smiling back. "And yes, someday, a long time from now, Zayn will get the privilege of being buried amongst our people. Much better than the alternative, though."

Zayn hid his eye roll as he caught her reference to the Tombs of the Seared, the elegant cemetary constructed on the Eastern side of the city. Pristine and well kept, only reserved for those fortunate enough to have one of the three giftings.

"Come on, Lyu. Our mother is buried there," Zayn said. "Give it at least *some* respect."

"You know what I mean," she said, lowering her head.

Tanyel shoved her back. "Don't stand there and lie to us that zero part of you has ever wanted to be a Healer. All those times you cut yourself scaling at the Docks. Not once have you wished you could heal those wounds? Or all the times we piss you off. Don't tell me you've never wished you could Incinerate us?" Zayn chuckled.

"I'm not a liar," she said, lifting her nose to the sky, holding back a smile. "Bandages work just fine... and I don't need flames to make you two bend to my will." Zayn and Tanyel both laughed, shaking their heads.

"But Lyu, our own family is Seared," Zayn said, poking back.

"As I've told you before, I love Mother and Father and Uncle Typher. But I hate that they are Seared, and I will stand by that until the storms are uncovering *my* bones." Zayn held a smile, but inside, he felt his throat clench at her words. Being Seared would beat living as a Drudge a hundred-fold. Nothing in him would ever agree with her.

"Speaking of Father," Zayn said. "If we don't keep up our pace, we're not going to make it on time."

"You're the one in the back," Tanyel said, laughing alongside Lyu.

Zayn sighed, catching up to walk beside them. He thought back to the first time he laid eyes on the Tombs. He was seven, and it terrorized him. Now, 13 years later, he was laughing as they passed. Somehow, no matter how horrific, constant exposure numbed the heart just enough to laugh.

The dirt path began to curve east, following the city's circular border wall. Thick brush and towering trees jutted out of the ground ahead, causing Zayn's excitement to build. A few leagues beyond the trees, he spotted the ridges peeking through the gaps between the branches. They were the only spot on the island that provided a perfect view of the Devastation Ruins, an ancient city of stone destroyed during the war, now heavily guarded by a troop of Levithe's closest followers. Despite the eeriness of the ruins, the view was spectacular and Zayn's favorite place on the island.

However, because of their duties at the Docks, and their father's Healing work in the city, getting time together as a family was rare. But on the first day of each moon cycle, their father made it a point to meet at the ridges to share the tale of the ancient ruins, have a meal, and be together. The time was perhaps the only part of Zayn's life he truly enjoyed. No distractions from the city. No ridicule from others. Just them.

Further to the east, Zayn saw the Northern Gates, one of the three entrances to Levitheton. His shoulders relaxed as he noticed the slow foot traffic in and out of the Gates. *The fewer people, the better,* he thought. As they got closer, warm blood flooded his face as he noticed two Seared, around his age, standing near the entrance.

"Stawb and Feeld," Zayn said, cursing under his breath. "I'm not letting those Shifters ruin this night." He grabbed Tanyel and Lyu by the shoulders and headed north, off trail.

"They don't have their incinerator buddies with them," said Tanyel, resisting. "This could be our chance to embarrass *them* for once."

"It's not worth missing our time with Father," Zayn said, gripping their cloaks tighter.

"Zayn's right," Lyu said, grinning. "We will have our chance, brother."

Zayn's face relaxed as Tanyel shrugged his shoulders and followed. Stawb and Feeld had taunted and tortured them with their words and giftings since he could remember. And they weren't the only ones. Everyone in the city seemed to have an opinion about them, one way or another. In the worst way possible, they were known and recognized amongst the entire city. Three Drudge children... with Seared parents.

"Even though the Drudge route is depressing, it beats the city route any day," Zayn whispered out of the corner of his mouth.

"Beats the Seared grave path as well," said Lyu.

"Finally," said Tanyel, winking. "One thing we can actually agree on."

Walking through the city was their worst nightmare, and passing the Tombs of the Seared was excruciating for many reasons. For all of them, a deeply painful reminder of their mother's death, for Zayn, an envious desire to be Seared, and for Lyu, a bitter rage laying eyes on the exquisite graves. All three paths from the Docks to the ridges were dreadful, but only one of them bearable. Either way, the end of the path, a night with their father, made the trip worth it every time.

As they headed north, the shade cast by the surrounding forest caused the sweat on Zayn's skin to cool. Sweet pine and damp grass replaced the smell of dirt and death. Insects screeched a repetitive melody that soothed his ears, and the empty path ahead allowed his breath to slow, giving his mind space to drift.

The evening before, his father gave them the typical speech about being on time and how important being together was for their family. After the speech, while Tanyel and Lyu headed off to their cots, his father's strong grip squeezed his shoulder, signaling him to stay back. *"I have something important to show you tomorrow, son. Promise me you will make it."* The words rang through Zayn's mind, causing his eyes to squint and his head to tilt. Since they started meeting, Zayn and his siblings had never even been late. What was so important?

Suddenly, the heavy sound of cracking branches boomed through the forest, causing him to stop mid-stride. Tanyel and Lyu froze. Without moving his head, his eyes crept toward the noise's direction. The thick brush hid whatever was approaching them. Zayn began backing away, looking for a tree nearby to climb in case of an attack. No branches within reach. Tanyel bent down to grab a large rock while Lyu backed up toward Zayn. His heart pounded through his forehead as the snapping footsteps beyond the brush drew closer.

His body went numb as he noticed Tanyel stretching his arm back to launch the heavy stone toward the bushes. Lyu lept forward, attempting to stop him, but she was too late. The rock flung from Tanyel's hand in slow motion, catapulting toward their stalker. As it crashed into the bushes, a loud grunt resounded from the unknown creature. Instead of fleeing, the footsteps dashed toward them at an alarming rate. Zayn reached for both siblings, but by the time he clutched their cloaks, the tingles in his arms and legs settled. A golden female *muwr* bounded over the brush, sprinting past them on all four hooves. One of the few harmless beasts on O'Varth. Zayn caught his breath as Tanyel and Lyu began to laugh.

"I knew it was harmless," Tanyel said with forced confidence.

"I'm sure," Lyu said. "You're lucky it wasn't a *shenrosh* or something worse. We would all be dead."

"Nah," Tanyel said. "*Shenrosh* are too rare. Besides, we're Drudge. Our lives should be threatened at least once a day." Zayn subtly crossed his arms at the truth and pain of the statement.

"Let's keep moving," Zayn said. "It's getting close to sunset."

The forest's density thinned as the path developed into an incline. It started mild, but as they continued, Zayn's legs burned as the slope became steeper with each step. With the forest clear, Zayn had a perfect view of the ridges ahead. His heart swelled as he saw the outline of a man waiting for them at the top. *Father,* he thought, picking up his pace. The sooner he got to his father, the more time they would have together.

Tanyel let out a howl, attempting to get their father's attention. Sure enough, the man at the ridge turned around and began waving his hands and howled back, causing their trot to turn into a full-blown sprint.

"You made it!" said Ryn, with arms wide, jogging down the ridge to meet them. He stood tall with dark brown hair scattered with specks of white. He wore a sophisticated cloak that tossed with the wind and a matching piece of cloth wrapped around his forehead. Attached securely to his belt was his large iron hammer with a tattered leather handle. His smile expanded as Lyu crashed into his arms first, followed by Tanyel and Zayn. They had seen their father the night before, but something about the special time together made it all the more exciting.

"How are you three?" Ryn said, with a tear in his eye.

"We're fine, Father," Zayn said. "Just another day at the Docks. Better now that we're here."

"We almost didn't make it," Lyu said, glancing at Tanyel. "But we've been looking forward to it."

"I have too, Lyu," said Ryn, looking back toward the top. "Tonight is important. Come, let's eat." Zayn's eyes squinted at the comment.

Waving them to follow, Ryn turned and hiked back up the ridge. Zayn kept by his side the rest of the way. He couldn't tell if he was making things up, but something seemed off with his Father. *Is this about what he told me last night?* He thought. As they neared the top, his thoughts wiped away as the smell of bread and honey engulfed his nostrils. His favorite meal, with his favorite people, at his favorite view. What could be better?

"There they are," Zayn said as he reached the crest of the ridge. "The Devastation Ruins."

He gazed at the massive ancient city of crumbled stone. Collapsed buildings covered in vines stretched as far as the eye could see. A gentle breeze from the north shore collided with his skin, causing the exposed hair on his arms to dance. He stared in awe at the colossal fortress wall surrounding the ruins below, a protective barrier scaling twice the height of any known structure on the island. A soft evening haze laid over the ruins as the sun set, causing the grayed stone to glow in an array of different colors. Zayn's heart slowed as he caught his breath. Every time he visited the ruins, they took his breath away. The incredibly grand city below, once rich and powerful, now stood silent, shattered, and absent of life.

"And the Ring of Ascent," said Tanyel, pointing west.

Zayn's spine chilled as he laid eyes on the massive ring of smooth dirt with metal pillars hovering in its center. The metallic structures were immovable, unbreakable, and the only other part of the island that brought more questions than the ruins themselves.

"Now sit," Ryn said, holding a wooden breadbasket. "Enjoy the view and rest. You deserve it." As Ryn unwrapped the cloth, steam soared upward, causing his stomach to groan. He passed a portion of the fluffy golden bread to each of them.

As Zayn took a savory bite, the warmth and taste fueled his body with instant energy and relief. It was obvious Lyu and Tanyel felt the same as they smiled back with stuffed mouths. Ryn remained standing, staring out towards the ruins. Zayn glanced at Tanyel and Lyu, knowing what came next.

"It happened three centuries ago," Ryn said poetically as the sun glistened off his olive skin and sand-colored cloak. "It all began with a war between the Seared and the Drudge. A war of giftings against swords, so bloody and vile, only one known survivor exists to this day, Levithe, god of O'Varth. His victory brought order to the people of O'Varth. Not only order, but a gift. Levithe recovered the Searing Stone from the war, now preserved in Levitheton's center for those who choose Searing. The mystery these ruins hold within instills fear, awe, and wonder in all who come near them. As you know, no one has entered them since the war. As horrible as their devastation was, they are our history. Never to be forgotten." Ryn paused. "As the story goes, that is." The last sentence created a small pit in Zayn's stomach, but he took a deep breath and tried to ignore it. Tanyel and Lyu sat in silence, smiling up at their father, embracing the view below. Ryn gazed towards the pink sky and began to whisper in song.

> *The city of old, torn by a grudge*
> *Destroyed by the war of Seared and Drudge.*
> *Peace came anew, and history lost*
> *Levithe saved O'Varth, no matter the cost.*
> *Seared serve Levithe for a chance at true power*
> *While Drudge toil to supply the Tower.*
> *Levitheton, our great city, our splendid home*
> *Holds the Crown Jewel, The Searing Stone.*

Zayn exhaled. The song always struck him differently than his siblings. Ever since his mother had died ten years ago, he had spent nearly every waking moment wishing he was Seared. The song was yet another reminder that he wasn't and never would be.

Lyu tapped him on the shoulder, bringing the bitter cycle to a halt. As Zayn shifted to glance at their father, his eyes squinted. The knot in his stomach returned and rose to the base of his throat. A worried look had crossed their father's face. Zayn was right. Something was off. With bent brows and chin raised high, Ryn's head bounced from left to right, fixated on the ruins. *What is he looking for?* He thought. Zayn checked on his siblings to see if they noticed, but Ryn's panicked voice interrupted, causing his heart to drop.

"I know I've told you this same story countless times," whispered Ryn in a hurry as he leaned in close. "But I need to tell you something." Zayn's brows descended as he focused on the words.

"The story," Ryn said, glancing around. "The great tale of the ruins. What if I were to tell you it isn't true?" Zayn's heart rate subtly increased as Tanyel let out an awkward laugh.

"What would make you say that, Father?" Lyu said.

"Because of our lineage, Lyu," Ryn replied. "The *truth* of this island has been passed down through our family for centuries, and I have proof." Ryn paused, looking back toward the ruins. "I've waited years to show you, and tonight, I finally get to."

The words from the previous evening echoed through Zayn's head. His lips dried as he tried to speak, but he was frozen in place as his heart thudded through his eardrums.

"Show us?" Lyu responded.

Ryn bent down and drew them in close, his face becoming increasingly more nervous. The wrinkles bordering his bouncing eyes creased before he spoke, and time slowed as the words left his mouth.

"Yes, Lyu. In the story I retell every year, I mention no one has entered these ruins. Well, tonight, that story changes. We are going to be the first."

Chapter 2

The Devastation Ruins

All three siblings' mouths hit the floor as they stared, speechless.

"What do you mean, *enter* the ruins?" Zayn asked, standing upright. "What could three Drudge possibly have to do with this place?"

Ryn placed one hand on Zayn's shoulder, easing the tension, and the other on Lyu's. Tanyel wore a face of excitement, clinging to the possibility of their father's words.

Ryn continued, "Myself and some others have been planning

this for a long time. I need the three of you to trust me. I won't let anything happen to you. Just stay close."

Suddenly, as Zayn's shoulders began to release, he gasped and threw his forearm towards his eyes. An explosion to the northeast battered against the stone walls bordering the ruins. Shouts from a group of people off in the distance flooded Zayn's ears. Ryn grabbed them by their cloaks. "This is it! We have to go now!" With no time to process, Zayn, Tanyel, and Lyu sprinted alongside their father. Zayn wondered if he was in a dream as his mind raced in all different directions. Nothing about it made sense. His life comprised early mornings and long days, skinning and scaling the catches at Netting Docks. Now he was supposed to enter the ruins? Zayn's lungs burned as he kept up.

Before he could question further, Zayn's heart jolted as he spotted a man dressed in Incinerator armor a hundred paces to the northeast. The man was staring right at them.

"Look out!" Lyu cried as a blinding, beam of fire propelled from the Incinerator's chest, blasting towards them. The warning cry wasn't enough. Instantly, his father's grip wrapped him and the others into his chest to protect them from the flames. The blast's awful impact collided into Ryn's back as the residual heat singed Zayn's cloak. Ryn screamed through his teeth as he shoved them out of the way. Zayn watched in horror as their father turned toward the blast's direction. Charred flesh was clinging to his back, leaving parts of his ribs exposed.

Ryn, flushed with anger, cursed as he reached over his shoulder, placing his palm on his burnt flesh. "Someone tipped off the Guard. We have to keep moving." Ryn's back began to heal as he screamed in agony, continuing toward the ruins. Zayn had seen healing before, but never a wound this atrocious. *The worse the wound, the more painful the healing,* he thought, remembering his father's words when he was younger.

Sweat dripped from Zayn's forehead as they sprinted even faster towards the colossal border wall ahead. As they approached the thick impenetrable stone, the guard was still shouting and not far behind. The wall towered above them with no means to enter. Zayn's lungs constricted as the thundering cries of the guard approached. A small amount of relief struck as his eyes detected the skin on his father's exposed back, perfectly healed.

"Remember, I need you to trust me," said Ryn, wincing as he moved towards the wall that soared above them. He slid his hand across a crack in the wall where some vines had grown, and knelt, grabbing the dirt beneath. Upon the skin of his left wrist was a branded marking, scarred over many years ago. It held the shape of a four-petaled flower. One of the Searing Symbols from the Stone in the city. With a hammer in one hand, he placed the other on the nearly dead vines below and whispered.

"The guard is fifty paces over the hill to our northeast!" Zayn warned.

"Zayn's right!" Lyu screamed. "You have to hurry, Father!"

"He said to trust him," said Tanyel, causing them both to settle.

Suddenly, Zayn's attention snapped toward the vines as each one began to burst and grow at a rapid pace. With the growth came the sound of stone hinges grinding. The crack in the wall became a gap, creating an outline of what used to be a door entering the ruins. The vine had caused enough space for them to slip through. Ryn took the iron hammer once they had cleared the doorway and crushed the stone wall hanging above the opening. The stone crumbled and closed the gap, making it nearly impossible for anyone to enter.

"That buys us some time. We can find another way out," said Ryn as his voice echoed through the endless stone ruins.

"Father," said Lyu, bewildered. "You are one of Levithe's greatest Healers! Why are they chasing us?!"

"It doesn't matter who you are or what rank you possess," said Ryn. "The command given to the Incinerator Guard is to kill anyone who comes within a hundred paces of the ruins, even if it is the Levithe himself. As for the rest, I promise you will all understand soon enough." Ryn turned and continued to march forward.

Zayn followed closest to their father as the two siblings staggered behind. Despite all his internal disgust living as Drudge, he still had respect and love for Ryn, surpassing any other in O'Varth.

Something in the back of Zayn's mind always wondered if there was a secret reason their parents chose this life for them. *Maybe this is it?* He thought.

"Father," Zayn said. "Why us? We are Drudge."

Slowing his breath, Ryn looked Zayn in the eyes and said, "As I have told you before. A man's gifting is only worth as much as the man. Just because you are Drudge doesn't mean you are useless, son. Besides, we have to do this together, as a family... for your mother." Zayn's eyes glazed over at the mention of her.

"Do what together?" Lyu said through composed breaths. "You still haven't told us."

"We have to use the other *Stones*... so we can defeat Levithe," Ryn responded with poise.

"Other Stones?" Zayn said.

"Yes, son. It may come as a surprise, but the Searing Stone in Levitheton is not the only one of its kind."

Zayn nearly tripped over a piece of crumbled debris as his eyes widened. "That can't be possible. The Searing Stone is the only artifact brought back from the ruins by Levithe himself..." Zayn stopped, recalling his father's words. *None of it's true.*

"I understand it's a lot," Ryn replied. "A convincing history created by the one who rules. Levithe is not the Savior of O'Varth, son. He is its demise, and he will do anything to keep it that way."

"But what about these *Stones*?" Tanyel said.

"It's why we are here," Ryn said, winking at Tanyel. "You're familiar with how Levithe sends brigades of his Guard out of the city daily?"

"Yes," Tanyel said. "But we've always been told the Guard are just keeping an eye on the Drudge working throughout the island."

"Again, another lie. That is exactly what *he* wants you to think," Ryn said. "But son, you and I both know Levithe isn't concerned with the Drudge."

Zayn winced at the comment.

"Levithe is searching and has been for the past three hundred years. And just like his secret history, he doesn't want anyone to find out about his search. It's the reason he sends the brigades out daily, the reason the ruins are protected. Levithe is looking for another Stone." Ryn said as they neared an entrance to one of the massive stone structures that still stood.

"And one of the Stones is in the ruins?!" Tanyel said with excitement.

"Not quite, son," Ryn said, leading them through the entrance. "This way."

Zayn's mind wouldn't stop spinning. *A new Stone? Does that mean I could finally become...* his theories crumbled as they entered the first room. Above them, once ceilings crafted for a glorious city, now shattered bits of stones barely hanging on, with light from the setting sun piercing through their broken gaps. After the fifth corridor, they entered a vast, open room. It reminded the four of their many trips to the deep caverns of the Tuskoth Caves.

"What do you think this place was, Zayn?" Tanyel said, gazing at the open room.

"I don't know," said Zayn. "Father, any idea?"

"I expect it was an old weapon barracks of sorts," Ryn said as he removed a flint from his cloak.

Ryn found some dead vines from the wall nearest to them. As he detached the vines, a swarm of insects flew out from beneath them and began gnawing into the flesh in his hand. He smashed some of them with the flint, shaking off the rest, causing them to buzz by Lyu.

Flustered, she swatted them away, saying, "Why do these useless bugs even exist?"

Ryn smirked back, responding, "I don't think we will ever get the answer to that one, Lyu. But I'm convinced that even what seems *useless*," Ryn paused, glancing at Zayn. "Can eventually serve a purpose." Zayn had used the word useless countless times, referencing his life as a Drudge. His father always tried to make him feel otherwise.

His jaw clenched as he wrapped the vine around his hammer's spike and used the flint to spark the flame. As the surrounding area became visible, they discovered some armor and broken weaponry scattered throughout. Ryn took three rusted spears found in the corner, wrapped them in vines, and gave one to each of his children. Zayn rushed forward to grab the first torch.

"You will need these as we head underground," Ryn said. "Not much further." Zayn bounced on his toes at the comment, noticing similar anticipation in Tanyel and Lyu. He kept the questions to himself.

They made their way through the expansive room with their torches, hearing only the sounds of their footsteps and breath. The damp air of the ruins thickened, causing sweat to form more rapidly. Scattered throughout the room were large shattered mirrors leaning up against the walls. The light from their torch flames reflected across the square-shaped room with a massive, domed ceiling. Suspended out of reach at the room's center was a massive stone chandelier. Carved into the ceiling were two perfect circles. The outer ring was large, taking up most of the ceiling, and the inner ring was small with the suspended stone directly in its center. Thirteen consecutive pillars on each side held the domed room in perfect balance. As they reached the end of the room, Ryn pointed to another cluster of vines on their last limb of life. Ryn healed the vines, but this time, the cracks expanded downward toward their feet instead of opening a gap for a doorway. The opening revealed a twisting stairway of stone held by a solid pillar leading down into the darkness.

Ryn sighed with a deep smile. "At the base of these stairs is a room even Levithe doesn't know about. Before the devastation, this was called the Forging Room. A place known only by dedicated Forgers of the time." Ryn wiped the sweat from his brow as he slowed his voice, "Luckily, our family lineage contained a Forger."

Shocked, Zayn glanced at his siblings. He realized he was not alone in the feeling.

Meeting their eyes, Ryn seemed to understand their confusion and said, "Perhaps this will help. When I was younger, about your age, my father gave me a scroll. It contains maps, symbols, a genealogy, and information assumed known only by Levithe. His father gave it to him, and so on. Until now, no generation of our known family has even attempted what we are about to accomplish. Your mother and I, before she passed, and others had been planning this for a long time." Ryn rarely spoke of their mother's passing, and none of the three siblings knew what happened to her. Zayn hated that he never got to say goodbye. Even more so, he hated not knowing how or why she died.

Removing a small tattered scroll from his cloak, he gave it to Zayn, whispering, "I no longer need this. This is what I was talking about last night, son. It is yours to keep." Zayn grabbed the scroll as his eyes descended and breathed slowly out through his nose.

"Father, this is almost unbelievable," Zayn said. "I don't know what to say."

"You don't have to say anything. Simply keep it close and

follow what it says." Tanyel and Lyu looked at each other in amazement.

The four of them made their way down the whirling stairwell, and when they finally reached level ground, they approached a large wooden door that opened to an enormous room, triple the size of the domed quarters above — not a single object in sight. No broken chairs, pillars, spears, vines, or even rubble. The utter emptiness of the chilling room made Zayn's bones rattle. Tanyel let out a whistle, causing his fear to dissipate. Lyu rolled her eyes, shoving him as Ryn and Zayn held back their laughter. *He knows what he's doing,* Zayn thought, noticing Ryn's worried face had disappeared.

They continued following their father through the vast space and approached what appeared to be the room's center. Their torchlights exposed a small boulder standing only about waist high. Hollow from the top-down, it held a similar appearance to a stone washbowl from home. There were four flat edges carved out of its top and engravings and markings along its exterior.

"Zayn. Tanyel. Lyu," Ryn insisted as noticeable excitement built in his demeanor. "Can each of you place your hand on one edge? I will take the fourth."

As they placed their hands on the cold stone structure, a soft smoke rose from the boulder. Zayn looked at Tanyel with wide eyes as their father signaled to hold their place. Lyu stood as steady as a pillar. Zayn was always impressed by her poise in the most intense scenarios. Then suddenly, the smoke flickered into a blue flame, which grew brighter until it encompassed the boulder's entire hollowed space. The immense heat from the flames caused Zayn and the others to lean their heads back as their hands remained on the stone.

Without hesitation, Ryn rolled up his cloak sleeve and reached into the flame. Before they could blink, he retrieved four small rods made of a metal they did not recognize. The rods measured a hand's length with the circumference of a writing feather. Ryn blew fiercely on his hands and forearms to cool them, bouncing the rods until they cooled.

With a gasp, Tanyel shouted, "How?! There was nothing in there!"

"I don't know for sure," Ryn said, staring at the rods. "But it was said that the Forging Stone contained a similar power to the Searing Stone."

Zayn pointed to the rods, saying, "What do you plan to do with those?"

Ryn paused for a moment with a slight twitch in his ears. He raised his finger to his mouth, stared at them with compassion, and said, "This is the Forging Stone. I need to forge these rods, which will require a bit of time. I need the three of you to go back to the stairwell and keep watch." Ryn paused for a moment, causing the siblings to lean in and listen even closer. "If you hear even the faintest sound, promise that you will sprint to me as fast as you can."

"We promise," they respond in unison. Ryn's eyes glistened in the torchlight, gesturing them to go.

They sprinted across the barren stone back to the stairway, Lyu arriving first, followed by Tanyel. At the doorway, Zayn looked back, noticing both his father and the blue flame were no longer visible. *He won't let anything happen to us,* Zayn thought as he turned and ran up the stairs to catch up with his siblings.

Nearing the top of the stairs, the three stopped and caught their breath. Once recovered, they sat in silence, waiting for the slightest movement or sound.

Tanyel's eyes squinted. He whispered, "I hear something."

"Me too," Lyu replied, tilting her head. "But I think it's from Father's hammer coming from down the stairwell." Zayn and Tanyel nodded.

"What do you think he's making?" said Tanyel. Zayn or Lyu didn't respond.

With a smirk, Tanyel continued, "I bet he is forging a weapon with that mysterious metal. One with the ability to repel Incinerator flames and destroy the Guard!"

"I think Father would need a few more rods for that," Zayn joked back.

"O'Varth's tiniest weapon," Lyu said, with a harmless eye roll. Turning her head, she signaled them to listen.

They sat on the stairs for what seemed like half a day's wait. Rhythmic clanking sounds of their father's hammer continued to reverberate through the empty deep stairwell. Zayn wasn't able to focus on listening as the overwhelming thoughts sped through his mind. He still couldn't believe they were in the ruins. Three Drudge. Wiping the sweat from under his eyes, his hands still smelled of fish. After today, he might never clean a fish again. For the first time in his life, the monotony of the next days would be non-existent. Somehow if they did escape the ruins alive, nothing would be the same again. *We have to do this as a family, for Mother,* he thought, recalling his father's words.

Suddenly, a faint voice shouted in the distance. One voice turned to more, causing Zayn and the others to leap to their feet in a panic. Following their father's instructions, they sprinted back down the stairs with as much speed as possible. As they reached the bottom, Zayn yelled, "Father, the Guard is here!"

Lyu, outpacing the brothers, arrived at the boulder where her father sat. Sweat dripped down his forehead as he looked up at her with a smile.

"We did it, Lyu," beamed Ryn. "It is finished."

Zayn and Tanyel stood by anxiously, out of breath, looking at Lyu and Ryn, waiting for them to run. Ryn quickly extended a closed fist to the three of them. Four unique symbols forged from the metal rods taken from the flame glimmered in the flame's light as his hand opened. Ryn gave one to each sibling, keeping the last for himself. Before their father ran, he raised the iron hammer, and with multiple heavy blows, he smashed the hollow boulder into pieces. The blue flame dissipated as the boulder crumbled.

Zayn's heart skipped, and his excitement rose as he gazed at the symbol in his hand. *Could this be what I think it is?* He thought. Looking up at the others, Tanyel shared in his excitement while Lyu stared at her symbol with disgust. *Maybe this is why our parents chose Drudge for us,* he thought. The glow of the blue flame brilliantly reflected off the symbols.

"Protect these with your life," Ryn declared as they ran. "Do not let *anyone* know you have them until we reach the new Stone. They are the key to the weapon that can finally destroy Levithe. Where we go next lies within the scroll. No matter what happens here, you must achieve what is written. You must keep moving and not look back."

The three followed their father in a hurry as he sprinted away from the approaching Guard. Reaching the other end of the colossal room, they came across another large wooden door. Ryn swung the door open, revealing an identical spiral stairwell to the one across the chamber. As his heart was racing, the screams from the Incinerator Guard pelted his ears as they closed in.

"To the top!" Ryn shouted as he slammed the wooden door, trying to jam some small boulders to keep it shut. "The Guard is halfway through the forging room. This won't hold long!"

Stone and vines blocked the exit at the peak of the stairway. Ryn healed the vines, causing the cracks to expand, leaving just enough room for one person to squeeze through at a time. Zayn attempted to send their father through first, but he refused and motioned them all to hurry. Lyu slipped through first as she reached down for Tanyel's wrist, pulling him up to safety. Once Tanyel was through, he grabbed Zayn and yanked him up with immense force. A moment of panic struck Zayn as his shoulders got caught in the opening. Before the panic consumed him, Tanyel pulled once more. Zayn gasped and sighed in relief as his body slipped through. Suddenly, the entire stairwell quaked as a blast of flame erupted below, exploding the wooden door into a hundred pieces of flaming kindling.

Zayn reached down to help Ryn, and his heart sank. The blast caused Ryn to lose his footing and slip down a few of the stairs.

"Father! Hurry! Grab my hand!" Zayn screamed as he stretched his arm out through the opening. Ryn regained footing and began to ascend.

Time slowed as the awful command from the Guard below resounded up the stairwell. "Fire again!"

Ryn was a step out of reach from Zayn's grip as the deafening sound of flames collided with the base of the stairwell. Ryn's eyes widened as the stairs gave way below his feet. With one last attempt,

Ryn sprang towards Zayn, reaching for his hand. Simultaneously, Zayn stretched his arm even further as he watched the stairwell crumble into a thousand pieces.

One brief moment of relief flooded Zayn's body as the firm grip of his father's hand tightened around his own. The muddled sounds of his siblings yelling from behind nearly deafened his ears. Everything seemed a blur as tears filled his eyes, staring at Ryn's body dangling above the destruction below, barely hanging on. The smoke from the flames flooded his lungs as he held back his cough.

Finally, as Zayn tried to muster the strength to pull his father up, a searing pain radiated through his shoulder as it dislodged from the joint. Zayn's eyes widened in terror at the awful feeling of his father's hand slipping down the length of his own.

"No!" Zayn pleaded as a mixture of tears and anger flooded his face. "Please! We need you, Father!" The possibility of saving his father dissipated as his shoulder continued to strip from the bone. He looked towards his father once more, expecting to see fear in Ryn's eyes. Instead, he saw the proud look of a father. His face was oddly calm, and with an assured voice, he whispered, "I'll be okay, Zayn. Take care of them. Follow the scroll. It is our only hope of escape." Immediately, Ryn released his grip and maintained eye contact with Zayn as he crashed into the rubble below.

Zayn's tears made it nearly impossible to see, and as he wiped his eyes clear, his last sight of his father was him lying at the bottom of the staircase, barely moving. Zayn's heart was pounding out of his chest as he saw Ryn look toward the shattered doorway. Then, time halted as a final beam of blinding flame swallowed Ryn and the rubble below. As the flames ceased and the smoke settled, the only remnants of his father were ash and the faint glimmer of his hammer. Zayn couldn't believe his eyes but continued staring in silence as his insides screamed in agony. The man who protected him his entire life, gone in an instant. His heart had shattered into more pieces than the crumbled stairwell below. He hung over the edge with his hand still outstretched. All he did was stare as the numbness of grief consumed his body.

Tanyel yanked Zayn out of the gap as Lyu collapsed into their arms, wailing in agony. Tanyel enfolded them both with an intense grip. The surrounding room's dark emptiness paled in comparison to the void Zayn carried within. Tanyel and Lyu's tears soaked his spring cloak as he wept with them. The faint smell of campfire and burnt hair flooded his nostrils from the incineration below, turning his stomach nearly to the point of vomiting. It seemed as if days had passed while the never-ending sounds of their pain echoed throughout the chamber.

He can't be dead, Zayn thought, having trouble determining whether his tears resulted from deep shame or bitter hate. Perhaps both. After all, if they were Seared, he would have killed the Guard, and their father would be alive. Zayn, once again, shook his head to release the hateful notions.

Zayn, coming to his senses, wiped his tear-soaked face as he released his grip on the others and stared back at them, unable to speak.

"Zayn," choked Lyu as she looked him in the eyes. "This wasn't your fault."

The shame he was experiencing both intensified and dissipated at her words while a waterfall of tears welled behind his eyes. Tanyel stared back with reddened, tear-soaked cheeks, nodding in agreement. His siblings loved him, and from this moment on, they were all he had. He mustered up only two words as he gazed back at them through his blurred vision. "Thank you."

As they embraced once more, Zayn softly cleared his throat and pointed towards the opening, whispering, "The Guard is below."

The three crawled in silence towards the opening as the Guards' muffled voices echoed up the stairwell. As they placed their heads onto the cold stone to listen in, a swarm of the insects burst out of the stairway's opening. Instead of attacking, however, they buzzed by without seeming to notice the three.

With their faces pressed to the stone once more, they held their breath in silence. Barely able to decipher the words, two Guards shouted at each other below.

"Excellent work," said one of them with a sarcastic tone. "Now, we can't even identify this sack of ashes!" Zayn's face flushed with hate.

"Don't blame me," spat the other. "We can't get the others because you destroyed the stairway!"

"Fair enough," responded the first. "But look at what we have here... An iron forged hammer and some sort of symbol? I bet Lord Levithe will reward us for these."

"Indeed. Let's get back to the entrance. They will need help with the explosion. The lookout will be on high alert around every square of this wall to eliminate anyone else who tries to enter."

Letting out a laugh, the other said, "Or *escape*."

Zayn exhaled, feeling his chest constrict at the Guards' words. Hiding the symbols was their father's primary command. Now, Levithe had one *and* the hammer. *Surely, they won't find out it was Father's,* he thought.

Zayn and the others continued to hold their breath as the rustle of footsteps below faded away, leaving them once again, alone with their grief. They sat up, pale-faced, at a complete loss about how they would escape.

Suddenly, Lyu gasped and pointed at Zayn, saying, "Brother, your shoulder!" Zayn's jaw locked as he became aware of the throbbing pain in his shoulder coupled with a terrible tingling sensation trickling down his neck. The rush from the grief and listening to the Guards had somehow delayed the memory of the pain.

"What do I do?" Zayn asked as his arm hung limp at his side.

"I've seen Drudge with shoulders like this after getting their arm caught in a rope at the Docks," Tanyel said. "They pop them back into place all the time. I could try to fix it, but it's going to be extremely painful."

"Do it. We can't go on like this."

Lyu agreed, saying, "Also, we can find a Healer to fix it when we get back to the city."

Zayn stood still while Tanyel grabbed his wrist. Without warning, Tanyel, with aggressive force, yanked the limp arm toward himself. Zayn screamed through clenched teeth as spit erupted through their gaps. He wasn't sure how it worked, but as Tanyel carefully released his arm, Zayn's shoulder snapped back into place. The pain remained, but Tanyel had succeeded.

"Good work, brother," Lyu said. "Now, how do we get out of this place?"

Zayn, still in pain, remembered the scroll and removed it from his cloak, making sure not to tear it. "Father said this would help us." Even saying the word father made him want to crumble to the floor. Noticing the same look behind both Tanyel and Lyu's eyes, Zayn knew acknowledging it was too much for that moment. He had to get them out of here.

As he carefully unrolled the parchment before them, the first words they read lined the top in large dark letters, "The Key to Our

Escape." Just below the title was a perfect circle drawn with ink. They read further and came across a map titled O'Varth, an intricate map of their entire island with several markings they didn't recognize. As their eyes scanned the scroll, the siblings found a genealogy that resembled a massive upside-down tree. There were poems, a few historical accounts they didn't understand, a set of symbols, and finally, a map of the ruins at the bottom.

Tanyel pointed to the scroll and said, "Look! It says, *The Forging Stone*. This is where Father... made the symbols. See here, just north of us. Those are docks! It says it right there, the Docks of Stone. There has to be a boat we can use to escape!"

"I don't think so," said Zayn. "There hasn't been a water vessel of any kind allowed on this island since before we were born."

Lyu grabbed her brother's shoulders and said, "I think you're both right. There might not be a ship, but I think it is our only chance. The guard said every part of the border wall would be swarming with Incinerators. If you look closely at this map, there's a tiny red marking where these Docks of Stone are located. It has to mean something important."

Zayn rolled the scroll back up to put in his cloak as he and Tanyel nodded in approval to their sister. When Lyu took the lead, she always reminded Zayn of their father. The pain in his chest sparked, causing his eyes to swell. Would every tiny moment be a reminder of his death? It seemed unbearable, but he had to keep going. They began to move at a quick yet steady pace, deeper into the ruins.

As they reached a large wooden door, a gentle wind poured through the cracks, causing their teeth to chatter. The old hinges screeched as Lyu pushed open the door, and the cool air flooded their nostrils. Light from the stars above exposed an enormous, elegant courtyard in front of them. Zayn's eyes adjusted as he detected a large stone arch in the courtyard's center, standing as a monument. He blinked rapidly as he saw how lush, green grass and vines had polluted every granule of the courtyard. As they neared the center, they spotted large stone benches covered in vines encircling the stone arch.

Suddenly, Zayn's eyes grew wide as he gazed back at the thousands of stones littered across the ground in front of him.

"Look," he said, lowering his torch to expose the horror below.

Lyu and Tanyel both leaped backward as Zayn remained still, realizing the pieces were not, in fact, stones. Instead, his torchlight revealed thousands of skulls and bones piled on top of one another. He diverted his eyes and stepped back towards his siblings.

"The war?" Lyu questioned. "More awful than I could have ever imagined."

"This doesn't look like a war," Tanyel said, shaking his head. "This was a massacre."

Zayn, remembering his father's words, responded, "None of

it's true, remember. There was no war. And if Levithe is capable of slaughtering thousands to keep his version true, Father is right. We must do whatever it takes to destroy him." Zayn's anger boiled as he stared blankly, picturing Levithe's body turned to ash.

Lyu took Zayn by the hand and signaled to Tanyel. She led them around the arch, keeping a significant distance between them and the pile of decay. The opposite of the courtyard revealed another wooden door matching the one behind them. As Lyu swung the door open, the grinding hinges caused Zayn to plug his ears, while the horrifying images of the boneyard continued to haunt his mind.

Finally, they reached another doorway leading to open air. Zayn glanced at the map to confirm they had reached the last room before the docks. Before he rolled up the scroll, his mind flashed to his father handing it to him. He held the tears back. Yet another reminder. He wondered if it would be better for his heart to turn to stone rather than feel anything at all. The wind struck Zayn's face as Lyu pushed open the door. Their torchlights exposed an expansive harbor. The sound of the waves battered against gigantic walls of stone jutting out into the water.

"The Docks of Stone," said Tanyel, as his emotion caused him to choke on his words. "It's incredible… Massive enough to fit every person from Levitheton. But where are the ships?"

"The red marking was at the end of one of the docks," Lyu said, signaling them ahead toward the eastern border wall. As they made their way to the end, something caught their eye floating in the water below. A small wooden vessel carved out of a single slab of wood rocked back and forth atop the small waves.

"A ship!" said Zayn. "I can't believe it! Tanyel, you were right!"

"That is not a ship," Tanyel said, lowering his head. "Ships fit hundreds. This will barely fit us."

"It will work for now," said Zayn, gripping Tanyel's shoulder. "Let's help Lyu down."

After they climbed down into the boat, Zayn squinted, seeing a small inscription carved into the side underlined by a red scratch mark.

For my Son, may it serve the Remnant. -AsR

"What does it mean?" Zayn said, showing the others.

Lyu lifted her hand to her mouth as her eyes darted open. "Zayn, Tanyel. I know who wrote this." She pointed to the initials.

Tanyel cocked his head with squinted eyes, and Zayn's mind was too busy to sort out the name.

Lyu continued, "A-s-R... A-s-R... Andyr, son of Roselyn! Grandfather! He left this for his son, Ryn!"

"But what is the Remnant?" Tanyel asked as Zayn was still awestruck by the realization.

"Father mentioned *others* when he talked about this plan," Zayn said. "What if it's what they call themselves?" Tanyel and Lyu stared back in silence.

Zayn's mind exploded as he attempted to perceive how the scroll had been hidden for generations. *"My father gave it to me, and so on,"* his father's words rang through his head. Zayn realized that Ryn's plan was more extensive than he assumed. Now, with no volition of their own, they were in charge of the scroll and a part of the *others,* whether they liked it or not. *The Remnant,* Zayn thought, pulling his shoulders back, looking at the stars.

The three tossed their torches into the water, causing a satisfying hiss. Finding their balance, they pushed off the stone to make their way around the eastern border wall. The ruins' walls protruded out over the water at least ten times the length of the longest stone dock. Drifting towards the wall, they came to the edge. As they peered around the wall, they saw the Guard standing back on land, ready to incinerate anyone who approached.

"If we paddle far enough east, we should be able to make it to shore without being seen," said Lyu.

"That should work," Zayn responded. "But we have to stay quiet. Lyu, you keep eyes on the Guard at the shore. Tanyel and I will paddle." She nodded, tears still stuck behind her eyes.

Before they began, the three siblings scooped some water with their hands, wiped their faces, and drank. Zayn reached down into the water and began to paddle, and the others followed his lead. The small waves pounded against the wooden vessel as they slowly made their way toward the tree line. Zayn glanced at the sky and absorbed the immense splendor of the flickering stars. It took them much longer than expected to paddle to a spot that felt safe.

They paddled towards the shore ahead, out of the Guard's line of vision. As their feet hit the sand, they tiptoed to the trees due south. With the main road leading to Levitheton within sight, Zayn was confident they would make it home before sunrise.

"This is only the beginning," whispered Zayn. "When we arrive home, we need to look at the map of O'Varth. I saw red markings similar to the one on the docks. I think they will lead us to where Father wants us to go." His chest hardened as the word father yet again, left his mouth. Taking a deep breath in, he turned and led the way.

After what seemed like a half day's journey, the sunlight's pale glow burst from the horizon, causing the sky and their surroundings to glow pink. Dawn's light exposed the Northern Gate's entrance a few hundred paces to their south. *Please no Stawb,* Zayn thought as he stared at the massive entrance. Two guards stood on high alert, making it clear to Zayn they had been warned about the breach to the ruins. His nerves rose as they approached, and he noticed Tanyel and Lyu looking straight ahead, attempting to blend in.

To their luck, the two guards were inspecting some Seared, allowing the three siblings to slip through with ease. Even though a breach occurred, no Seared would ever expect it to be from the Drudge. Zayn released his shoulders as he walked under the towering gates. Tanyel looked over at him and sighed, shaking his head.

Their home was in the south-central part of the city, still a long way off. Exhausted, Zayn, Tanyel, and Lyu walked past the mud-shacks that made up most of the city's outer edge. The Drudge within the city outnumbered the Seared tenfold. Grime and sweat painted the faces of everyone they passed, children included. Because of the lack of resources, a hazy yellowish cloud constantly shrouded the city's outer edge. Zayn coughed, covering his nose, as the putrid scent of feces and waste filled the air. Looking to his right, a decaying pile of human waste swarmed with insects. Two burly men, one of which was missing a leg, and another missing a hand, were loading the pile into a cart with shovels.

As they made their way deeper through the shacks, a crippled woman tugged at Zayn's cloak. With wiry black hair and pale, wrinkled skin, she foamed at the mouth, only able to utter mumbles and groans. Her sunken eyes stared at Zayn. He attempted to force a smile, then turned, yanking his cloak from her hand. Most Drudge were the throwaways, the forgotten, and Zayn wanted nothing to do with them.

"I wonder if Ganya is home," said Tanyel, staring at one of the mud shacks. "We should see if he wants to travel with us."

"He usually has his hunter's net hanging out to dry if he is home," Lyu said, pointing to the empty drying line stretched across the front of Ganya's house.

"It would be nice to have a hunter with us," Tanyel said.

"It's okay," Zayn responded. "Father trusted us enough to do this by ourselves."

"Yeah," Lyu said. "It would honestly attract more attention if he were with us."

As they made their way closer to the center of town, the houses became more and more elegant; from homes and shops made with mud, then wood, then stone, and finally, buildings made of metals mined from the Tuskoth Caves. There wasn't a single part of this city that Zayn didn't hate walking through. In the mud-shacks, he felt bitterness, and here, amongst the Seared, everyone always recognized them because of their parents. As they would pass the homes of the Seared, all they received were constant glares and head shakes. A daily reminder of his pathetic status.

Finally, the three reached the center of town. Zayn gazed at the two most powerful structures within Levitheton. The first was Levithe's Tower with its spear-like peak clipping the low-hanging clouds. Built with extreme elegance entirely of bright silverish metal, the tower reflected the sunlight, causing the innermost part of the city to glow. Zayn scanned upward toward its peak and saw dozens of balconies jutting out like daggers. Only a few floors up was Levithe's main portico. The massive balcony overlooked the city's center and the second powerful structure, the Searing Stone.

"Look," Tanyel said, pointing to three families standing in a line before the Stone.

"I hate watching these," said Zayn, glaring at the Stone. He was forced to walk past this structure daily as a painful reminder of his life as a Drudge.

"I have to agree with you," Lyu responded, but for the opposite reason.

Zayn gazed at the enormous Stone boulder before them. It held the shape of a small elongated building with rounded edges on its sides. It appeared as if a portion of a circle had its top smashed off by an enormous hammer. Surrounded by a blue, never-extinguishing flame, it contained three symbols carved into its side. Each symbol represented one gift. One for Healer, like their father. One for Incinerator, like the Guard. Most peculiar of all, one for Shifter, like their uncle Typher.

Every time Zayn looked at the Stone, his heart filled with resentment. Parents were the ones who decided their child's gifting, just as their parents had decided theirs. A rule Levithe had created to maintain control of the gifts. Each set of parents had one year after their child's birth to determine if they wanted to choose their children's gifting or forgo the Stone and give their child the life of a Drudge. If parents chose to Sear their child, it meant a life-long oath, bound to serve Levithe. If parents chose to forgo the Stone, it meant a life of survival and toil without gifts. The Drudge worked jobs as fishers, crafters, hunters, and other common trades. Because of the significant divide between people, some Drudge looked down upon those who chose Searing. However, even rarer were Seared parents who chose to forgo the Stone. The only reason Zayn knew that Seared parents would ever choose to forgo the Stone for their child was if the child had an ailment, birth defect, or mental block. It was an act of disownment. Parents would simply drop their crippled children at the mud-shacks and consider them cursed. But not Zayn's parents. From what he understood, their mother and father were the only Seared parents on O'Varth who had ever chosen to forgo the Stone *and* keep their children. Zayn constantly pictured them allowing his first year to pass without choosing to Sear him. He hated he didn't have a choice in the matter.

Even though the Seared were forced to serve Levithe, they typically lived a life of luxury and plenty. Zayn would have much rather had that than calloused hands and the constant smell of fish.

The sounds of infants wailing filled his ears as he examined each of the three symbols on the glowing Stone. The first, a three-tongued flame, caused both envy and hatred to rise. Incinerators were the bulk of Levithe's Guard, and they were his means of keeping order in the city. Deep down, Zayn knew if he were one, his father would be alive. He pictured having the ability to propel an immense beam of flame from his chest, disintegrating Levithe and his Guard to ash. He would be unstoppable. As he looked at the second symbol, his heart sank as he pictured his parent's wrists. The four-petaled flower. The gift of Healing. Perhaps the most desired gift on the island. Most parents in O'Varth chose Healer for at least one of their children because of their ability to fix even the bloodiest of wounds. Images of Ryn's scorched back, pulling itself together, flashed through Zayn's mind. However, once a person's heart stopped, no power on O'Varth could bring them back. Lastly, Zayn stared at the third symbol, the half-face. Shifters could take on the form of any human they laid eyes upon. They were among the wealthiest on the island because they existed mostly as entertainers and pleasure providers for Levithe, his Guard, other Seared, and even the Drudge when they could afford it. There were the good ones, like his uncle Typher, and the vile ones like Stawb. It would have been Zayn's last choice as a gift for himself. But he would take being a Shifter over a Drudge any day.

    Zayn directed his eyes toward the armor-clad Guard standing upright with the glowing Stone at their backs. The Searing Stone was protected with more ferocity than the ruins themselves. Zayn had heard stories of many parents over the years attempting to slip past the Guard, trying to give their babies multiple gifts with none succeeding. Not only was it deemed treason against Levithe himself, but even the few babies that had been illegally branded with multiple symbols, only the first Searing worked. However, one person existed on O'Varth with more than one gift. Levithe had all three.

They all stopped to observe the scene as the three infants were brought to the large Stone one by one. The first parent chose Healer. The Guards of the Stone grabbed the baby and held it facing the Stone. One guard took an iron rod with the metal symbol fastened to one end. The guard pressed the brand to the Healer symbol on the Stone and then forcefully branded the infant's wrist. Simultaneously, every guard shouted the gifting's ancient name, "*Keha!*" The infant wailed, and the parents wept, but from that moment on, the child was a Healer, sworn and bound to serve Levithe for the rest of its life.

The next set of parents handed their baby over to the guards and branded it with the Incinerator symbol. "*Eshe!*" the guards chanted.

Suddenly, an ear-piercing horn blast interrupted the ceremony, and every person in the surrounding area fell to their knees. An insufferable darkness seemed to enter the air as Levithe, the island's insufferable god, exited the tower, advancing toward the Stone. He was taller than all men in the kingdom and wore a thick white cloak. Impenetrable metal armor made of the same silver as the tower covered most of his body except his chest and scolding yellow eyes. His bright hair, the color of golden sand, flowed out beneath his helmet on every side. Despite being alive for centuries, he had a beauty that attracted both men and women of all ages on the island.

THE SEARING STONE

His smile either drew people in or instilled fear in their bones. He was the island's leader and brought order to the people, but all feared him. Before them, he stood, the vilest savior O'Varth had ever seen.

The center of town was silent, and Zayn slowly raised his eyes as Levithe approached the Stone. Grabbing the infant by the ankle and holding her above his head, Levithe glared at the child's parents with a chilling smile.

"You see here," said Levithe, looking at the surrounding crowd. "This is a family I remember vividly. The father serves in my Guard as a Healer, and the Mother is a Shifter."

Looking at the mother with rage, he said, "It came to my attention you denied my request for company last evening."

"I... I was..." cowered the woman.

"Have you forgotten?" Levithe said with a voice that rattled the center of town. "You're sworn to me. All Seared are mine to use, however I please. When I call you to my Tower, you obey."

"Yes, Lord," she whimpered, with her face to the dirt.

The husband interrupted with a desperate shout, "Lord Levithe, the fault is my own. When the Guard came to retrieve her for you, she was only asleep, and I... I forgot to give her the message when she woke."

Levithe looked at the man and didn't say a word. Handing the infant back to the mother, Levithe's face swelled into an awful rage. Without hesitation, he turned to the mother holding her infant and propelled flames from his chest. The screams of the mother and child echoed through the city as every person within view knelt, frozen in complete silence. As Levithe released the flames, the charred flesh on the mother's back barely gripped her bones. Even worse than Ryn's back. She was taking tiny whimpering breaths, nearly alive. Zayn gasped as he noticed black ash scattered over the mother's chest. *The infant,* he thought.

"Heal her," Levithe said to the husband, glaring at the crowd. "And remember who I am and who you serve."

The father, in shock, still having no words, looked at his wife, grabbed her smoldering hand, and began to heal her. Zayn's face paled as the mother's skin turned from black to red as the tendon and skin latched back onto the bone until finally, she appeared normal. Barely breathing and unable to speak, the husband carried his ash covered wife away from the Stone and out of the city center. Levithe re-entered the tower looking back to the crowd with a grin on his face.

Zayn placed the back of his hand to his mouth as the bottom of his throat lunged toward the roof of his mouth. The sight was both unbearable and nauseating for even the mightiest Seared.

"It wasn't even treason," Tanyel responded in horror, shaking his head. "She simply didn't respond to his request, and their baby was decimated? This has to be why our parents chose to forgo the Stone for us."

"Exactly! Why would anyone surrender their child over to Levithe!?" Lyu said, rage in her voice. "This is what happens... I swear, if Levithe were giftless too... I would execute him in front of all of Levitheton!"

With a fiery scarlet face, Zayn snapped at Tanyel and Lyu, "They were wrong to forgo the Stone for us! We wouldn't be in this position today if we were Seared. Father would still be alive!" As the words left his mouth, Lyu and Tanyel looked at each other, emotions overwhelming them to the point of tears.

"You are both wrong," Tanyel said, wiping his eyes. "Mother and Father were Seared, and they never once resented it. If we truly trust them, we have to believe they chose what's best for us. We have to be together in this."

In his mind, Zayn knew Tanyel was right, but his heart didn't feel it. Before Zayn apologized, he glanced up toward the main portico and saw Levithe leaning against his throne. For the faintest moment, it appeared as if Levithe was staring directly at them.

He clasped his elbow as his eyes tightened, whispering out of the corner of his mouth, "Lyu, Tanyel, I think we're being watched. We need to get home." They nodded and followed.

"Also," Zayn paused as the pain in the back of his throat loosened. "I'm sorry."

Chapter 3

Levithe's Alarm

LEVITHE LEANED AGAINST HIS THRONE atop the portico, observing the city's center. The city of Levitheton was meant to be temporary. A holding cell to allow enough time for his Guard to grow and find the other Stone fragments. As the years went on, Levithe found the search to be more and more of a waste. After all, it took almost two hundred years to grow a sufficient population and build the great city of Levitheton. In the early years following the *devastation*, the search for the fragments was what drove him. However, his motivation had severely declined over the last one hundred years, while his hatred for the *Ones Beyond* grew tenfold year after year. *Three hundred years, almost to the day and not a single clue,* he thought, as the deep pit of anger bubbled within. The fragments were his only chance at escaping the wretched rock.

The dawn's cool air whistled through his shining helmet as he looked to the sky. His face seethed with resentment as an array of different colors reflected off the horizon far off in the distance. No one but him understood the true reason the sky surrounding the island shimmered at certain points throughout the day. To them, it added to O'Varth's beauty. To him, it was an unbreakable cell door, locked for eternity. *They sent me here to serve. Giftless. Only to trap me here forever,* he thought as his upper lip shuddered from the rage. His attention shifted below to the city's center. His eyes fell on a group of young Drudge that caused an odd suspicion to flood his veins. On a typical day, nothing about the Drudge caught his attention, but he recognized these three. Everyone in Levitheton did. The *Drudge* children to Seared parents. As he leaned in to examine closer, the three looked away, and a shout from inside the tower stole his attention.

Labarth, his main Shifter, entered the portico. Kneeling before him, Labarth wore an elegant cloak containing colors matching the forest surrounding the city. Along with his cloak, metal armor protected his wrists, legs, and throat. His eyes held a perpetual look of deceit while his smile was like a *nachash* approaching its prey. He was fair-skinned with graying golden-brown hair. His eyebrows were in constant descent, and surrounding his lip was a perfectly shaven bristled goatee. Labarth had served Levithe faithfully since birth and did not tolerate the other Seareds' slightest offense. Levithe enjoyed the executioner's duty, but for offenses he didn't wish to handle himself, he sent Labarth.

"Lord Levithe," Labarth said with his head bowed. "There has been an attempt by some of our own to breach the ruins. We have captured the few who tried to destroy a portion of the border wall. The Healers have been killed already, while the others are being held within the tower's prison, awaiting execution."

"Why do you waste my time with this?" said Levithe, walking towards his servant. "There have been thousands of attempts from many people over the years, and all have failed. Do not interrupt me again."

"Yes, Lord," Labarth spoke with hesitation. "But I also must inform you... four individuals entered the ruins at a location different from the explosion. We believe the explosion was a distraction."

"And you had them killed, I assume?" Levithe's eyes descended, heart rate steadily increasing.

"We... I... the Guards killed one intruder but have yet to find the other three."

Levithe's insides strained. *No one on this island knows the true history,* he thought. It was why he had the ruins protected. Levithe needed both Drudge and Seared to believe his revision. It gave him control and was perhaps the only reason he was viewed as the island's savior.

Levithe's chest glowed as he approached Labarth. He removed a razor-sharp dagger from his belt, thrusting it into Labarth's rib cage. Blood and air spewed from Labarth's lungs as he gasped for breath. Levithe clutched him by the throat and healed him as he said, "I will have every Guard, including yourself, slaughtered if you do not find them by this evening's sunset."

"As you wish," Labarth panted as he kept his head towards the floor, regaining the color in his face. Pulling an iron forged hammer and a metallic symbol from his cloak, Labarth choked on his words, "One of the guards found these on the incinerated body."

Reaching for the hammer and symbol, clasping them tight, Levithe analyzed them in excruciating detail. His squinted eyes shot open as they fixated on the symbol, and his face swelled with fury. "Call for an immediate count of every Seared in the city. I want the names of all who were outside the walls last evening."

Impossible, Levithe thought, continuing to gaze at the symbol. He knew this symbol well, but no one else should have had the faintest idea of its existence. With raised eyebrows, he gazed at the symbol, and for the first time in two hundred years, a small glimmer of hope surfaced in his mind. *If someone found this, they may have found others,* he thought.

The hope turned to urgency as Levithe paused for a moment,

then looked at Labarth. "It looks as if the prisoners will not be a waste of my time after all. Go, now!" Labarth leaped up and sprinted back into the tower.

Levithe hurried up the tower's winding stairs to the prison. Containing countless cells with bars made of the strongest metals, the prison was inescapable even for the Seared. Levithe desired the prison to appear like a pristinely kept palace to contrast the punishments that awaited the prisoners.

It's more torturous to be slaughtered while your surroundings are magnificent than in a dark depressive cell, Levithe thought as he approached. The former created a sense of what they would lose, while the latter caused begging for death. He found it much more appetizing to slit a throat while someone begged for life.

The prison was simply another means used to maintain order and control on the island. Occasionally, to remind people of his unyielding dominion, Levithe would ask for even innocent Seared to be brought to the prisons. Control and fear were his greatest allies, and he had used them daily for the past three hundred years.

As he arrived at the prison's entrance, Levithe sneered as he breathed in the treasonous prisoners' terrible smell. He paced toward the three cells at the end of the hallway that held the groups responsible for the explosion at the ruins. Without saying a word, his chest glowed as he opened the first cell door and completely incinerated the first person he saw. The young female Shifter didn't

THE SEARING STONE

have a chance to say a word as her flesh, along with her sand-colored cloak, disintegrated into black ash. The other prisoners backed up against the outer edge of the cells, staring at Levithe in horror.

"Now," said Levithe, removing his helmet and exposing a deadly handsome grin. "The first person to name the man and his companions who entered the ruins will leave this Tower innocent. It appears there are four of you. Perfect. I will give you one count per person before turning every one of you to ashes. One... Two..."

"Wait," said a man as he shifted his weight off the wall, stepping towards Levithe. "Lord, we were unaware of others. We acted alone in our attempt to enter the ruins. We..."

Blood sprayed across the room, dousing the immaculate walls, as Levithe's dagger sliced the man's throat. Staring at the others with anger, he shouted, "I did not come here for lies or for you to waste my time. Three..."

Before he finished, a beam of flame propelled from one of the prisoner's chests towards Levithe. Instantaneously, the man's flames collided with the massive beam of fire bursting from Levithe's chest. Levithe held the flames as he stepped toward the prisoner. With a shout that rattled the prison, Levithe poured forth all his power, engulfing the offender in flames, turning him into a pile of soot.

Levithe's rage released as he reached into his cloak, removing the hammer given to him by Labarth. "Enough of your foolishness! Every one of you will die a slow and excruciating death!"

As he raised the hammer to strike his first victim, he paused, noticing something peculiar about the handle. The leather was coming loose. As he unraveled it, a bone-chilling smile swelled across his face. At the base of the hammer's handle, there were three engraved letters.

R-Y-N

He let out an awful laugh and lowered the hammer as he stepped out of the cell. He took one last terrible moment to eye the rest of the prisoners in the additional cells. "It appears as if *all* of you are in luck. I will return to deal with you properly."

Ryn, son of Lora. He knew the Healer well. And his wife. *How did he get the symbol? Or enter the ruins?* He thought, squinting his eyes. Somehow, Ryn, one of his closest and best Healers, had committed treason right under his nose. Levithe's mind flashed to the time before the Devastation. The time he had incited his own rebellion. It brought a spoiled smile to his face. No one on O'Varth has matched his deceit. Even if Ryn had planned this, it had already failed miserably. After three hundred years, Levithe had finally discovered his first clue to possibly finding the fragments. He only needed to deal with the other three. *The three Drudge below,* he thought, as his heart raced with excitement.

Before leaving, he recognized a prisoner in the final cell. He let out a whistle to get the prisoner's attention. As the treasonous man made eye contact, Levithe held his stare for a moment and then winked. The prisoner began to tremble and yell as Levithe marched toward the stairway to find Labarth. The prisoner's screams caused Levithe's lips to coil into a menacing smile.

Ŏ

Lyu swung open the wooden door to their stone house, and the three rushed inside. Zayn breathed through his nose as he entered, and the familiar smell jolted his body. His chest caved as he laid eyes on their father's cot towards the back of the home. The crinkled blanket left from the day before lay perfectly still, a scene frozen in time. He felt his limbs weaken as his eyes bounced to the cooking area. Pots and bowls lined the wooden countertop, organized in their typical fashion. All he could picture was arriving home after a long day at the Docks and Ryn standing behind the counter cleaning and smiling back at them. The pressure built in his chest as he forgot to breathe.

The awful silence lingered as they all stared. Tanyel's face held a slack expression while Lyu's head dipped low. Zayn knew what would happen if they even glanced at each other, so he held off as long as he could.

Lyu stepped towards the back of the home, causing the floorboards to screech an unpleasant tune. Zayn's mind tried to numb as she slowly turned to face him. Her lips were pinched together, and her clouded eyes focused inward. *Not now, Lyu. It's too painful,* he thought. She reached for the pillow on Ryn's cot. As soon as it touched her hand, her legs buckled, and Lyu crashed to the floor. Clutching the pillow tight, her knees pressed to her chest as she leaned against the cot's wooden frame, weeping. Tanyel fell toward her, landing on one knee and throwing his arm around her shoulder. Zayn stood motionless, watching their tears crash into the knotted wood flooring. He fought to keep the pain buried, never wanting to feel the anguish again. But seeing Tanyel and Lyu gave him no choice. The terrible hurt he had been avoiding bubbled into an explosion of grief, crumpling him to the floor as tears poured from his fastened eyelids. Both hands covered his mouth, muffling his wailing and his curses.

Lyu's hand grabbed his good shoulder, causing his bawling rage to increase even more. He could barely make out her words as she spoke.

"Feel it, Zayn," she said as her voice rasped. "We can't keep this in. It will kill us if we do. Just keep feeling it until it stops. We've got you."

Her words both magnified the pain and supplied hope for it to end. *I made it through the ruins, I can make it through this,* he thought, clenching his fists.

The tears kept flowing as Tanyel and Lyu both sat and wept with him. As Lyu said, each heave became softer after a while, and each wail became shorter until finally decreasing into the occasional sniffle. Zayn never enjoyed crying, let alone weeping. The odd part was that anytime he did, it always seemed to bring relief.

Finally gathering the strength to stand, the three washed the soot and grime from their faces and hands and then collapsed into their cots. Zayn laid in silence for a few moments, crossing his hands behind his head, keeping his eyes closed. As he focused on his breath, a subtle wave of peace washed over him.

"Zayn," Tanyel said. "What did you mean when you said you thought we were being watched?"

Zayn shot up out of his cot, remembering the portico. "I'm not completely certain, but I could've sworn Levithe was staring right at us."

"How would he ever suspect us, though?" Lyu asked, sitting up placing both palms on the wooden frame.

"I don't know, Lyu," Zayn said, lowering his head slightly. "But what if somehow he knows? And even if he doesn't, the Guard found the hammer *and* the symbol."

Lyu gripped the cot tighter as her eyes turned to a darting gaze.

"Zayn's right, Lyu," Tanyel said. "I think there is a good chance Levithe will never find out it is us, but I don't think we should waste any more time in the city than we have to."

"In that case, we need to check the scroll again," Lyu

responded. "You two focus on the map, and I will make some fish stew."

Lyu stood and stretched, wiping her blushed cheeks as she headed to the cooking area. She grabbed a few dried fish hanging from a string that stretched across the counter. Lyu sliced the fish in even parts as she started a small fire under a stone bowl, adding water, fish, some greens, and spices. The aroma of the stew filled Zayn's mind with memories of his parents' cooking during the springtime. Zayn's posture relaxed as he watched Lyu prepare the meal. All he could see was their mother's strength and beauty.

Tanyel took the tattered scroll from Zayn and spread it across his cot.

As Zayn stood up, his teeth chattered as the pain in his shoulder crawled up his neck. He placed his opposite hand on Tanyel's shoulder to keep his balance. They began examining the section of the scroll displaying the map of O'Varth.

"Zayn, you mentioned the red marks by the Docks of Stone here," Tanyel said as he pressed his finger against the map.

"Yes. It may have been a coincidence, but those markings are what led us to the vessel," Zayn responded.

"Look," said Tanyel, frowning. "There are red markings all over this map. The Ring of Ascent, the Netting Docks, all major lakes and marshes, the Tuskoth Caves, even the Barren Plains. It doesn't seem to be much help for our next step."

THE SEARING STONE

With the steaming smell of fresh greens and fish in the air, Lyu stopped stirring the stew and walked over to examine the map. She placed her hands on Tanyel's shoulders and leaned over. Her eyes widened as she pointed towards the bottom of the scroll. "Here, you see!" she said, tapping the parchment. "The poem!"

> *The spring is quenched here alone*
> *do not look back to towns of stone*
> *continue on until you parch*
> *toward wooden docks do keep the march*
> *many dark doors they may appear*
> *choose the one you hold most dear*
> *the mist you feel will stir your heart*
> *looking back to see the start*
> *always move towards what is known*
> *there you'll find a missing stone.*
> *Andyr son of Roselyn (Incinerator)*

They stared, speechless, as the words seemed to echo off the room's walls. "Grandfather at it again!" Tanyel said, staring sparkle-eyed at the scroll. "Just like on our boat, Zayn!"

"It's just the clue we need," Zayn responded. "Now read it again, slowly." The Remnant's plan seemed too perfect for them to fail. *We will find it, Father,* Zayn thought. It seemed incredibly strange, talking to his father in his head as if he were standing beside him. But surprisingly, it helped the grief.

They read the poem a hundred times over, trying to decipher where it led. Tanyel was the first with an idea.

"The O'Varthian *spring* quenches at two places on the island, according to this map. The marshes and the Barren Plains. There are tons of watering holes in the marshes. Perhaps the Stone is underwater?"

"Possibly," said Lyu. "But what if spring means the season and not the river? There isn't any mist near the marshes. And..." Lyu paused as she lifted the scroll for a closer look. She glared at the words as her mouth swelled to a smile. "Remember what Father used to say to us when we were younger?" She slowed her voice and repeated the words in her father's tone, "*If you look back, you can see where we started...* The Tuskoth Caves! It's the only spot where you get a view of the entire island!"

"But what does the rest mean? There are hundreds of entrances to the caves. How would we know where to go?" He stopped for a moment and reread the words. He nearly leaped out of his cot. "*Toward the docks.* It's saying to go south! *The dark door you hold most dear.* Where did we always go as kids? The southernmost entrance of the caves! It says to *move towards what is known.* It has to be it!"

The three stared at each other with a sense of triumph. Once again, their father had given them exactly what they needed. Lyu, with tears welling, held a faint smile. As she walked back to the steaming stew, she swatted at some insects hovering over the bowl and dished up three separate portions. As she handed the meal to her brothers, the sound of their growling stomachs echoed through the home. Taking their first sips, their shoulders fell, and they experienced a momentary sense of relief and comfort. Tanyel reached for the scroll, rolled it back up, and handed it to Zayn.

"Tanyel, you focus on the packs, clothing, and bedding. Lyu, will you gather the rations, flints, and waterskins?" said Zayn. "We need to leave as soon as we can."

"What are you going to do?" Tanyel asked with a hint of mockery

"You'll see," Zayn said, winking back.

The glare from the sunlight flashed directly into Zayn's eyes as the others began to stuff the three packs full. As he took a few steps toward the cooking area, the wooden floorboards screeched the same familiar tune, increasing his pulse and sending a rush of energy through his chest. He bent down, and with one arm, he pried open the boards of his parents' storage area and peered inside. His mouth spread into a wide grin as he reached down and removed a cloak with heavy items wrapped inside. Unraveling the cloth, he accidentally breathed in the dust, causing an outburst of coughs.

"Zayn, are you okay?!" Lyu asked.

"I... was packing... and the dust..." Zayn said, still coughing.

Both Lyu and Tanyel's eyes gleamed as they immediately noticed the stash of weapons and tools in Zayn's hands.

"Good eye, brother. These are perfect," Tanyel said as Lyu nodded.

Zayn reached down as his cough dissipated and grabbed the wooden bow and quiver. As he carefully raised it to his left eye with one arm, it reminded him of all the times his father and Ganya would take him *muwr* hunting. Fishing was Zayn's typical trade, but hunting was for pleasure, even though he had little time for it. Lowering the bow and plucking the string with two fingers, he looked at his siblings with his chin high and said, "I'll take this one."

Lyu reached for the stash and grabbed Erym's short sword. The blade had multiple engravings, and when she raised it to the sunlight, hundreds of tiny beams of light scattered across the room. "I don't remember much at that age. But I do remember when she gave me this." Lyu swung it fiercely in a circular motion in front of her chest and over her shoulder.

Lastly, Tanyel stumbled over to the stash and raised an iron forged hammer with a leather handle. A replica of the one their father lost in the ruins. Strong enough to crumble stone, it had a long thick spike on the back that could pierce even the strongest armor.

Before Tanyel claimed it as his own, he detected something

on the handle causing the color in his face to dissipate. Raising it to the light, Zayn stared in horror as he noticed the letters *R-Y-N* engraved into the handle. Zayn's bow contained the same carved letters. Examining her sword, Lyu lost her breath when she saw her mother's name. They stood in shock as Zayn realized they had reached the same conclusion.

Suddenly, Zayn's heart nearly left his chest as a rhythmic pounding at their door froze every part of his body. He raised his hands to his siblings' chests, signaling them to remain absolutely still. Inhaling through his mouth, Zayn quietly shoved the weapon stash under the flooring and hid the travel packs behind them.

"Children of Erym!" shouted a guard. "Open immediately, or your home and everything in it will be incinerated."

Lyu headed towards the door as the others tried to stop her. She looked at them and took a deep breath, motioning them to calm down. She opened the door and bowed as she said, "How can we serve you today?"

Zayn's anger rose as he recognized Labarth standing at their front door, scowling down at Lyu. The perfectly shaven man seemed to slither through the door, accompanied by an Incinerator and Healer. "Fine place you have here. We are looking for your father, Ryn. Are you aware he is missing?"

Zayn tried to speak, but Labarth interrupted with an unsettling rage, "Choose your words wisely, Drudge. There is a good chance your father has committed treason against both the city and Lord Levithe. Now, you must be keenly aware of the punishment for treason, considering who your mother is."

Zayn recoiled in confusion at Labarth's piercing words. He had never interacted with Labarth before, but it reminded him exactly of his interactions with Labarth's son, Stawb. They were the same. Both Shifters, both vile as could be, and both despised the Drudge.

Labarth paced across the room, mocking them with his smirk, gliding his fingers across the dusty furniture. As he walked past the three, Zayn's stomach dropped when he saw Labarth eyeing the packs. The slow draw of Labarth's voice was clear as he said with a smile, "Packing for a trip?"

Zayn, Tanyel, and Lyu stood together with no words as Labarth drew closer.

"Do you think the Levithe, the *god* of this island, can be lied to!?" screamed Labarth, grabbing Lyu by the chin and licking his lips. "He is all-knowing and is always three steps ahead of the treasonous! No one has or will ever get the best of him!"

Before he spoke again, his eyes twitched, and his face shimmered. His grizzled goatee disappeared as his long nose shortened. The shape of his face and body shrunk as his leathery skin changed to smooth olive. All three of the siblings' eyes widened. Standing before them in all of her beauty and grace was Erym, their mother, with Larbarth's armor dangling off her body. Labarth, in the form of Erym, looked at Zayn with disgust and said, "My firstborn, what a complete waste of a human you have turned out to be. I assumed you were pathetic, and your father and I would often discuss how we wish you never existed. In fact, the main reason we chose to forgo the Stone was that you would never be worthy of being Seared." Zayn fought the urge to rip Labarth to shreds, then the form of his mother turned to Tanyel. Erym's voice echoed through the room. "My sweet middle son. I was actually pleased when I died, knowing I wouldn't have to be around you any longer."

Zayn and Tanyel couldn't contain their tears, even though they knew the truth. Every fear and insecurity came rushing forth as they listened to the words pouring out of this false Erym's mouth.

Erym removed a dagger from the armor that hung loosely off her body. She touched the blade to Lyu's throat and hissed with a smile, "My dearest daughter. Your father and I never loved you. We wanted a third son, and you were quite the disappointment. Now answer my question and live. Where is your father, dear?"

As Zayn watched Labarth's blade press toward Lyu's neck, his insides screamed. *I have to do something,* he thought, but he was frozen in place. Sweat formed on his forehead when he saw Lyu wince as a drop of blood formed on her neck. Zayn perceived Tanyel's rage, and just before Tanyel spoke, a shout from outside the home caught everyone's attention. Labarth shifted back to his appearance, continuing to hold the knife to Lyu's neck.

"Zayn, Tanyel, Lyu!" A familiar voice yelled. A man, slightly taller than their father, burst into the room out of breath. With golden hair and fair skin, he was nearly a spitting image of Ryn. Hope flooded Zayn's heart as their uncle stared back at them.

Typher caught his breath, surveying the room, noticing their packs. "Where have you three been?!" he yelled with a hint of anger. "I've been trying to find you all morning and tell you your father is in the main market. He packed three packs for you so we could all go visit and honor Erym at the Tombs of the Seared."

Tanyel looked at his uncle with new confidence and said, "We were just out along the roads to the Netting Docks. The forest along those roads usually provides some good greens and berries for our rations."

Labarth looked at Typher and said, "Shouldn't you be performing your mindless street acts for the Drudge? You are a sorry excuse for a Shifter with your foolish story-telling and witless acting."

"You know me," Typher smirked, looking at the siblings. "I'm the best actor Levitheton has ever known. Besides, I rather enjoy being around the Drudge. They feel like family to me. Shouldn't you be washing Levithe's feet instead of threatening the innocent?"

Suddenly, the awful resounding sound of Levithe's horn boomed in the distance. Labarth's eyes twitched as he turned towards the exit, shouting at the two accompanying guards, "To the market, immediately!" As Labarth stepped toward the door to exit the home, he looked behind him once more and said, "When we find your father, we will make you watch his death." Zayn's shoulders released as Labarth and the guards left. The sound of the slamming door shook the house as Zayn looked back at his uncle.

Typher met his gaze and said, "Ryn told me he was planning something, but I didn't think it involved you three."

They took a few deep breaths as the fear wore off. The smell of fish from earlier still lingered in the air. Typher filled some water skins and handed one at a time to the siblings, saying, "You know as well as I do Ryn isn't at the main market. So where is he?"

"I will tell you," Zayn said, closing his eyes. "But you may want to sit down for this, Uncle."

Chapter 4

Out of Levitheton

ZAYN RETOLD THE EVENTS as best he could, while Typher stared back in astonishment. With his hand inside his cloak, Zayn thumbed the metallic symbol his father gave him and continued, "Father found a way inside the ruins, Typher. We had no idea what was happening as the Guard pursued us, but Father asked us to trust him, so we just kept following him."

"Wait, wait..." interrupted Typher, standing up as he scratched his chin and angled his head with a modest gesture to the right. "Hundreds of people have tried to enter over the past three hundred years, and not a single person has come close to those ruins. How did he find out about the entrance?" He continued to stare at them, still scratching his chin. Exposed on his wrist was the seared flesh displaying the two-faced Shifter symbol.

"It's a lot to take in, Uncle," said Zayn, sipping his waterskin. "Trust me, we're in the dark almost as much as you are."

Lyu made eye contact with Typher and said, "Father told us we were searching for something... something that would help us defeat Levithe." Zayn's cheekbones gritted. *She can't tell him. No one can know about the symbols,* he thought.

"A scroll, Typher... an ancient scroll, hidden deep within the ruins." She paused and eyed Zayn and Tanyel. Zayn hid his sigh as he realized Lyu's lie. Ryn gave no exceptions for people knowing about the symbols, but the scroll would be just as believable once Typher saw it.

"A scroll?" Typher's voice boomed.

Lyu continued, "Yes, Uncle. One with maps, symbols, poems, and the clues to the *real* history of our island." She paused, seeming to gather strength for her next sentence. "After we found the scroll, we heard the Guard pursuing us. We thought we had lost them, but somehow, they found us. Father led us up a stairway to escape, and..." she choked on her words.

Tanyel, with tears flowing down his face, said, "The Guard destroyed the stairway, Typher. All of us had made it up except... Father." Tanyel's tear-soaked face glistened with rage. "Then they incinerated him... murdered him in cold blood. He didn't even have a chance to speak. Father spent his whole life serving Levithe as a Healer, and this was his reward?!" Tanyel shook his head, staring towards the floorboards. Zayn's anger and grief bubbled within as Tanyel spoke. He couldn't shake the image of Ryn's face just before he let go. *You were so calm, so sure. How is any of this going to be okay?* Zayn thought.

Noticing Typher, his spinning thoughts halted. Typher stared back with a cold gaze. He seemed to be staring right through them. His eyes became glossed over as his brows held the slightest decline, making it seem as if he were ruminating about thousands of ideas at once. Zayn and the others attempted to move closer and comfort Typher, but the cold look remained, even as they embraced him.

He stepped back and looked down at them with tearless, bloodshot eyes. Zayn looked at Lyu, and she raised her shoulders, sharing in the confusion at Typher's response.

"Uncle," Zayn said, pointing to his wounded shoulder, "I tried to save him. I tried to pull him up. It wasn't possible." Zayn's throat tightened as the words came out.

Typher took a quick breath through his nose, shaking his head. He seemed to be fighting to re-center himself before he spoke. Then finally, with a calm voice, he said, "Whatever is in that scroll must be worth it. Your father wasn't just my brother. He was my best friend. I promise to be with you wherever you go. Whatever you need, I am here."

Even though Zayn didn't understand Typher's way of grieving, he and his siblings had always viewed their uncle as a second parent. He was with them their entire lives, always there to listen and to make them laugh. Typher was the only person they trusted to help them carry out their father's wishes.

"Labarth will be done searching the main market any time now, and when he is finished, this will be his next stop," Typher said. "We need to find a way out of this city. Where did your father tell you to go next?"

"The Tuskoth Caves," said Tanyel, subtly chewing on his lip. "A journey just like when we were younger. You always loved sticking back with us while Mother and Father kept ahead." He forced a smile, but even Tanyel couldn't hide his emotion when he spoke of their parents.

Typher's mood seemed to shift as he grabbed Tanyel by the shoulder, giving him a slight shake. Reaching for the three travel packs, he said, "I'm a new man, Tanyel. This time, you will be the one who needs to keep up."

"Especially since you'll be carrying my pack until we can find a Healer," Zayn said, attempting to lift the mood. It had been one of the worst days of their lives. But if they could laugh by the Tombs of the Drudge, they could figure out a way to smile even during their own grief.

"Only because you're my brother," Tanyel said, rolling his eyes, bending down to grab both packs.

Typher tossed the remaining bag to Lyu, then reached for the door handle to exit the home.

"Wait," said Lyu, reaching for the floorboards below. "We can't leave without these." Light scattered across the room as she lifted the short sword above her head. Zayn stood tall as he took his bow and watched as Tanyel snatched the hammer. Lyu extended the stash towards Typher, and he picked a small dagger that slid easily into his cloak pocket.

As they packed up their final belongings, Zayn noticed Tanyel and Lyu placing their symbols into a rolled blanket and shoving it into their travel packs. He reached into his pocket, thumbing the symbol, and decided to leave it there, keeping it close. Typher stood at the door. Pressing it open, he signaled them out towards Levitheton's stone-paved streets. As they exited, Zayn paused and looked back at his home realizing he might never see it again. The laughter, love, and memories built within these walls would far outlast the stone that held them. Yet, the pain, tears, and grief he experienced there would always remain. "*Grief softens but never disappears*," Ryn's words after their mother died echoed through Zayn's head.

Typher tugged at Zayn's pack, saying, "We need to stop by my place to gather a few things before we leave the city. I have a plan to get us out of here. If Labarth knows about Ryn, then so do the guards at the entrance gates. Lyu, lead the way."

Zayn ran behind as Lyu led them north, back across the city center. Because of Typher's success as an entertainer, he was fortunate enough to live in one of the most luxurious homes in Levitheton. The bustling sounds of the surrounding city momentarily distracted Zayn from his grief. Sweet smells of perfumes and oils flooded his nostrils as they passed through the most elegant part of the city. Small street vendors were shouting as street performers caused people to gasp in awe and tear up with laughter. Because of his parents, he had always gotten a taste of the extravagance surrounding him. But the constant tease of the Seared life was torture. The taste had never been enough. It only caused him to starve.

As they continued towards Typher's home, they once again passed the Searing Stone. More infants were being brought before it to receive their Searings. The tower to the north reflected the Stone's blue flame off the metallic homes and shops surrounding the city's center. Zayn exhaled with relief when he realized Levithe was not on his throne on the portico above.

Continuing north, the chattering sounds of the city's center faded. The homes surrounding them were made of exquisite metallic architecture, leaving anyone who passed by with a sense of envy.

A nagging, familiar voice shouted from behind them just before they arrived at the alleyway leading to Typher's home, causing

Zayn's body to tense. *Not now,* he thought. *Any time but now.*

"If it isn't the *Drudge* children of Erym," sneered the voice.

Zayn turned his head and laid eyes on none other than Stawb and Feeld, accompanied by an Incinerator. Their pristine purple cloaks draped over their bright white buttoned shirts and pants. With golden hair that laid perfectly straight across his forehead, Stawb wore a scowl just like his father, except for a large blotch of darkened skin near his lip. He was shorter than Lyu and frailer than a decently fed Drudge. Feeld had black curled hair and bleach white skin. With a voice even more shrill than Stawb's, Feeld's bright red freckled cheeks glowed like an Incinerator's chest as he glared at Zayn. He hobbled behind Stawb with an ever-increasing limp and because of the ailment, he should have been a throwaway. However, his parents were in denial and chose to Sear him anyway.

Eyeing Zayn, Stawb said, "Have you gotten a chance to visit the Tombs recently? The Tombs of the Seared that is... I hear Erym was buried there a few years back... well, what was left of her, at least."

Tanyel stepped forward with an enflamed face, reaching for his hammer. "Say her name one more time." The Incinerator's chests glowed, causing Tanyel to freeze.

"Ah, yes," Stawb said, smiling. "A hammer won't help much if you are ash now, will it?"

"Still need others to fight your battles, Stawb?" said Lyu,

approaching. "Now step aside, or I will shred you with my bare hands until you cry for your useless father."

Stawb ignored her and kept his eyes on Zayn. "What about you? The eldest. Aren't you going to stick up for your sweet baby sister?"

Zayn was fuming inside but remained composed and spoke, "You have it all backward, Stawb. You see, unlike yourself, my sister can fend for herself. I just can't wait to watch."

Stawb's scowling face darted towards Lyu. "Sweet Lyu. We will never take orders from a soiled Drudge. I think I will take you up on your challenge."

Stawb's body shimmered as he changed form. Lyu shook her head as she realized what he was doing. Zayn took a few steps back as he looked at his own appearance standing before him in Stawb's clothing. He glanced over at Typher, who was rolling his eyes.

Tanyel chuckled, taunting Stawb, "Trust me, Stawb, that will only make it worse. She is always at Zayn's throat. You've only given her a better target." Zayn smiled as he saw the anticipation on Lyu's face. She was the strongest woman he knew. He wasn't worried about her for a moment.

A pitiful voice came from Stawb's new form, "Lyu, please... please don't hurt me. I need protection." Then, without warning, he threw a punch directly at her face. Lyu ducked and gave him a quick jab to the center of his stomach. Stawb's eyes shot open as he coughed and placed his hands on his knees. With immense force, Lyu leaped and spun, smashing her left heel directly into Stawb's jaw. Spit flung across the road as he slammed onto the paved street, causing a small cloud of dust to kick up around Lyu. She drew her sword, standing above him, pressing the blade to his throat. She glared down with the most taunting smirk on her face.

"I told you we would have a chance to embarrass them," she said, winking at Tanyel.

Tanyel laughed, shouting in victory as he pulled Lyu back and dusted her off.

The Incinerator and Feeld helped Stawb to his feet as he shifted back into his form. His eyes blazed at Lyu as blood poured from his mouth.

"As Tanyel said, your Shifter trick won't work on me, Stawb. Do you want to go again?"

Stawb attempted to lunge for her once more, but his companions held him back. As Zayn and the others tried to move forward, Stawb continued to order his crew to block their path. Clearly fed up, Typher pulled his hood over his head and stepped in front of the siblings, bending to Stawb's level. Zayn witnessed Stawb's eyes turn to terror as an awful voice poured from Typher's mouth. "Move!"

Stawb and his posse nearly fell to the ground as Typher pulled his hood back down and walked past them. Zayn and the others followed quickly behind.

"What was that, Uncle?!" Tanyel asked.

Typher turned to them and smirked. "I may or may not have turned into the person he fears the most." Zayn looked at Tanyel and Lyu, and they fought to hold back their laughter. A shared enemy seemed to always bring them closer. Especially when they won.

"Now, let's keep moving," Typher said under his laugh. "We have had too much of Labarth's line for one day." Zayn nodded and followed. Lyu took a quick right to a small alley and approached Typher's front door. Typher swung the door open for the three siblings and rushed them in with the wave of a hand.

"I always loved this place more than ours," smiled Tanyel. "The decor is better, the beds are more comfortable, and it doesn't always smell like fish." Typher smirked back at him.

"What is the plan?" Zayn said in a hurry, eyeing Tanyel. "Every moment we waste gives Labarth and his guard more time to find us." The words brought them all back to reality.

Typher walked across the main room, glancing around. On the walls hung fabric of all different colors, along with several creatures' skeletons. One in particular always caught Zayn's eye. Mounted in the center of the wall hung the skeleton of a *baraqra* queen. It had razor-like armor and one massive socket where the eye once was. Individually, *baraqra* were only the size of a pillow, but everyone knew their shells were as efficient as an axe.

"Did you kill that, Typher?" Tanyel said, pointing to the hanging *baraqra* skeleton. "Or did our favorite Drudge, Ganya, gift it to you?"

"No," Typher said as he winked. "It was a gift. I'm sure you could kill one with ease, though. I'm not nearly as brave as you are."

The kitchen area was built of pure metal with well-defined edges, giving it an elegant appearance. Instead of the two bedrooms they had at their home, Typher had three. The cots' bases were made of stone, and instead of grass for sleeping on, there were bundles of cloth about a fist's width, providing extremely comfortable padding.

At the far end of the room, Typher shuffled through his belongings and let out a sigh of relief. He bent down and opened a massive wooden chest. Inside were many types of costumes, dresses, and armor for his entertainment. Typher took his work as a Shifter seriously and was the best storyteller the three had ever known. Shuffling through the garments, Typher pulled out what he needed.

"Lyu, Zayn, wear this," he said, tossing some Incinerator Guard armor and two helmets. "Tanyel, you will be our Healer." Typher threw a sand-colored cloak with a small matching headband across the room to Tanyel. "Lastly, I will be our Shifter." As Typher spoke, he lifted an elegant cloak with colors matching the forest's, along with some metal armor. Something about the cloak was familiar to Zayn.

"This is how we will leave the city," Typher said as he

squinted at the siblings, adjusting the armor around his throat.

"I don't understand," said Zayn, but before he continued, his eyes widened with both fear and hope. Typher transformed his appearance before them into none other than Labarth.

"We will exit this city as Labarth and his crew. The Guard would recognize me, but this city contains countless Incinerators and Healers who will never notice you. Promise you will follow my every move."

"We promise," the three said in unison as they changed into their outfits.

Lyu's face displayed her distaste for the disguise as she placed the heavy armor over her shoulders. Tanyel, on the other hand, swiftly threw on the Healer cloak, wearing a large grin. Despite his fair skin, dressed in full Healer garb, Tanyel looked just like their father.

Zayn smirked as he grabbed his own armor, flinching in pain as he slipped it over his hurt shoulder. They hadn't had time to find a Healer. He would have to manage. Securing the armor, he noticed the giant hole in the center of the chest piece. Ironically, the most vulnerable part of an Incinerator was exposed at all times. *If I had my bow, I could have sent an arrow through their chests,* he thought as he placed the helmet over his head. He couldn't let go of the what-ifs. Thousands of details led up to Ryn's death, and Zayn could have stopped any one of them.

Zayn's heart steadily increased as they followed Typher out of the house. They planned to exit the city through the Southeastern Gates. The entrance was in the opposite direction of the main market, where Typher had led Labarth and his crew astray. They headed south and passed through the center of town once more. Just as they reached the southeastern edge, Zayn looked back towards the Levithe's tower. Faltering mid-step, he felt a dense knot form in his throat, not allowing him to swallow. Levithe stood at the portico's edge, glaring back and forth, appearing to be searching for something. Zayn shouted towards his family ahead, "Levithe is back at the portico!"

Suddenly, a horn sounded that shook them all to the core. Zayn's eyes shot back to the portico, and to his horror, Levithe was staring directly at them, yet again. Zayn's heart raced as he saw Levithe nod and turn back to march inside the tower. The awful horn was the sound alerting the city Levithe was leaving his tower to make an example of offenders. *There is no possible way he knows,* Zayn thought.

Lyu grabbed Zayn by the shoulder, breaking his attention, and said, "We have to go now!"

Zayn trailed behind as they walked faster than normal, but not at a pace that would cause suspicion to those around them. They wound through alleys and streets to make sure no one would follow them. The surrounding air smelled of fish and dust with a hint of cedar, oddly calming Zayn's nerves. As they made their way past the stone and wood-built homes, something caught Zayn's eye.

"Lyu, Tanyel, look," Zayn said, approaching one of the wooden buildings and pointing. Just above the doorpost of a home was a scratch mark.

Lyu gasped as she realized the red color of what Zayn was pointing at and said, "It's the same mark as the ones on the map!"

"It has to be a coincidence," Tanyel said, looking around and examining the other homes. Suddenly, a look of excitement rose on his face as his eyes fixed on a building across the street. "Or maybe not?"

"You mean the map from the scroll?" Typher said, confused.

"Yes!" said Lyu. "These exact marks were scattered all across the map of O'Varth."

Typher's brows descended as he responded, "You can show me once we make it out of here."

Zayn eyed his siblings as they treaded forward. He knew they were just as confused as he was. *Are the marks a trail? Or maybe they identify the Remnant?* He thought as ideas swarmed his mind.

They eventually reached the mud-shacks of the Drudge, the final section of the city before the Southeastern Gates. Because of their clothing and armor, the Drudge people fled into their homes at the sight of them. Zayn sensed an odd power overwhelm him as the Drudge ran. For a moment, he got to savor what it meant to be

Seared. Ashamedly, he loved it. The Seared normally didn't bother the Drudge, but whenever a group of them entered the mud-shacks, it didn't end well. They kicked more and more dust up with every footstep they took. Finally, Tanyel said with excitement, "The gates! We made it."

"Not yet, Tanyel," said Typher. "This will be the most difficult part. The Guards at the gate will want a specific answer for why we are leaving the city. It is Levithe's order for all Seared attempting to leave these walls."

Zayn remembered the times they left the city with their father. The Guard always inspected Ryn while ignoring Zayn and his siblings.

"You're right," Tanyel said, lowering his chin. "I wasn't thinking about how we would make it through them. So, Uncle... I mean, Labarth. What's your plan?"

"Let me do the talking."

They continued to follow their uncle as he moved towards the gates. Zayn's heartbeat pulsed through his neck, just below the ear. Lyu marched alongside her siblings with a cold face. Tanyel walked directly behind Typher, looking at his feet and hands as his sand-colored cloak swayed below, probably imagining what it would be like to heal.

As they approached the city's exit, one Incinerator guard accompanied by a Healer stood below an enormous opened gate that spanned the height of the walls surrounding the city.

Typher, with the voice of Labarth, spoke, "Fine day, my ladies. We require a visit to the Tombs of the Seared. It has been brought to our attention that a man wanted for treason may be headed there. We have brought our packs if there is a need to pursue the criminal further. It is by strict order of Lord Levithe, now out of the way and let us pass." Zayn was shocked at how perfect the impersonation was.

The two female guards marched up to Typher, showing no sign of intimidation. "So, it's the god's pet, Labarth, aye?" smirked one of the guards. "I didn't realize Lord Levithe allowed you to have pets of your own," she said again, maintaining eye contact with their uncle.

"We don't have time for games," shouted the voice of Labarth. "We need to get to the Tombs immediately." Zayn stared ahead through his helmet, avoiding any eye contact with the guards.

"Relax," said the other guard, smirking as she scratched her temple with her finger. "We will perform our normal inspection, and you can be on your way. Simply show us your Searings."

Zayn felt his cheeks burn as his heart spiked. *We are done for,* he thought, just waiting to be arrested.

"You can't be serious!" Typher protested. "Let us pass. There is no time for nonsense like this."

The Incinerator's chests glowed as she stood up tall, walking closer towards the four. "We will ask you one more time. Show us your brands, Seared."

Just before their uncle protested again, Zayn noticed something familiar about the two guards. As he opened his mouth to speak, Lyu said with conviction. "We are not Seared; we are Drudge. Our names are Lyu, Tanyel, and Zayn, children of Erym, and I beg you, please let us exit."

Typher, Tanyel, and Zayn glared at her in horror. "What is she doing?" Tanyel whispered to the others. With one final attempt to change the story, Typher yelled, "She is out of her mind, we…"

The two women removed their helmets as their glowing chests dimmed. Without their helmets, Zayn recognized them instantly. Old friends of their mother and father's, who they remembered meeting when they were young.

"Enough, Labarth," said the guards as they stepped closer to Lyu, leaning down to whisper. Zayn listened closely. "Lyu, daughter of Erym. You must not speak of this to anyone, but we are a small part of your father's plan. Many in this city believe in his work, not just those who helped with the explosion. A few days ago, your father gave us instructions to secure the Southeastern Gates the entire week following the explosion. We weren't sure why until now. You may pass, but we fear Labarth is too dangerous of a choice for traveling."

"Don't worry," Lyu said, sighing with relief. "It's our Uncle Typher, not Labarth. We are forever grateful for your service."

As Typher changed back to himself, the guards smiled and embraced him. "It's been so long," said Typher. "I barely recognized you two."

"Whatever you accomplish, it will be well worth the treason," said the guard as she stepped back under the massive gate. "We got your back at the gates. Now go. Levithe's horn sounded not too long ago."

As they turned to leave the city, Lyu paused, looking back at the guards, and said, "Remind me of your names... and is there any chance you could heal Zayn's shoulder?"

"Of course," said the guard in the Healer's cloak.

The guard walked towards Zayn with an enormous compassionate smile. With skin the shade of rich bronze and eyes as dark as Lyu's, she seemed to glow as the midday sun struck her face. The bulk of her thick dark hair was wrapped tight into a knot that sat perfectly on top of her head. A few of the loose curls sprung out to the sides as she placed her soft hand on Zayn's shoulder. Her eyes squinted once she looked at him with tears welling and said, "My name is Naye, daughter of Sheen, and I knew your mother very well before she died. Your mother and I cut off being close as your father started developing his plan. We didn't want there to be any suspicion of a rebellion. I used to care for you as babies when your parents would travel. Your mother would have been so proud of you." Zayn stared back at her as the pain in his shoulder both intensified and soothed all at once.

"Thank you, Naye," Zayn said. "Did I do okay at hiding the pain?" Naye's mouth opened wide as she let out an unforgettable laugh, hitting Zayn on his healed shoulder.

"Anytime, Zayn. It's so good to see you again."

"Deshome, daughter of Phee," the other interrupted, beaming at them. "Your mother was my mentor at a young age when my parents passed." With beautiful dark skin, incredibly kind eyes, and hair curled tight to her head, Deshome gave off a presence that made them comfortable and at peace. However, behind the kindness laid a fierceness even the toughest of men would not dare to challenge. She bowed slightly, maintaining her smile, and nodded toward the gates. "Now, please, will you get out of this forsaken city? We can't have you getting snatched up by guards who aren't as gracious as us." She paused and bowed her head, placing her hand over her chest, and saluted them with three final words. "For the *Remnant.*"

"Thank you," the four said with immense gratitude. A crisp breeze swept through the entrance as the four passed under the massive gates. Zayn exhaled with a new sense of confidence and hope, pondering Deshome's final words and remembering the red scratch marks from earlier. *The Remnant. The note from Andyr on the canoe. The name of the rebellion. How many people are in on this?*

Chapter 5

The Tombs of the Seared

GANYA, WITH HUNTING DAGGERS in each hand, knelt behind the creek's bank. His calloused palms began to sweat as he spotted a pair of *muwr* approaching his position. Adjusting his gripping on the knives, he felt his feet sink into the mud as he waited patiently to strike. Even a single female *muwr* would be enough for a monthly ration, but Ganya had found two males, and he was going to attempt to kill both at once.

Luckily for him, *muwr* were not dangerous like many other beasts on the island. However, their impeccable hearing and sense of smell made them spook and dash at even the slightest warning. Ganya had prepared well by covering his arms and legs in mud to mask his smell. He remained perfectly still as the two beasts continued toward him. With deep golden coats that glistened in the sunlight, the *muwr* walked on four impressively muscular yet thin legs. Their backs approached about chest high compared to the tallest of men on the island. A beautiful white mane stretched from the base of their chin straight down the middle of their chest. The most spectacular and valuable portion of these creatures, however, were their unique horns. Two ivory-colored spikes pointed directly to the sky, with no curve or angle. Just before the point, two more spikes forked at a perfect angle, and so on. Ganya licked his lips as he noticed that the approaching *muwr*'s horns each had four forks. *These will sell for a quarter year's wages,* he thought.

They were so close he could hear their breath. He knew to take them both he would need them to come to him. As the *muwr* lowered their heads to eat, Ganya bent down to the bank, grabbing a smooth stone. He would only have one chance, but he had to act now. Taking a small breath, he flicked the stone over the backs of the *muwr,* remaining silent as time slowed. As the stone hit the brush, an eruption of clomping hooves dashed toward him, sending tingles through his arms. *This is it,* he thought as a smile swelled across his face. Just as the *muwr* reached the bank to jump the stream, Ganya gripped both knives, thrusting them upward with immense force, aiming for the hearts. Warm blood splattered across his face as both *muwr* bleated in agony, crashing into the stream. Ganya leaped toward them once more, dodging their massive legs, sinking his blades deep into their throats. He took a massive breath, wiping the blood from his eyes as he stared at his catch in victory. "The greatest hunter this island's ever seen," he whispered to himself.

Catching his breath, he gutted and cleaned each *muwr*. As he sliced a perfect line down their white manes, the smell of guts and blood engulfed his senses. To him, the smell wasn't the least bit putrid. Instead, he inhaled the beautiful scent of pay, of survival. Ganya breathed deeply through his nostrils as he daydreamed what he would do with the hefty wage. Then, a faint sound in the distance caused his eyes to squint as he turned his head toward Levitheton. *Levithe's horn? Again?* He thought, confused. The first blast had occurred earlier that morning, just as he was leaving the Southeastern Gates. However, the second blast caused his heart to drop, realizing he had almost never heard two blasts in one day before. *Ryn?* He thought, squinting his eyes.

Ganya reached into the chest wall of each *muwr,* removing the blood-soaked organs and tossing them aside. He thought about his peculiar encounter with Ryn the day before. While the kids were working the Netting Docks, Ganya had stopped by Ryn's home. Ryn was frantic and talking to himself as he sorted through the home, preparing for what seemed like a trip. Ryn was mentioning things that confused Ganya. *Forging Stones? Healing vines? The ruins?* Ganya was used to Ryn's worries. After all, Ryn was one of the main leaders of the *Remnant*. As the sound of the horn blast replayed in Ganya's mind, something terrible twisted inside him.

As his worry increased, he forcefully carved the horns off the skulls, placing them in the soft mud, then using his knife, he stripped the golden coats from the carcasses. Reflecting on the day Ryn had recruited him to the *Remnant*, he specifically remembered his mind shattering into pieces as Ryn revealed the island's truths. He was no longer just a Drudge tossed aside by his parents. The *Remnant* gave him the chance to be a part of something so much more significant. Ryn and Erym and their kids had always been like family. If they were in danger, he needed to return to the city as fast as possible. As he finished removing each cut of *muwr* meat from the bone, his heart seemed to palpitate. *Please don't let it be him.*

Ŏ

Zayn absorbed the beauty of the rolling grassy hills as he gazed at the road leading east toward the caves. The cool breeze filled his nostrils with the aroma of a fine spring evening. Most of the area surrounding Levitheton was a vast, grassy meadow that spanned multiple leagues in all directions. The area was cleared of trees because of the city's need for lumber. A few hundred paces to the northeast were the Tombs of the Seared. Compared to the massive Tombs of the Drudge, which were located outside the western side of

Levitheton, the burial ground ahead was much smaller, more intimate, and incredibly ornate. Large carved stones and statues marked the tombs of each Seared who had passed away. His mother's included. In one sense, ten years had felt like an eternity. At the same time, though, her death seemed like yesterday. Zayn turned his attention back to the road. A few leagues ahead was the tree line to the beautiful, dense forest covering most of the island.

Typher removed his disguise as he motioned them to toss their armor aside. Zayn hesitated to do so but understood the armor would be too much weight and even more of a distraction. Even though his time acting as Seared was brief, Zayn thoroughly enjoyed every moment. Tanyel kept his Healer cloak but ditched the headband. Lyu, on the other hand, nearly leaped out of her armor, chucking it to the wayside, aggressively dusting her entire body off.

Zayn was still fixated on the encounter with the two guards at the gate. Their father had once again provided them with aid to their escape. First the boat, then this. A hint of relief stroked his body as he paced along the wide dirt road.

"Can you believe we made it out, Lyu?" said Tanyel as he walked with a bit of a skip. "Look at this view!"

"I know, brother. I'm just as surprised as you," Lyu responded with a wide grin.

Zayn interrupted as he kept up with Tanyel, "If Father set up the guards at the gates for us, I imagine that won't be the only time we will see his help on our travels."

"We can only hope," Lyu said, breathing in the fresh air with her eyes closed.

The rush from the escape momentarily distracted them from their father's death. Zayn's stomach tightened as they continued to get closer to the road leading to the Tombs of the Seared. He hated that his Father would never get a proper burial or a place at the Tombs. *I wish he were here,* he thought. Lyu and Tanyel noticed the change in his demeanor. Zayn turned around and saw Typher walking behind them, staring off into the sky with an inattentive gaze.

Zayn tapped Tanyel and Lyu and whispered, "We aren't the only ones who lost someone last night. This must be just as hard for him as it is for us. Let's give him some time." Tanyel and Lyu nodded in agreement.

As they continued their march east in silence, they crossed paths with many people coming and going from various places along the island's eastern part. A handful were Seared returning from their visits to the Tombs. However, the bulk of the foot traffic comprised the Drudge. Along the stream to the south, dozens of families gathered water in stone and wooden bowls. Companies of miners were rolling massive hand carts containing materials from the caves. Most fascinating of all included brave hunters, both male and female, carrying the meat, skins, and carcasses of O'Varth's most terrifying beasts.

Tanyel slapped Zayn's shoulder, frantically pointing, and said, "Zayn, there's your *shenrosh!* I can't believe she got one!"

As Zayn looked toward where he was pointing, his eyes shot open as he saw the large fur-coated carcass of a *shenrosh,* deadly fangs and all, draped over the back of a female hunter. He had always heard the stories about them, but this was the first time he had ever seen one up close.

Zayn's head tilted as he realized he had never quite seen the Drudge in such a fierce fashion before. The crippled throwaways surrounding them had no giftings, but perhaps they did have something special. Zayn reflected on how his mother and father always reminded him of his worth, even as a Drudge. He never quite believed them, but perhaps for the first time since his mother's death, seeing the Drudge before him with fresh eyes brought a small sense of appreciation.

Zayn saw Tanyel peeking back at their uncle again as they passed by the Tombs of the Seared. Something in him knew what he was about to ask.

"Uncle," Tanyel said with hesitation. "Why did Father never tell us about how our mother died?" Zayn tensed at Tanyel's words but had always wondered the same.

Typher didn't respond and continued to stare ahead as his spinning thoughts projected through his eyes. Tanyel looked back at Lyu, raising his shoulders, and she signaled him to try again.

"Typher," Tanyel said louder. "Did he ever tell *you* what happened?"

Typher snapped out of his trance, glaring at Tanyel, and said, "What did you say?"

Tanyel stepped back, responding, "Uncle, I was... just trying..."

Instantly, Typher's neck quivered, causing his glare to fade, and he said, "I'm sorry, Tanyel... I just can't believe he's gone."

"It's okay, Uncle," responded Lyu with welling eyes. "We can't believe it either, but he has saved us many times already." She paused, looking back at Zayn and Tanyel. "I don't think the pain will ever go away, but knowing that he had a plan to rescue us gives me enough strength to keep moving."

Typher wiped his hand across his eyebrows, looking at the dirt below. A moment later, he lifted his head, making eye contact with Lyu, and gestured to her with a thankful stare. He glanced back to Tanyel and said, "Your mother... she was a woman of even greater integrity and stature than your father. As we pass by the Tombs, you may honor her as I share her story." Zayn wasn't sure if he was ready to listen. If their father never dared to speak of her death, it certainly wouldn't be an easy tale. As he saw the eagerness in Tanyel and Lyu's eyes, he kept a straight face and leaned in. He wouldn't rob them of hearing the tale because of his own fears. They needed the story, not having nearly as many memories with her, especially Lyu.

"Ten years ago, when you three were still at the age of innocence, Erym and Ryn were two of the greatest Healers Levitheton had ever known," Typher said, glancing at the tombs once more. "Healers, as you know, normally focus on one of two things. Either they are healing themselves so they can live longer or healing the Guard per Levithe's order. Your parents were different. They never saw much use in extending their lives, especially since healing doesn't keep you from aging. So they focused their efforts elsewhere. Yes, they fulfilled their duties to Levithe, but they spent their spare time and energy tending mainly to you three and the Drudge. While most Seared look down on the Drudge, your parents always had a heart for them."

"It was obvious to us," said Tanyel. "From what I remember, our parents looked beyond what people possessed. So yeah, it would have been great to blast fire from my chest, but I'm okay with their choice for me. It doesn't matter whether I'm a wealthy Seared or a poor fisher with calloused hands. It matters what's in here. They taught us that." Zayn stared at Tanyel's hand as it pointed towards his chest. Tanyel *was* right, but Zayn's jaw still clenched at the words. Out of the corner of his eye, he saw Lyu's face tense as well, most likely for the opposite reason.

"That is exactly how they wanted you to feel, Tanyel," said Typher with a dim smile. "Caring for the Drudge was something Levithe never wasted his time with. To him, they are merely necessary pawns to support the city's most undesirable crafts. He normally doesn't bother with them unless they are distracting his Seared or causing trouble in the city."

"Is that why she was executed?" Lyu exclaimed, glaring at Typher. "She was too distracted by the Drudge?"

"No," replied Typher with a straight face, stepping aside to allow a mining cart to pass. "Erym was killed for committing treason. No one in the city knew why, except for your father and me." Zayn's eyes squinted. Labarth had mentioned a similar accusation against his mother earlier that day. Zayn would never have believed his words to be true.

"What do you mean?" Lyu asked, coughing on some dust kicked up by the cart. "Are you saying she was actually a criminal?"

"I would *never* call Erym a criminal," Typher said as he stepped towards the siblings. "She was anything but in my eyes. However, what she did is assuredly punishable by death. Levithe makes the law. He is the judge, and he decides who dies."

Typher paused to take a deep breath. He stood up straight and continued to share. "Do you remember your mother's friend, Sara?"

"Sara..." Lyu replied with a surprised stare. "She was a Shifter who lived in the house across the road from ours. Her parents died when she was young, and our mother treated her like family. She was basically my older sister growing up. However, after Mother's death, I never saw her again."

Typher nodded and continued, "Because she had no parents, Sara was one of Levithe's preferred picks for entertainment. He would perform horrendous acts of abuse on her just for pleasure. She would often return on the edge of death after serving Levithe, and your mother would care for her. It was awful to watch, and night after night, the anger and desire for revenge filled Erym's veins. When she couldn't take it anymore, she developed a plan she kept solely to herself."

Zayn wasn't as close with Sara but remembered her well. At the time, she was around Tanyel's current age. She would normally come over late at night, and Zayn remembered pretending to be asleep. His mother would care for her and, most nights, heal her. The tears and pain on her face were something Zayn would never forget. All these years later, Typher's explanation of what was truly happening caused his stomach to twist into knots.

Typher stopped and looked at the three with wide eyes as he whispered, "Your mother planned to kill Levithe."

Zayn, Tanyel, and Lyu shook their heads as their eyelids fluttered in confusion and terror. Zayn's heart pounded through his eardrums.

Lowering his chin to his chest, Typher raised his eyes toward them and said, "I'm sorry. Maybe it's best if I conclude. I don't want to cause you three any more grief."

"Please," said Tanyel. "No matter the pain, we deserve to know what happened to our Mother."

"Alright, but let's keep walking," Typher replied as he continued east on the dirt road. "The next time Levithe summoned Sara to his quarters, Erym went with a blade in hand, hiding inside the massive chest containing Sara's Shifter outfits. The Guard would help Sara carry the chest to Levithe's quarters, so she had everything she needed for her performances. Apparently, Sara blindfolded Levithe to surprise him while Erym crept out of the chest and slowly removed the blindfold. Before he spoke again, Erym thrust the dagger into his throat, hoping to finish him once and for all. Flames burst from his chest as he fell to the ground, gasping for air. Furniture and tapestries that hung throughout the room caught fire, alerting the Guard outside his room. When the Guard entered, it is said that Levithe had healed himself and began shouting with rage as the slit in his throat closed. A smoldering corpse was on the floor with remnants of a Healer cloak beside it. Before they reached the other person, they saw a flash of a brightly colored outfit leaping out the window."

The story was more painful to hear than Zayn ever could have imagined. Erym receiving the penalty of death would have been more bearable than outright slaughter. He recalled Levithe's terrible grin after he had incinerated the infant and mother at the Stone. Hate flooded his veins as he pictured him wearing the same grin after killing his mother. No words left his lips, only visceral hostility toward the island's *Great Savior*. All of them paced in silence.

Wiping a tear from her reddened cheeks, Lyu eventually broke the silence. "What happened to Sara, Typher?"

"The next day, when the Guard came to tell your father, I was there as well. They told us that Erym was dead and that we were to tell no one of what happened in Levithe's quarters. They threatened the punishment of the Tower prison and even death. I was shocked Ryn's death wasn't called for on the spot. Perhaps he was spared because Levithe didn't want any word going around about an assassination attempt. Or perhaps it was because Ryn was one of the best Healers Levithe had. When we asked about Sara, they said she was pursued toward the ridges north of Levitheton, and they found her body at the base of one of the cliffs. I'm so sorry, you three."

"Thank you, Uncle," Tanyel said, looking at Typher with bent brows. "It helps to know the story, but it doesn't make sense to me. Why would she try to kill him? She had to have known it was suicide." Zayn was asking the same questions in his head, and from Typher's look, he didn't seem to have any idea. As Zayn's mind settled, a single thought gave him a small amount of relief. *In the most terrible ways, I now have two parents who proved their love for me through their deaths.*

Zayn and Lyu grabbed Tanyel by the shoulders and embraced him. Typher continued to walk and motioned them forward with a head nod.

Not long afterward, they finally made it to the tree line. The more distance they put between themselves and the city, the better Zayn felt.

"We need to make camp soon," said Lyu. "We have a head start if the Guard knows which direction we went, but being close to the main road is too risky. I say we head through the forest due south and find a place to rest there." They followed without needing to respond.

As the four of them stepped off the road, Zayn looked around as the sun eclipsed the horizon. The last light of the day reminded Zayn of the evening before. Everything had occurred so fast. *I will protect them, Father. We will find the Stone,* he thought.

The trees' branches cast shadows across the forest as the clouds covered a portion of the sun as it set, causing a glowing fiery effect. Exhausted and out of breath, the four ascended a small ridge that led to a cliff with one of the river's streams below. The ridge gave them a pleasant view of the surrounding area. Zayn sighed as they reached the top, realizing the ridge's height just surpassed the tall pines below.

Lyu set her pack down, removed her short sword from her belt, and sat as she said, "This will work fine. We have a view of the road, and the trees provide suitable cover."

Zayn, Tanyel, and Typher sat down next to Lyu on the damp

grass, removing their weapons and packs.

"Now let's see that scroll," Typher said, removing some bread from his pack. "I haven't been able to stop thinking about it since you brought it up earlier."

Zayn removed the rolled parchment from his cloak and carefully tossed it to Typher, saying, "Perfect. I will put some food together for us."

Both Lyu and Tanyel scooted across the grass, racing toward their uncle, peering over his shoulder as he flattened the scroll across his lap. Zayn knew this was just the distraction they all needed to move on from both the grief of their father and story of their mother. He removed four portions of bread and dried fish and handed them to the others, positioning himself directly behind Typher for the best view.

Typher read out loud the title of the scroll, "*The Key to Our Escape.*" His finger slid down the fragile parchment, landing on the map of O'Varth. Zayn noticed something he hadn't realized before.

"Off to the side," Zayn said, pointing. "It's a magnified version of Levitheton, drawn with elegant detail."

"You're right," Lyu said, surprised. "Every home, shop, and mud shack seems to be accounted for."

Tanyel let out a faint gasp as he pressed his finger to the scroll. "Look at our home..."

Zayn immediately perceived what Tanyel was pointing at. A

faded, tiny red scratch mark was etched across the drawing of their home.

"And another one here," Tanyel said, pointing at Typher's home. "And Ganya's, and Sara's, and…" His words faded as they all gazed at the map. *The Remnant. This has to be them,* Zayn thought. A truly committed group of rebels all united to overtake Levithe right under his nose. Pride swelled in his heart for his parents. As his eyes fixed on the faded scratch marks scattered across Levitheton, he smiled at the plan's intricacy and extensiveness. A small part of him was beginning to believe that their plans for him were just as intentional.

"Deshome and Naye's homes are marked as well," Typher said, concerned. "There are close to a hundred houses marked on this map, and I'm actually familiar with most of the occupants."

"Can you imagine if Levithe ever got a hold of this?" Lyu said, shaking her head. "The *Remnant* would be eradicated."

"I don't think so, Lyu," Tanyel interjected. "There seem to be enough people here to end Levithe at any moment's notice. If Levithe dies, I'm willing to bet his faithful followers wouldn't remain so faithful."

"It's a valiant thought, Tanyel," Typher said. "But Levithe's Guard still outnumbers these scratch marks ten to one. There is a reason we haven't tried to take Levithe by force yet. It would be a bloodbath. The *Remnant* would never succeed."

Confused, Zayn said, "So what do you know of the Remnant, Typher? Why wouldn't Father tell you about his plans for the ruins."

Typher paused, looking up and to the right before responding, "Some are more involved than others. I, for one, happen to be a more passive member. I wait for instructions to come my way and follow once they do. Other than that, I'm not clued in on much."

The answer caused somewhat of a stall in their conversation. Subtle darkness consumed the camp as the sun eclipsed the horizon.

After a moment of brief silence, Typher adjusted the scroll on his lap to display the next main section. The giant, tree-shaped genealogy. Zayn's eyes immediately darted to the name at the top of the tree. *The one who started the rebellion. The original member,* he thought, reading the name aloud.

"Aven," Zayn mumbled. "Who is she?"

Notated just above the genealogy were the words *Post Devastation.* To the right of her name was a year marked 1 *p.d.* – followed by a blank. His eyes landed on a name halfway down the tree. *Abra son of Ninna 103 p.d. – 174 p.d. Every name from her lineage accounted for. A perfect way to breed a rebellion. Slow and controlled,* he thought.

Typher's head bounced back and forth as Tanyel spoke, "As you get about two-thirds of the way down, most names start to have symbols below, matching the ones from the Searing Stone in the city. However, why do some of the names have two?" Zayn looked again at

Aven's name and a few of the names toward the bottom. Sure enough, just below her name was the symbol for Healer and another he did not recognize.

"Maybe it's to represent some sort of status or ranking?" Lyu said. "Multiple giftings don't work. It's been tried a hundred times over..." She paused as she gasped, pointing to the bottom of the lineage. "Mother and Father's names, and yours, Typher!" Erym's name was on the far-left side of the scroll, whereas Typher and Ryn's were on the far right. Incredibly distant cousins from the same lineage of rebellion. The perfect match.

"And look!" Lyu said. "They both have two symbols. Their Healer symbols first, and then accompanied by a secondary symbol, each different."

Typher finally spoke with a hint of bitterness. "Lyu, your rank theory makes sense. Your parents were at the forefront of the plan and look at my name. Only the Shifter symbol."

The blackening sky made it almost impossible to see the scroll any longer. Despite the remaining questions, it was a perfect way to end their evening.

"We can look at the poems and stories another day," Typher said. "And I am still curious about the map of the ruins at the bottom. Thank you for indulging me." Tanyel and Lyu let out a sigh of discouragement.

Before Typher rolled it up, Zayn asked him for one last look.

THE SEARING STONE

Grabbing the scroll, he glanced back and forth at his parents' names on opposing sides of the parchment. *Erym, daughter of Hicho 260 p.d. – 290 p.d.* and *Ryn, son of Lora 259 p.d. –.* The numbing grief returned as he stared at the dates next to his father's name. He knew Ryn never expected for his dates to be completed this soon, and every fiber of Zayn hated that they now were. He reached into his pack and took out a writing feather, bringing the point to Ryn's name. Focusing on each stroke of the feather, he wrote the year 300 p.d. as tears rolled down his face. He missed his father so much. If only he were here to explain the scroll to them. Taking a deep breath in, he rolled up the scroll and placed it in his pocket.

The four of them ate their fill and eventually laid down with their hands crossed behind their heads, staring at the sky above. Tiny specs of light burst through the black night, taking their breath away. Because of the exhaustion, they laid in silence as their eyelids started to blink heavily.

"Sleep well," Lyu said before she dozed off to sleep. The soft chirping of insects mixed with the stream's flowing waters below caused the four to fall asleep in peace.

Before the sun rose, when the sky was dark and stars still provided more light than the dawn, Zayn's entire body went numb as he felt a hand grab his shoulder. Once he saw Tanyel, Lyu, and Typher sleeping soundly within his view, a sharp tingle ran down his back. The fogginess of sleep was making it extremely difficult for him to distinguish dreams from reality, yet the feeling of the hand's grip remained on his shoulder. As he gathered the focus to turn his head and look, a familiar whisper nearly made him pass out.

"Keep going, son. Protect them, and keep them hidden."

Chapter 6

The Traveler

AS ZAYN WHIPPED HIS BODY around to find out where the voice was coming from, the grip of the hand released. But nothing was there. The cliff's edge was a few paces off, accompanied by the sounds of insects and the stream below. Zayn blinked and plugged his ears multiple times as his heart raced. *It was just a dream,* he thought. *Father is gone.*

As he sat up and caught his breath, he watched his family sleep soundly next to him. The sounds of their breathing were distracting him from his feelings caused by the perceived dream. "It was too clear and felt too real to be a dream," he whispered to himself. Zayn figured it didn't matter, as long as the words helped him continue. *Keep it hidden*, he thought, remembering his father's command in the ruins. He had almost forgotten he had kept the symbol in his pocket. He reached into his cloak and handled the cold, hard shape of the metallic symbol. Zayn continued to whisper to himself, "This has to be it. My chance to finally become Seared."

With the sun still below the horizon, the others began to stir as the sky turned from black to a hazy blue. Zayn had been awake for a while, not able to shake the words from his dream. Tanyel stood and stretched with all his might as he let out a giant sigh. He reached down to grab his water skin and realized they were all nearly empty. The stream below flowed further south, and the only way to get water was to walk down to the base of the ridge and intercept the stream about fifty paces south.

"Let's draw straws for the refill," said Tanyel with a smile. "Or do you want to volunteer, Zayn?"

A branch cracked behind them, and Zayn jumped. Lyu and Tanyel laughed while yawning as Lyu held up a small rock like the one she had just thrown.

"Hilarious," said Zayn. "And no, I wouldn't want to steal such a courageous task from my valiant brother." Lyu let out a laugh as Tanyel smiled back.

Typher held out his hand, showing the ends of four small twigs. "Here you go. Let the twigs decide our fate."

One by one, they grabbed a stick. First, Tanyel drew and held it close, then Lyu, and finally Zayn. Zayn looked at his stick, annoyed, comparing it to his siblings'. Typher opened his palm, exposing the final twig, the longest of the four. Zayn shook his head and begrudgingly rose to his feet. At least it would help him take his mind off the dream.

"This isn't fair," he said as he picked up his bow and quiver. "I am taking this just for precaution."

Typher, Lyu, and Tanyel burst into laughter as they looked at Zayn. Zayn knew they loved him with all their hearts. It had been the most difficult two days of his life, but on his worst days, he was certainly glad he was with them.

"You got this, big brother," said Tanyel. "Give us a shout if you see anything out of the ordinary."

Zayn breathed through his nostrils with a quick breath and headed towards the ridge's base. He had one arrow knocked, ready to draw on anything that moved. As he reached the bottom of the ridge, he took quiet steps, eyes bouncing back and forth. It reminded him of the times he would hunt with Ryn and Ganya. As he approached the rumbling crystal stream, the lush forest grew extremely dense. The thick bushes and wet grass were up to his waist. His family's faint laughter back on the ridge caused a smirk to expand while he examined the rich sunlight reflecting off the dense clouds. As he raised his bow above his head, shifting himself towards the stream, he finally broke through the thick brush onto the soft mud of the stream's bank. He removed the four waterskins from around his shoulder, lowered to one knee, and filled them up one by one. Zayn took a slow deep breath and watched the water sweep over the stones, broken tree limbs, and boulders. He noticed some shallow areas full of debris and others deep enough for a swimming hole. The rushing sounds of gently flowing waters calmed his mind, and for a moment, peace washed over him.

Still kneeling, Zayn reached into his pocket and took out the symbol his father gave him. The dawn's initial rays of sunlight reflected off the symbol in his hand. He stared in admiration and realized his hypothesis in the ruins was correct. The symbol held the exact shape and size of the ones used on the Searing Rods. Yet, as he stared at the weaves and lines of the design, Zayn did not recognize the symbol itself. After scratching his head, he securely placed it back in his pocket and peered at his reflection in the water below. Before he stood, a soft breeze brushed against his face, and suddenly a terrible sound flooded his ears, causing chills to radiate through his entire body. A slow, repetitive clicking sound. He raised his head with as little movement as possible to see where the sound was coming from. Just across the stream, his eyes met those of one of the rarest and fearsome beasts on O'Varth. *Shenrosh*. Not just one, but an entire pack, staring at him with fangs exposed.

The clicking sound of the *shenrosh* pack grew louder with every breath Zayn took. With thick hind legs and arms that mimicked humans, the *shenrosh* crept closer toward Zayn on all fours. Even at 20 paces across the stream, the *beasts'* spines stood chest-level to Zayn. The pack's piercing yellow eyes didn't blink as they stalked forward, and their stunted snouts poured forth venomous saliva that was sourced from their hollowed fangs. The coarsely matted fur of these vile beasts blended in with the brush that surrounded them. One drop of *shenrosh* venom could paralyze an adult for days.

Zayn crept backward with immense caution, trying to slow his breathing and raise his bow for a clear shot. The sound of his heart pounding in his eardrums nearly drowned out the clicking noise around him. Just as he was drawing his bow to fire, the sound of a branch cracked beneath his feet. His heart stopped for a moment as he glanced down, and to his horror, the clicking noise became silent. Before he lifted his eyes to look, the battering sound of the stream's water and the charging noise of the *shenroshs'* shriek forced him to release the arrow blindly. With his luck, one of the six beasts yelped and crashed into the water as the arrow pierced matted flesh. Without hesitation, Zayn turned and sprinted back towards the ridge.

"Help!" Zayn shouted as he approached the base of the ridge. "*Shenrosh*! Behind me!"

His sister's distant scream taunted his ears as he sprinted.

"Zayn, don't look back! We're coming!" Lyu, Tanyel, and Typher were charging directly toward him with weapons drawn, ready to take on the vile pack of beasts.

Zayn leaped over some rocks that lined the ridge and knocked another arrow as he continued sprinting toward the camp. As he glanced over his shoulder, he saw the *shenrosh* in full pursuit, with water dripping off their darkened, soaked fur. The beasts' fangs were terrifying, but the most bone-chilling part of the pack was the way their hind legs elevated the back end of their body to nearly twice the height of their shoulders. The sharp descending angle of their spines as they sprinted was a site that gave the bravest of men nightmares. With each step Zayn took, shrieking and clicking filled his head with madness.

Knocking a second arrow, he swung around and stopped to get a perfect shot. Zayn drew the string, held his breath to steady himself, and released. Momentary relief overwhelmed him as the second *shenrosh* released an agonizing yelp as its body smashed into the dirt about forty paces down the ridge. The other four beasts paused for a moment to observe their fallen kin flailing violently in the dirt, yelping and shrieking to its death. The slow clicking sound pulsated as the yellow eyes fixed on Zayn. Instead of sprinting, the horrifying beasts slowed to a stalking motion towards him. He reached for his quiver, but before gripping an arrow, Lyu grabbed his shoulder while Tanyel and Typher spread out alongside them with their weapons drawn.

"I killed two already," Zayn said, wiping his brow, maintaining eye contact with the beasts below.

"Good shooting, brother," Tanyel said, with both hands gripping his hammer. "Now it's a fair fight. Four against four."

"Don't be so sure," said Typher while catching his breath. "A half dozen hunters have difficulty taking down one *shenrosh* unless they have a bow. Our best bet is to back away slowly and avoid a fight."

Fixing another arrow to his string, Zayn backed up and said, "The stream below! I know we're pretty high up, but parts of this stream are deep enough to make a jump for it." Tanyel's brows raised in anticipation.

"What choice do we have?" Lyu whispered, maintaining eye contact with the beasts.

Zayn responded confidently, "Stay at my pace and don't take your eyes off them. If they charge, we have to make a run for it. It's about a hundred paces to the top."

The family continued creeping backward, keeping a suitable distance from the beasts. The clicking sound remained consistent, and there were no signs of disturbance. Tanyel's knuckles were turning bright red as he gripped his hammer. Lyu maintained her graceful steps with one hand on Zayn's shoulder and the other on her mother's short sword. Typher kept a steady pace with the dagger still in his cloak. He appeared to be the most skeptical of this plan and seemed ready to dash towards the jumping spot at any moment.

While pacing back towards the cliff, they arrived at their

camp. Without stopping, each of them grabbed their pack, eye's forward, with no sudden movements. Zayn hesitated for a moment and remembered the scroll and symbol in his pocket. If he jumped, he would lose them in the water below. As he continued backward, he removed both symbol and scroll, burying them as deep as he could into his pack.

Suddenly, a deafening shriek, far-off towards the river, caused the *shenroshs'* ears to fly back as they whipped their heads around to inspect. Zayn's heart sank as he discovered the scream's origins. Ferociously sprinting up the hill with copious amounts of speed and adrenaline was the *shenrosh* he had shot in the stream. Blood was gushing out of its soaked body, and venomous foam was pouring from its mouth. As the pack became aware, they all let out a bone-chilling screech and immediately bolted towards Zayn and his family.

"Run!" Zayn yelled with every fiber of his being.

Zayn had time to release one last arrow as the rest of his family turned and ran towards the cliff. All he saw was the arrow pierce the dirt next to one of the ravenous *shenrosh* below. Losing hope, he hung the bow strap over his shoulder and ran to catch up with the rest of them. The sounds of the beasts gained on him. The cliff was only thirty paces ahead, but being an uphill grind made it even more difficult and exhausting for them. Twenty paces. Zayn looked back and saw the terrifying yellow eyes fixed on his. They were closer to him than he was to his siblings. Looking back towards the cliff, he saw Tanyel leap off, then Lyu, and finally Typher.

Ten paces. Zayn was gasping for air, thinking to himself the jump would be impossible. Five paces. The awful stench of the beasts' breath twisted his stomach as the clicking noise pounded through his ears. Finally, one pace was all he had left before a piercing pain jolted through his right ankle. The pain caused him to trip and stumble off the cliff. His mind went delirious as he fell, eventually crashing face-first into the cold stream.

Ŏ

A burning pain jolted upward through Tanyel's calves as he hit the water. As he swam upward, thousands of bubbles clouded his vision as Lyu and Typher crashed into the water next to him. *Why hasn't Zayn landed yet,* he thought as he reached the surface, clearing the water from his eyes with the palm of his hand. Horror rattled his teeth as he watched his brother's limp body plummet toward the cold water. His mind replayed the scene of himself staring over Zayn's shoulder, watching his father fall with the shattered stairwell. He couldn't lose anyone else. Zayn and Lyu were everything to him. Tanyel was the closest to where Zayn landed and swam to him with dread in his eyes. Zayn was lying face down, floating in the water with the four waterskins and his bow tied around his body and not moving. Typher and Lyu grabbed Zayn's pack before it floated away and helped Tanyel pull him to shore.

"Zayn!" Lyu yelled as they turned him over on his back. Zayn's flesh was as pale as the sand-colored cloak Tanyel wore. There were bruises all over his neck and arms. He looked like a day-old corpse lying stiff and wet before their eyes.

Tanyel's heart pounded as Typher began pressing on Zayn's chest and yelling at Lyu to find help.

"Look!" Tanyel stopped him and pointed at Zayn's heel. "There is a cut or some type of gash on his leg. The *shenrosh* must have bitten him before he jumped!"

Typher looked closer and nodded to Tanyel. "I'm not certain, but from the looks of it, there might not be enough venom to be fatal."

Tanyel's throat tightened as he bent down to hold his brother. "I thought he was gone." Tanyel hugged his brother's seemingly lifeless body as he clenched his jaw, with tears pouring down his face. *Why did I have to make them draw straws?* He thought as the shame overwhelmed him.

Typher looked up to check for Lyu, but she was already far off towards the nearest tree line, looking for help. "Stay here with Zayn, Tanyel. I'm going to find something that will help with the venom."

Tanyel gently removed the waterskins from Zayn's body to shift him into a more comfortable position. He removed the bow as well, setting it next to his side, whispering to Zayn, "You are an excellent shot and an even better friend. Stay with me, brother."

Tanyel looked up as Typher sprinted off in Lyu's direction, looking frantically towards the ground. Even though Zayn was beside him, unspeakable loneliness overwhelmed him. As the middle child, he hated the feeling. It was why he resorted to always being the peacemaker during Lyu and Zayn's fights. It was why he constantly attempted to make light of most things in life. His greatest fear was that if he didn't do those things, he truly would be alone. If arguments got too out of control, Zayn and Lyu would leave. Just like his mother... and now his father. A pit swelled in his stomach as bitterness overwhelmed him. Though Tanyel would never admit it out loud, he had always held it against his mother for dying, and he hated himself for it. He inhaled, expanding his stomach as far as he could, trying to crush the bitterness back into the depths of his heart.

It had seemed like nearly a half-day since Lyu and Typher left. Tanyel kept his eyes forward, waiting anxiously for their return. He hoped it would be soon. For it was becoming unbearable to make eye contact with Zayn's pale, frozen face.

Ŏ

Up ahead, Lyu found a perfect tree to climb for a viewpoint. She launched herself upward to grab the first branch and swung herself up, panting as she landed. The next few climbs were challenging as she scaled the tree, grabbing a small branch and pulling herself up with speed and intensity. She knew she needed to get to the top to see if anyone or anything around could help them. Almost to the top, the leaves were extremely thick, making it almost impossible to see. Sweat was dripping from her brow even amidst the cool morning breeze. Lyu made one last leap upward and grabbed a thick branch with both hands. Her momentum allowed her to use her body weight to swing upward, landing her feet directly on top of the highest limb.

Taking a deep breath in, she wiped her brow and gained her balance. This was her first time being alone in the past two days, and the emotion struck her all at once. Her father incinerated before her eyes. The story of her mother being slaughtered by Levithe, and now Zayn. Her beloved brother, poisoned to the point of complete paralysis and possibly death. Her chest heaved in and out faster than it ever had before. Her vision blurred as darkness closed in on the edges. A shooting pain expanded throughout her chest as if it might explode. The panic consumed her body as an impending doom swept over her, as if she would die at any moment. Her only relief came from focusing on the branch that held her weight. Before long, the terror dissipated. Her heart returned to normal, and the pain stopped. *What was that? It felt like my body was attacking itself,* she thought as her vision cleared. She missed her father immensely. She wouldn't allow Zayn to share the same fate.

Lyu squinted her eyes as she swirled her head in all directions, looking for help. The view allowed her to see the walls of Levitheton in the distance and the road that led south to the Netting Docks. To the north, she saw the main road that led to the Plains. Besides the normal traffic of Drudge, nothing seemed helpful or out of the ordinary. Finally, she looked to the East. About two hundred paces away was the faint appearance of smoke drifting upwards near another one of the river's streams. Lyu leaned closer and placed her right hand above her eyes to get a better look. As she examined the campsite, a glimmer of hope burst inside her. A man dressed in a sand-colored cloak. A Healer.

As Lyu gathered her breath to let out a cry for help to the man below, a sudden, horrifying noise caused her to freeze. The terrible sound of Levithe's horn. The sound came from the main road just to the north. Her eyes shifted to the location of the noise's origin. Only five hundred paces away was a Guard made up of a dozen Incinerators, each accompanied by a Healer. She expected to see Labarth in the center of their march, but the dazzling silver armor and the height of the man walking with the Guard gave her absolute certainty the Levithe had actually left the city. *He may be after us, but he doesn't know where we are or where we are going,* she thought.

Lyu took a breath, gathered her focus, and descended the tree. Seamlessly falling from branch to branch, she made it to the bottom in a fraction of the time it took her to climb. When her feet hit the ground, she made a dead sprint toward the mysterious Healer's camp. Focused and maintaining her breath, she dodged shrubs, leaped over tiny boulders, and weaved throughout the trees. Just ahead of her, Lyu saw smoke beyond a thicket of leafy bushes that spanned twice her height. She didn't have time to go around the wall of the thicket, so she gritted her teeth and lowered her head as she increased her speed. Lowering her shoulder at full speed, she smashed into the thick wall of lush shrubbery. The pain of the thorns piercing her flesh as she collided with the bushes remained unfelt. When she broke through, she hit the ground, rolling onto her side with her arms and legs covered in tiny red slices, trickling small droplets of blood. She rose to her feet, and as she wiped her cloak free of debris, an unfamiliar voice called to her.

"Little girl, what are you doing?" the voice said, surprised.

Lyu turned around to lay eyes on a man with a perfectly bald glaring head and a wide, mysterious grin. His teeth were large and gapped right down the middle, giving him an awkward, curious look. At about ten paces away, he towered over her with a height nearly matching Levithe's. The old man awkwardly stepped forward with his feet pointing away from each other. His stomach pressed his cloak out further than the average person, and he held the appearance of a man who resembled a great-grandfather. Healing could keep a man alive for a long time, but no amount of healing had the ability to stop the signs of aging. Except for Levithe.

"I need you to come with me now!" Lyu said. "Please. My brother has been paralyzed by *shenrosh* venom."

As she begged, he continued to stare at her with bent brows and a wide smile.

"I am glad to help," he said, slowly reaching for his pack. "But you should know, *shenrosh* bites can be healed. But the venom within the blood cannot."

"It wasn't a full bite," Lyu said. "Please, we have to hurry!"

"Lead the way," said the smooth-headed, curious man. "As you can see, I don't move as quickly as I once did. I will come at my pace. What is your name, girl?"

She didn't appreciate the belittled title but expected nothing less from an arrogant Seared. No matter how kind they were, the Seared always seemed to speak to Drudge as they would to a pet. Lyu's face turned red in frustration, and she was about to protest, but something about the small twinkle in the man's eye caused her to hold her tongue. "I am Lyu, daughter of Erym. And you?"

The man's grin closed as his eyes widened slightly. Hesitating, he looked around in several directions before answering, "My name is Wilso, son of Barhb. By Erym, you mean Erym, the Healer?"

"Yes," Lyu said with a furrowed brow.

"I can see the resemblance," he replied through his gapped

teeth grin. "Are we going this way?" He pointed behind her. Lyu nodded.

Wilso's eyes bounced around before reaching down to grab his bag. He lifted it onto his shoulder and signaled Lyu forward. "Let's go see if we can help this unfortunate son of Erym." Lyu nodded.

"Oh, I almost forgot," said Wilso as he reached for a pot of water near the fire. Slowly, he doused the flame, creating a thick pillar of smoke that reached the treetops and beyond.

Lyu, mildly annoyed, turned to head back towards Zayn's location. A series of questions bounced through her mind as she marched forward. *Who is the peculiar man? Why is he alone?* Despite her curiosity, she knew Zayn needed help, and if this man could give it, she would accept it for the time being.

Chapter 7

The River

"TYPHER! WHERE ARE YOU?!" Tanyel shouted as he sat with his motionless brother. His uncle was nowhere in sight, and Tanyel became increasingly nervous with every moment that passed. Zayn's face was still pale as ice, with no sign of improvements since they pulled him from the stream.

The subtle crushing of leaves and branches caught Tanyel's ear, and his head darted up, expecting to see Typher. His eyes squinted, and his head tilted to the left as off in the distance he saw an unfamiliar man wearing a Healer's cloak walking towards him. Lyu was trailing the old man with a scowl on her face. Tanyel's heart lifted, and he jumped to his feet, waving her and the stranger near.

"Over here! Zayn hasn't woken yet!"

Lyu picked up her pace, passing the bald man, who maintained his steady, unhurried stroll. When she reached Zayn, she fell to her knees and wrapped her hands around his stiff neck to examine his face. Lyu shook her head as she looked behind her to find the man sauntering toward them with a puzzled grin.

Tanyel noticed Lyu's annoyance and shouted at the bald Healer, "Sir, we don't have any more time. We need you to heal him!" Lyu placed her hand on Tanyel's shoulder, nodding to him to calm his tone.

"He is just like all the other Seared, brother," she said, shaking her head. "They only help if it helps themselves."

"But who is he?" Tanyel asked.

"His name is Wilso. He claims to know our mother."

His face burned as he brushed her hand away and stood to meet the strange man. Wilso was still fifty paces away, maintaining his curious grin. In a fury, Tanyel sprinted towards the Healer. *I'll drag him with my bare hands if that's what it takes,* Tanyel thought.

"Easy, my boy," said Wilso as Tanyel charged.

Before Tanyel reached Wilso, he tried to come to an immediate stop and slipped, slamming straight onto his back, crushing the damp terrain beneath. The force of the impact shattered his senses, momentarily causing him to lose the ability to move or breathe. His eyes looked towards Lyu, trying to get her attention, but she was too caught up caring for Zayn. A moment later, Wilso's figure came into view, blocking the glare of the sunlight above. He stared into Tanyel's eyes.

"Another son of Erym, I presume?" said Wilso calmly. "As I told your sister. I am willing to be of help. But using the gift of healing on a *shenrosh* bite is no easy task, nor is it recommended." Wilso adjusted the bag stretched across his shoulder as he continued moving towards Zayn's position, leaving Tanyel lying in the dirt.

Before Tanyel attempted to stand, he looked to his left and spotted Typher heading toward him with a collection of lush green leaves in hand. His uncle stopped, reached his hand down, and pulled him up with ease. As he brushed the grass and leaves off his back, Tanyel detected Typher gesturing towards Zayn's direction with a faded smile. "Don't worry, nephew. I've met this man. Exceedingly difficult to relate to, but he is harmless. Let me do the talking." Tanyel stretched in confusion as the bruised pain radiated down his back and followed Typher back towards Zayn's paralyzed body.

Ŏ

Near the stream, Lyu knelt with Zayn and fought back the tears each time she looked into his eyes. She lowered her head to his mouth, and the weak, warm air expelled from his lungs, tickling her ear. Lowering herself further to his chest, a steady heartbeat drummed against her ear, giving Lyu the hope she needed for the tears to cease. As her head remained on his chest, she saw Wilso approaching, followed by Typher and Tanyel. *You're going to be okay, Zayn. Just hold on,* she thought.

The old Healer finally managed to arrive at Zayn's feet. He stood still, surveying Zayn's body, seeming to have no intention of speaking. Typher brushed past the man in a hurry, bending down towards Lyu to help.

"Lift his foot. We need to apply some directly to the wound," Typher said to Lyu as she stared over his shoulder at Wilso in confusion. "It's been a long while since the bite."

"But Typher, he is a Healer. Can't you get him to help us?" Lyu whispered out of the side of her mouth.

"As I told your brother," making a nod to Tanyel, who was brushing the remaining debris off his back. "He will only do what he wants to do. Only Levithe can command him."

"Pardon," Wilso said in a peculiar tone. "I'm not sure that we have met, Shifter. I may be of old age, but my hearing happens to work just fine. What may your name be?"

"I am Typher, son of Lora," he said as he seemed to tense. "Am I wrong, Wilso, son of Bahrb? Now, is there anything you can do to help?"

With a slight eye roll, Wilso replied, "This boy is receiving just the help he needs. Your herbs will work much better for a proper healing than my gifting. He should be back to himself by this time tomorrow."

"I hate to admit it," Typher said, looking towards Lyu and Tanyel. "But he's right. I've never seen a *shenrosh* bite before, but my Healer friends, your parents included, have often mentioned that it's best to let the wound drain and heal on its own. If it's healed instantly, it has been known to cause all sorts of complications."

"Precisely," Wilso added. "And even after a natural healing, a full dose of venom will severely hinder both their physical and gifting abilities for the rest of their lives."

Tanyel's face turned bright red as his neck trembled. Lyu noticed Tanyel's rage and lifted her arm to his chest to hold him back. Tanyel breathed through his nose and released his frown as he stepped backward, wincing as he held his lower back. Instead of acting on his urge, he returned to their packs and began pulling out everything to dry. Lyu sighed as the tensions softened. She knew Tanyel hated standing by in any situation, even more so than herself. She, just as much as the others, wanted her brother to be healed immediately. However, Typher's words confirming Wilso's gave her the patience to endure.

As Tanyel sorted the packs, Lyu saw their father's scroll fall from Zayn's pack and unravel before Wilso's feet. A curious glare swelled across the Healer's face as he eyed the scroll. Lyu's expression tensed as Tanyel leaped forward, snatching the scroll before Wilso could get a closer look. Tanyel didn't even acknowledge Wilso and continued separating the travel items. Wilso's shoulders bounced as he looked away.

Lyu sighed and turned back to her uncle to assist with Zayn. As she lifted his ankle, she removed the wet sandal from his foot. A single deep gash the size of her fingernail was trickling a yellow and white foamy substance. A bright purple circle surrounded the gash, creating a rash that crept halfway up Zayn's leg. The paleness of his skin exposed his bluish veins in a way that made her stomach churn. She didn't dare imagine what a full *shenrosh* bite would do.

Typher was preparing the medicine with some rocks he found nearby. When he crushed the leaves to release the healing oils, it brought memories of her scrapes and cuts being treated as a child. She held Zayn still as Typher took a waterskin and cleaned the wound with care. *You're going to be okay, Zayn. Hang in there,* she thought.

Typher handed the crushed leaves to Lyu and said, "This will help with both the absorption of the venom as well as the dilution of it. If his veins take it properly, Zayn should have a quick recovery, and most of the pain should be gone when he wakes."

Lyu sighed as she dabbed the wound over and over until Typher gestured to her to stop. At that point, all they could do was wait. As she finished wrapping Zayn's leg with some cloth, her stomach let out a growl, reminding her of her desperate need for some food. She looked up and realized Tanyel was one step ahead of her with a fire started. As she got up to help her brother, the midmorning air mixed with the charring smoke flooded her nostrils. Her stomach grumbled all the more, and Typher followed.

As Lyu was eating, her mind recalled the terrifying sound of Levithe's horn from the treetop. Her heart raced, conceptualizing how close Levithe and his guards were to the north. They needed to move soon but were stuck there until Zayn woke. Even with Typher and Tanyel's strength, it would be useless to try and carry him. She and the others ate their fill, then Tanyel rose to his feet, grabbed all the waterskins, and headed towards the stream. Sensing the look of shame in Tanyel's eyes, Lyu walked over to him and tapped him on the shoulder.

"It's not your fault, brother," Lyu whispered, making eye contact. "We drew sticks. It could have happened to any of us." Lyu saw the tears well in his eyes.

"Just promise you won't leave me, Lyu," Tanyel said, lowering his head.

His comment shocked her, causing her to grab him by the shoulder and respond gently, "I would never, and neither will Zayn. We are in this to the end, Tanyel." As he looked up at her, she detected the doubt in his eyes. No optimism or sarcasm. His fear was on full display.

"I'm so sorry, Tanyel. You've never told me this was something you worried about."

"It's okay. I've never really given myself the chance to say it... or feel it. First, Mother left. Then Father. I can't be alone, Lyu."

Lyu hugged him tight, and they both wept. She kept whispering over and over, "He's going to be okay. We are with you, Tanyel."

Eventually, they walked back to the camp together and sat as Typher spent the next while readying their packs for departure.

Wilso remained in his same position, peering down at Zayn. Occasionally, his head would dart around as if he was waiting for something. He finally sat as he pulled a half loaf of dry bread from his cloak and ate. By the time he finished devouring the loaf, he had a pile of crumbs gathered on his lap. As Lyu sat, she kept her eyes on the old man. She wasn't afraid, threatened, or even worried. Her main cause of suspicion was the old man's awkward uneasiness. Lyu nudged her uncle and whispered, "Ask him what he wants and why he's here."

Typher nodded and turned to Wilso as he set the full pack down and said, "Wilso, why are you camped south of the main road? If you offer us no help, why stay at our camp?"

Wilso looked past Typher. "I am too old to be of use for Lord Levithe's service. May I not camp and travel where I please?" He picked some loaf crumbs off his lap and heaved them into his mouth. "And as I stated earlier. I would love to be of any help I can." He paused. "I will ask you the same question. Three Drudge and a Shifter in the woods, running from *shenrosh*? What brings you off the main road?"

Typher stumbled over his words, saying, "We are traveling to the Tuskoth Caves. It's a family tradition in the spring." Lyu glared at Typher in shock. *How could he reveal this to a stranger?* She thought.

"Traveling, I see," Wilso said, staring at the sky, maintaining his awkward grin. "As I said, I remember Erym. I was ashamed to hear of her plight years ago. But what of the father? Where might he be? Or is this a lovely trip with just the uncle this spring?" Lyu's body tensed at the question.

"Speaking of family," Typher grinned back and spoke with sarcasm. "Your daughter, the Incinerator. You must be proud of her service to Levithe. Also, what of your wife, Judi? I don't remember seeing her for some time." Lyu knew Typher had just struck a deep nerve.

"You are correct," Wilso stumbled over his words. "My daughter proudly serves as an Incinerator, and as for my wife…"

Wilso's face contorted, and eyes widened to display a slight sense of shame. He went silent, and his uneasiness softened. Typher gave it a rest and turned back to Lyu, shrugging his shoulders.

"I'm going to check Zayn's wound again and then search for some more herbs," Typher said as he stood. Lyu watched as Typher bent down to examine Zayn once more. He placed his hand on Zayn's shin, carefully lifting the bandage to inspect. Shaking his head, he stood and trotted back into the forest. Lyu stared at Zayn as her heart fell. *Just hold on Zayn. You're going to be okay,* she thought.

The sun warmed the ground around them, drying everything in its path. As Tanyel and Lyu rested in silence, time turned slower than normal, but the curious man, Wilso, remained. The birds flying and singing overhead mixed with the streams' soft sounds brought more awareness of the company's exhaustion. Even a full night's sleep wasn't enough to fill their energy. Wilso drifted to sleep as Lyu and Tanyel fought to stay awake. Typher had still not returned.

After some time, the soft rumbling of Tanyel's snoring began, causing her to roll her eyes and toss a rock at him, jarring him awake. Both of them stretched as they rose and moved toward Zayn's body to check how he was progressing. Lyu let out an immense sigh as she realized Zayn's color had begun to return. She was shocked at his speedy recovery. His breath was still weak, but her nearly hopeless heart began to fill. She stayed with Zayn as Tanyel moved back towards the camp to wake the others. They would be able to leave sooner than expected.

Without warning, a scolding shout thundered from the woods behind them, "Don't move, Drudge!"

Lyu instantly recognized the voice. Staring back at her with a bow drawn was the golden-haired nuisance, Stawb. Beside him stood his other Shifter buddy, Feeld, holding a long sword pointed directly at them. The bottoms of their elegant, purple cloaks were covered in dirt and mud. They crept closer as they glanced around, observing the camp.

"No uncle to save you this time, sweet Lyu," Stawb said.

"He'll be back," Lyu shouted as she noticed Tanyel stepping closer toward her. "I see you ditched the Incinerator and brought actual weapons. Typical of Seared. Claiming superiority, yet using the very weapons us *Drudge* crafted." Tanyel let out a faint laugh.

"You would never even have the chance to *craft* weapons if the Seared didn't allow you to," he responded in anger. "Your tongue is quite loose for someone who has an arrow pointed at their throat." Lyu's neck tensed as she swallowed.

"After our little run-in earlier, I decided to find my father. He clued me in on your treason, so Feeld and I have taken it upon ourselves to find you and return you to the city."

"Speaking of that run-in," Tanyel interjected with a wide smirk. "How's your jaw feeling?" Lyu's eyes darted open as she attempted to hold back her laughter.

"Final warning!" Stawb shouted, stepping closer, pointing the bow down towards Zayn's body. "Hold your tongue, or this arrow will finish your pathetic waste of a brother." Lyu placed her hand on Tanyel's shoulder, realizing Stawb's threat. Stawb stared with an awful grimace.

She ached for Typher to return. As her mind raced, Stawb and Feeld crept forward, focusing intently on Lyu and Tanyel. At about ten paces away, they stopped.

"Now," said Stawb. "You will come with us back to the city." Lyu spotted a slight quiver in Stawb's hand as he held the bow. *He is terrified,* she thought. Then suddenly, Stawb's eyes widened as an extremely tight grip clasped around her arm just above the elbow. Glaring back, she stared into Wilso's curious eyes, noticing his opposing hand clutching Tanyel's arm even tighter than her own. Before she and Tanyel reacted, Wilso dragged them towards Stawb and Feeld.

"Goodday," Wilso whispered with a calm face. "I have served Lord Levithe for a long while, and I am well aware of the rewards he gives for helping capture the treasonous. So how about I help you take these *Drudge* back to the city, and we can split the wealth?"

In shock, Lyu fought the man's grip, immediately causing Stawb and Feeld to rush to help the old man. Tanyel and her were no match for three Seared, and before she knew it, her face smashed into the damp ground as they bound her hands behind her back. Tanyel's screams echoed off the cliff's walls as she tasted mud creeping through her clenched lips. *Typher, where are you?* she thought as there was still no sign of him.

"I can't wait to watch your execution, sweet Lyu," Stawb whispered in her ear as he tightened the straps. The weight of his body, along with the soft mud, made it nearly impossible to respond or move. Because her head was jammed into the mud at such a fierce angle, all she saw was Wilso standing behind them.

As Stawb let up some pressure, suddenly, Lyu saw Wilso wink and reach for his knife. *What is he doing?* She thought in horror as she watched Wilso thrust the dagger into Stawb's lower back. Stawb let out an agonizing scream, and a moment later, Feeld's scream deafened her ears. As she rolled over to check on Tanyel, her insides tensed as she stared wide-eyed at Stawb and Feeld, covered in blood. Wilso remained behind them both, with a blood-soaked dagger in hand. His knees cracked as he knelt, causing Lyu's heart to race as the dagger approached her chest. To her relief, Wilso cut the straps that bound her and then did the same to Tanyel. They both stared at the man in shock as the sounds of Stawb and Feeld's screams turned to whimpers.

"I told you I would be of help," Wilso said with a smirk. Tanyel and Lyu were speechless as Wilso broke eye contact and moved towards his victims. He grabbed Stawb's bow and Feeld's sword and tossed them into the deep stream.

"Now, as for you two. I'm afraid you will not be receiving your reward today or following us any further. In fact, with that type of knife wound, I expect you to have a half day's worth of life left to make it back to the city." He paused and smirked curiously at Lyu and Tanyel. "I would find a Healer if I were you. And I wouldn't waste any more time with your whimpering here."

Stawb and Feeld stumbled to their feet, clutching their

backs, and headed back toward the city, wincing with every step. Tanyel shouted at them as they left. "That's twice, Stawb! Twice made a fool by us *pathetic Drudge*. Go tell your father for us!" Lyu shook her head as she moved back towards Wilso to thank him. He still held the dagger in his hand and raised it towards Lyu, motioning her to clean it with the straps.

Before she took the knife, a familiar booming voice shouted, "Put it down, now!"

Lyu and Tanyel looked up in shock as they saw Zayn standing upright with his bow drawn, staring directly at Wilso.

"You have one more chance. Drop the knife, or I release this arrow into your heart," Zayn commanded.

"Zayn!" Lyu shouted, waving her hands. "It's okay! He's with us. But how are you awake?" Zayn's brows bent as she spoke. He didn't lower the bow.

"Seriously, brother," Tanyel yelled. "We were just ambushed by Stawb, and this man saved us." Lyu felt relief as Zayn released the string and set the bow on the ground. She and Tanyel sprinted to him and threw their arms around him as they smiled through tears.

"You're okay!" Tanyel said.

"I'm okay," Zayn responded. "Actually, I feel pretty great."

Lyu bent down and removed the bandage from his leg and realized the wound looked remarkably better than before.

"Looks like it must have been a smaller dose of venom than

we thought. We didn't think you would be awake until at least tomorrow," Lyu said with a wide grin.

"So the eldest son of Erym is awake, and my words have deceived me," said Wilso with a confused look. "I will have you know. It has been quite a pleasure getting to spend some time with the children of one of O'Varth's finest Healers." Lyu nodded back.

"Thank you," Zayn said. "For saving them."

"And for making an absolute fool of Stawb," Tanyel added.

"You're very welcome," Wilso replied, looking past them toward the tree line. "It appears your *family trip* seems to be a bit more important than you are letting on. Stawb accused you of treason, but I see no possibility of that from the likes of you three."

As Lyu was about to respond, the familiar voice of her uncle approached.

"You're exactly right, Wilso. These three wouldn't recognize treason if it were right in front of them," Typher said, with more herbs in hand. "Also, Zayn, you look good! I guess I didn't need these after all."

"Ahh, Typher. It seems the great Shifter has missed the show." Wilso smirked back.

"I can't wait to hear about it," Typher responded. "In fact. Why don't you join us? It would be especially useful to have a Healer on hand."

Lyu and Tanyel agreed. Wilso saved their lives, and despite

him being Seared, something in the man's eyes made him trustworthy. As she looked at Zayn, his face wasn't as optimistic as theirs. After all, he had been unconscious, so it made sense that he would seem leery of the old Healer.

"As I have said from the beginning. I am happy to be of help," Wilso responded.

They packed their remaining belongings, and they followed Wilso back to his camp to the east. Wilso shoved the last few items scattered around his camp into his pack.

"Let's head south," said Tanyel. "We need to make our way to the coast, anyway. Might as well get as far from the road as possible and then cut east through the plains."

"Might I suggest a different route?" Wilso asked. "If we follow the river, we will maintain a constant supply of water and shade. There is a stream branch that heads southeast. A much quicker and wiser route."

"You are right," Typher said. "We take the river."

"Are you sure?" Tanyel asked, taking a step back. "Levithe's horn blew not that far north of us. It would be nice to be as far away from his as possible."

"I understand that," Typher said. "But Levithe has no idea where we are, and I am confident he and his Guard will stay along the main road." Tanyel nodded.

Wilso didn't speak. He simply started trotting off to the

southeast, assuming the family would follow. Lyu adjusted her pack and marched towards Zayn. She noticed a slight limp in his step and let him hold her by the shoulder as they marched. It was midday, and if they moved fast enough, they could make it to the caves within the next two days.

A faint smile drew across Lyu's face as the five of them reached a massive stream of water. The way the water sped over the boulders caused large sections of white jostled rapids. Crashing sounds from the river were much more intense than those of the stream they jumped into earlier. At about fifty paces wide, the vast river had numerous break-offs that transitioned into creeks and small channels as Lyu looked ahead. The forest surrounding the river was a stunning lush green with a hint of color as the buds of spring bloomed. No matter how Lyu felt, the river was their new road, their source of life, and the path that would lead them to their father's key. She grinned at her brothers and uncle as Wilso walked ahead. Without saying a word, she experienced the deep comfort of her family's love, knowing they felt the same.

Ŏ

Ganya, rushing back to Levitheton, dragging the large bag of *muwr* meat, looked up and detected a terrifying troop ahead. Along the main road, carts and large wooden wagons crafted by the Drudge were rushed off the dirt by their owners. The horn that blew a few moments before alerted all who traveled in the surrounding area. As he stared in disbelief, his head lowered, and his body seemed to shrink in terror. He raised his eyes and gaped at the approaching Guard. The troop's circular formation spanned across the entire road. Twelve Incinerators made up the outer edge of the band. The inner circle, twelve Healers. Directly in the center, wearing a dazzling white cloak and glimmering silver armor, was Levithe. As they marched east, the Seared Guard shot eyes of disgust toward the Drudge.

Ganya darted off the side of the dirt road and looked toward Levithe, expecting to see vehement anger. Instead, his eyes expanded as he witnessed the most diabolical smile he had ever encountered. He bowed to the ground and broke eye contact. It both chilled his bones and made him want to vomit. A hunter, like himself, shouldn't experience that kind of fear. *Why is Levithe outside of the city?* He thought. As the guard passed, he heard some Incinerators at the back bickering amongst themselves.

"Whoever we are after, I will make sure to be the first to Incinerate them," said a shorter man carrying a large axe.

"Are you sure you can handle a few Drudge?" said a female Incinerator, strong in stature and intimidating in height.

"If they are as weak as their father, it will only take a few seconds," the short man responded. Ganya's ears perked, and he leaned in closer.

"You mean the weak man you let enter the ruins?" she responded, glaring.

"It wasn't my fault! We would have captured them all if..."

"Enough of the excuses. The children of Erym escaped. You killed their father. Now you have a lot to make up for." Ganya's heart sank as the woman paused. "And you wonder why you find yourself in the back of this formation."

"Then why do you find yourself here, woman?"

She smirked. "To make sure you don't hinder any plans with your loud mouth and indolence. Lord Levithe's order."

"Who do you think you are?" scoffed the short man, nearly stumbling over his boots.

"I am Behk, daughter of Judi," she said, looking ahead and keeping her poise. "You will not say another word unless spoken to." The man's face swelled red as he continued his march.

Ganya, on the verge of panic, rose to his feet after the guard passed with no notice of him. He fought back tears as his mind spun. *Ryn is dead? What about the kids?* he thought. They had to be terrified. All on their own, grieving their father and being pursued by Levithe. Ganya was shocked they were still alive. Brushing the dirt from his knees, he sprinted back toward Levitheton as his net dragged behind. The irregular beats of his heart caused him to clutch his chest as he ran. Between heavy breaths, he whispered to himself, "I have to warn the others."

Chapter 8

The Bridge

THE DENSE FOREST TOWERED ABOVE as Zayn's feet sank into soft mud while he paced along the river's bank beside his family and the Healer named Wilso. The afternoon sun glistened off his bronzed skin and golden hair, and the warmth dried all his belongings. Despite the *shenrosh* attack, he was feeling surprisingly energized. Lyu and Tanyel filled him in on the events he had missed as Typher and Wilso walked ahead. His breath was steady, and the conversation distracted him from any remaining pain in his leg.

Zayn still couldn't believe how long he had been unconscious. To him, it was only a moment of bizarre dreams. So when he woke to find Wilso pointing a knife towards Lyu, his instincts caused him to reach for his bow to stop him. *Sometimes, things are not what they seem,* he thought as his shoulders relaxed, looking toward the bald man walking ahead. Initially, Zayn found it difficult to trust Wilso. However, the fact that Typher invited the man along gave Zayn enough confidence to accept the company. After all, the man had saved both Lyu and Tanyel, and in such an extreme way. If he was willing to betray Labarth by stabbing his wretched son, he must have been trustworthy in helping with their travels.

Suddenly, a wave of nausea overwhelmed Zayn. He placed his hands on a fallen tree log as Lyu stopped and bent down. Tanyel, Typher, and Wilso stopped and turned around to inspect.

"What is it, Zayn?" she said, placing her hand on his back.

The ground under Zayn's feet seemed to swirl around him as he clung to the dried tree bark. He found it difficult to remain balanced, let alone speak. His knees hit the dirt, and his elbows crashed through the log.

"It's the venom, dear," Wilso said. "He may experience this type of effect for the next few days. Each spell should only last a few moments."

Zayn's head pounded as the ground continued to spin. His breaths slowed until finally, the nausea let up. He felt the color rush back into his face as his stomach settled. Looking up to the others, he said, "I think I'm okay. How often will this happen?"

"It's always different," Wilso replied. "If I had to guess, I would assume with such a small amount of venom, it shouldn't occur more than once a day, perhaps less."

"Well, that's good news," Tanyel said, helping Zayn to his feet. "Need me to carry you, brother?"

"I'll be fine," Zayn replied, laughing and shaking his head.

As he reached for his pack, his body quivered as he noticed a white scaley *nacash* shed loosely coiled inside the broken log. Tanyel reached in and pinched one end with two fingers, slowly lifting it from the hole.

"Seems you found a small one," Wilso said. "Typically, *nacash* can grow up to five paces long."

"Should I keep it, Lyu?"

"Put it down," Lyu said, laughing through her nose. Tanyel dropped the filmy shed, and as it hit the dirt, he stomped on it, crumbling it to pieces.

Before lifting his pack to his shoulders, Zayn waited for the others to turn and walk. Discreetly reaching into his pack, he sighed as he gripped the cold metal in his fingers. *I need to keep this close,* he thought, removing the symbol and placing it into his pocket.

As they continued, Tanyel stepped closer to Zayn. His demeanor shifted, and his head hung lower than normal, hardly making eye contact as he spoke. "In all seriousness, I shouldn't have let you go to the stream by yourself."

THE SEARING STONE

"It's no one's fault, Tanyel," Zayn said, looking his brother in the eyes, attempting to release him from the noticeable shame. "And it doesn't matter. I'm okay now. Just a small limp and occasional nausea. I'll take this over the soreness from a long week at the Netting Docks any day."

"But I..."

"I said it's not your fault."

Tanyel sighed and said, "Thank you, Zayn. I'm glad you're fine."

"Me too. But I do wish I could have seen Stawb and Feeld's faces as Wilso's knife pierced their backs."

"Hard to believe we humiliated them twice in one day. Us. The pitiful Drudge!" Tanyel said with a smile.

Zayn nodded back with a half-smirk. But within, Tanyel's last two words struck him. Tanyel seemed to be fine boasting about their Drudge status. Zayn didn't allow himself to get there. Most likely because the worst parts of him agreed with Stawb. He truly believed Drudge were pitiful. Even his siblings, and especially himself.

As Wilso maintained his steady lead, Lyu looked back at Typher and said, "Do you think we should show Wilso the map?"

Zayn's eyes squinted and ears raised. It was one thing to show their uncle Typher, but no matter how trustworthy, Wilso wasn't family.

"No," Zayn whispered. "The Remnant has clearly kept this a

secret for hundreds of years. Just because he saved you both doesn't mean we should share it with him."

"Share what with me?" Wilso said, staring back at them. Zayn hadn't noticed him stop as they were talking. His mind froze as he tried to think of a response.

"It's about your campsite," Lyu interjected. "Your rations seem a bit low for the remainder of our trip. I suggested we share with you, but my lovely, *shenrosh*-bit brother here disagrees." Tanyel laughed as Zayn gathered his thoughts.

"I just... we barely packed enough for ourselves," Zayn said.

"While I appreciate the gesture, for a man my age, I don't need as much as you'd think." As Wilso spoke, he smiled, causing the wrinkles near his temples to deepen into the shape of tiny strikes of lightning. The man was certainly old, but the way the light struck his face made him seem older than anyone Zayn had ever seen.

"How old *are* you?" Tanyel asked, catching Zayn and the others off guard.

"I will have reached my hundredth year," he said, unoffended. "But let us continue ahead. We must find a way to cross to the river's southern side."

Zayn saw Tanyel and Lyu's jaws jut open as he processed Wilso's answer. He had heard of Healers keeping themselves alive into their sixtieth or seventieth year but had never met anyone this old. Drudge were lucky to make it past fifty.

"O'Varth's oldest Seared," Typher interjected. "I have never understood why you would put yourself through the misery of staying alive this long."

"Well," Wilso responded as his eyes bounced from left to right. "Let's just say I still have someone to live for."

"Your daughter," said Lyu.

"Yes, Behk is my youngest and my last surviving kin. I find it difficult to leave her."

"But last I heard, she won't talk to you," Typher pressed.

The old man's eyes glossed over, and it appeared as if rage and hatred consumed him all at once. He snapped, grabbing Typher by his cloak just below his throat. Typher remained still as Zayn watched with bent brows. Until this point, Wilso had shown no sign of hostility. Even in Lyu's description of the stabbings, she specifically recalled his calm face. But just before Zayn and the others could step in to help, Wilso's regular expression returned, and he released his grip, shaking his head.

"My apologies, Typher," Wilso said, taking a deep breath and looking at his feet. "She blames me for her mother's death, and she's right. I was so focused on using all my energy to keep myself alive. I couldn't protect her."

Zayn lifted his hand to Typher's chest, signaling him not to press any further. He knew what it felt like to blame himself for his father's death. Even more so, how painful it was to talk about. Even so, Wilso's rapid change in behavior brought more caution to Zayn's trust. He figured it best to change the subject.

"So, Wilso," Zayn said, "You must know more about O'Varth's history than most. Tell us what it was like being Seared a hundred years ago?"

Wilso raised his head as he looked back past Zayn and said, "Well, it is one of my greatest honors to have been given the opportunity to become one of the first Seared."

Zayn and his siblings' eyes squinted. Typher remained unaffected by the comment.

"What do you mean, one of the first?" Zayn said.

"Well, to put it simply, all those before me were just as you are. Drudge."

They all stared back, speechless.

"Ahh, it's curious how history finds itself forgotten. Especially amongst the Drudge," he said with a smile. "After the war, Levithe built his city with Drudge and only Drudge. It has been said that after two hundred years, the Drudge became so beat down and discouraged, they lost both the will to live and to procreate. So, a hundred years ago, Levithe introduced the Stone to the city. He instituted the Searings, giving Drudge the ability to choose a gifting for their children. A new motivation for childbirth. I... Wilso, son of Barhb, am one of the first Healers on O'Varth since the war." Zayn's brows raised. Why hadn't he been told this? Perhaps this man would help them fill in the pieces of history, along with the Remnant.

"Typher, did you know this?" Tanyel asked, leaning in.

"Yes," he responded. "Seared learn of it when their oath is reinstated once you pass the age of innocence. Most Drudge don't speak of it." A twinge of bitterness rose, but it paled in comparison to Zayn's curiosity.

"Isn't it beautiful?" Lyu said. "As I see it, it only proves my point. Levithe needs Drudge, no matter how much he doesn't want to admit it."

"But why wouldn't our parents tell us?" Zayn said, trying to keep his cool.

"Add it to the list," Tanyel said. "And honestly, I don't think it matters. It doesn't affect us or what we're trying to do. What's important is they had our best interest in mind and have certainly proved it enough already." Zayn and Lyu nodded.

As they continued, Zayn noticed the rapids had calmed, giving the water a glass-like appearance. Bugs danced on the water's surface, sending subtle ripples in every direction. Birds sang a rhythmic tune, causing Zayn to notice his exhaustion. It reminded him of the evening before, and suddenly he remembered the dream. He still didn't understand, but something about the memory still felt so real — both haunting and hopeful at the same time.

After a while, he was startled by Tanyel's shouting. "Look, way up there. A bridge!"

Zayn squinted as he stared ahead. About a league away was a giant crossing point, leading them south across the river. Wilso stumbled ahead to observe. As they approached the crossing, he said, "Not quite a bridge, but an appropriate place to cross."

Wilso stood with his shoulders hunched over in his sand-colored cloak, glancing at them for a quick moment. Looking back towards the river, he pointed.

They noticed the river narrowing at the spot Wilso had noted. To their luck, stretched across the entire span of the river, were a few broken-down trees creating a crossing point. The waters still poured forth at a swift speed, but looking ahead, Zayn didn't see any other way across.

"You first, Shifter," Wilso said, waving his hand towards the logs.

Typher rolled his eyes and stepped onto the first tree, stomping his foot against the dry bark to check the stability. To Zayn's surprise, the wood didn't budge. Typher placed his entire weight on the log and jumped to double-check. Looking at the others with eyebrows lifted, he gave them a nod and a subtle shrug of the shoulders.

"Just be careful," Typher said. "There could be dead spots."

Tanyel jumped up first, followed by Lyu, then Zayn. Zayn looked back at Wilso, who was staring at his feet, walking more cautiously than normal.

Zayn observed as Lyu and Tanyel stepped over the rotting bark areas. For the most part, the bridge was sturdy and provided them with an easy crossing point. The crystal water took his breath away. Zayn spotted a few large fish fighting to swim upstream despite the river's speed but remaining in the same place. His left eye twitched as he realized he may never gut another fish again.

A violent crash and scream from Lyu caused his eyes to dash forward. Her left leg had smashed through some rotten bark. Without thinking, Zayn leaped forward to help. As his feet hit the wood, it collapsed, causing him to crash through the hallowed bridge.

"Are you hurt?!" Typher yelled to them.

Zayn felt relief as Lyu climbed back up onto the solid log.

"All good here," she said. "Zayn?"

"I think I'm okay," he responded.

Tanyel stepped toward him, stretching out his hand to help him. Zayn placed one foot on the solid opening and pulled himself up.

"Looks like I'm the responsible sibling," Tanyel said, laughing. Lyu and Zayn shook their heads.

Suddenly, Zayn witnessed Typher's face turn from laughter to wide-eyed shock. His uncle was staring directly past Zayn's shoulder. Turning slowly, Zayn's bones shivered as he saw Wilso lifting a metal symbol to his eyes. His father's words echoed through his head as his entire body froze. *Keep it hidden.* Wilso's face was almost ravenous as his eyes fixated on the symbol. Zayn couldn't move. A tingling fired down his arms as helplessness overwhelmed him.

"You seemed to have dropped something from your pocket, son of Erym," Wilso said as his expression eased. "Where did you get this, my boy?"

Zayn checked his pocket, and sure enough, his symbol was missing. *I have to make up something,* he thought in a panic.

"Did you not hear me? It appears to have a similar shape to *the* symbols on the Searing Rods. Where did you find this?"

Zayn was out of words, and the longer he waited to speak, the more suspicious Wilso grew.

Tanyel broke the silence and said with sarcasm, "I can't believe you brought that childish piece of metal, brother. I swear, we have enough to carry, and mother and father gave that to you years ago!" Wilso's eyes descended, staring at Tanyel and then back at the symbol.

"I just wanted to have a part of them with me," Zayn said, forcing the act as best he knew how. "It *is* just a toy, but it helps me remember them."

"I remember when they made that for you, Zayn," Typher interjected, not breaking eye contact with Wilso. "Give it back to him, old man, and let's be on our way."

Wilso's teeth were exposed again as his eyes glanced around. He didn't seem to buy the story, and he responded with a calm smile,

THE SEARING STONE

"Of course."

Wilso slowly stretched his arm towards Zayn. Zayn dashed his arm toward the symbol, grabbing it and turning away without saying a word.

Before he took a step, Wilso's scream interrupted. Zayn saw a look of horror on Lyu's face as he turned around. Wilso was slowly backing up towards the log bridge's opposite end. To Zayn's shock, he laid eyes on the source of Wilso's fear. A slick black serpent with a ridged spine uncoiled itself out of the rotted hole created by Zayn. *Nachash*, Zayn thought, terrified. The *nachash* began to let out a hiss as it raised its head towards Wilso, steadily approaching. Its smooth black skin peeled away from its ridged spine, revealing razor-sharp barbs across the entire length of its body. The *nachash* were known for wrapping their prey tight, and as they squeezed, each barb would pierce deeper into their victim until they died. Zayn and the others watched as Wilso continued to back away, causing the serpent to hiss even louder. Then, without warning, the *nacash* struck.

Wilso's eyes shot open in horror as the thick black serpent wrapped itself around his waist. Zayn saw Lyu and Tanyel's face pale as Wilso fell to his knees, wailing in agony from the *nachash* barbs. Zayn had never heard a man scream in such pain before. Wilso's face grew paler with each stab of pain as blood trickled down his legs.

"Zayn, move!" Lyu shouted as she dashed towards Wilso.

Zayn stared wide-eyed as Lyu gracefully removed her sword

and lunged toward the serpent. With one clean cut, the *nachash*'s head fell to the ground, releasing one final tortuous hiss. Its body fell limp, releasing Wilso from the barbs.

Tanyel, Zayn and Typher, hoisted Wilso onto their shoulders and carefully carried him to solid ground. Wilso crashed to the mud, covered in blood, blinking rapidly. Zayn clutched the symbol in his hand and stared as Wilso, in agony, placed his wrinkled hands on the barbed wounds covering his body. When he removed his hands, the redness disappeared, and his skin returned to normal.

"Are you okay?" Lyu asked as she gazed down at Wilso.

"It's hard enough to keep myself from dying because of my age," Wilso responded, discouraged yet calm. "Any additional healing drains every ounce of my energy."

"Can you manage a few more paces?" Lyu said.

"I should be able to with a helping hand," Wilso responded, reaching both hands up. Lyu and Tanyel each grabbed an arm and assisted Wilso to his feet. He stumbled as he grabbed hold of their shoulders. Before Zayn turned to walk, he noticed Wilso staring back at him. *He knows about the symbol,* he thought. Zayn still refused to say anything more about it, even if Typher or the man asked. The symbol was better left hidden in his pack than to fail his father's promise even more. They were getting close to the plains, which meant only one more day until they reached the caves. *We are so close,* Zayn thought, walking in front of the others. Typher reached for his shoulder and tried to speak.

"I can't, Uncle," said Zayn with his head bowed. "Father told me no one was allowed to know. Now all of you do. Please don't press any further," he said it loud enough for the others to hear, hoping none of them would bring it up again, especially Wilso. Typher released his grip and squinted. Zayn knew the face well. The face of a man who was holding back his anger at yet another thing Ryn kept from him.

Before long, slight gusts of wind swirled at random, and the air changed from warm to a slight chill. The dense clouds above increased in speed as they held a mixture of light and dark greying surfaces scattered throughout.

"We need to find some cover," Lyu said, glaring up at the sky, sniffing the air. "It's not quite dark yet, but we can't afford to have all our supplies soaked before our trip through the plains."

"She's right," Typher said. "We can get a fire going to cook up some stew before the rain hits. Zayn, can you gather some kindling?"

"On it," Zayn said, immediately looking around for a dead tree.

Wilso staggered behind, still clinging to Lyu and Tanyel. His eyes were sunken in, barely able to keep them open. Looking ahead, he winced as he raised his arm and pointed towards a thick portion of forest just fifty paces south. The area contained about a dozen lush giant trees huddled together with entangled branches. The others approved without saying a word, and they moved towards the cover.

Wilso spoke, pointing to the earth, "Feel the leaves and debris below this herd of trees as compared to out in the open."

As Lyu walked under the trees, the sounds of her steps changed. The dried leaves and sticks cracked beneath her feet as she smiled, looking up at Wilso. "A great guide, even while exhausted. Thank you, Wilso."

Wilso coughed out what seemed like a chuckle and said, "I don't enjoy getting wet just as much as the next person." He moved closer toward the center of the covered area. As he sat on the dried ground, his long awkward legs crossed, and he leaned back against his pack, closing his eyes with a faint smile across his face.

"We have all the kindling we need right here, Uncle," Tanyel said, bending down and gathering leaves and sticks. "We can build a fire, eat, and then get plenty of sleep. Hopefully, it will give us an early start to our morning."

The stew's smell churned Zayn's stomach. Wilso refused to eat their food and stuck to the dried rations he had within his pack. As they finished their meal and sighed with bellies full, the gentle pattering of rain approached from afar. He could see the wall of rain approaching until, eventually, the torrential downpour engulfed the forest surrounding them. Occasionally, raindrops crept through the leaves above, landing on their packs and causing the coals to sizzle.

THE SEARING STONE

The darkness of nightfall mixed with the black clouds above brought a sense of weariness to them all.

Tanyel yawned with an exaggerated stretch and said, "This rain could last all night. I don't know about you, but I am tired."

"I agree," Lyu said as she rummaged through her pack to set up for sleep. "Sleep well, everyone."

Wilso and Typher were already half asleep with bloodshot eyes, nodding off as they leaned against their packs. A few raindrops struck the fire's last glowing ember, and darkness consumed the camp.

Zayn's heart sped up, dreadfully anticipating the idea of sleep. *It was just a dream,* he thought, taking a deep breath, pondering the evening prior. He brushed some leaves and sticks out of the way to make a soft spot to lie. As his head hit the blanket, his heavy eyes clamped shut, and he did not fight them. The day's exhaustion outweighed his worry once again.

After what seemed like only a short period of deep sleep, Zayn's eyes shot open, and he realized what woke him. The rain had stopped. The empty sound of the forest at night amplified his awareness tenfold. His surroundings were still nearly pitch black, but his eyes had adjusted. *How long have I been asleep?* He thought, laying back down on his soft tattered blanket. As his eyes blinked again, he looked at his siblings, sound asleep. Typher's heavy breathing caused his shoulders to relax, but then he sensed something. He squinted his eyes to find Wilso's sleeping spot, and his heart nearly stopped. Wilso wasn't there.

Zayn remained still, lying on his blanket, as he darted his eyes around the camp, looking for the old man. Left-over raindrops falling from the branches above thundered through his ears as they crashed into the damp leaves. Random gusts of wind whistled by, causing his heart rate to increase. *Where did he go?* He thought, panicking.

Then, suddenly, the hairs on the back of his neck shot up as his ears caught an alarming noise in the distance. *Voices*, Zayn thought as he angled his head in their direction. He could only make out mumbles until abruptly, they stopped. Zayn waited as the sounds of insects chirping and heavy breathing flooded his ears. Without warning, a terrible voice, not belonging to Wilso, spoke loud enough for Zayn to hear. His heart jolted as he recognized the voice, "She will die."

Levithe, he thought, terrified. His worst fears had been realized. Wilso was working with Levithe. Zayn gulped for air as the three dreadful words gripped his every though. He grasped in his mind for any inkling of what to do next. He was too worried that waking his family would cause an ambush of sorts, so he kept still. As the distant mumbles stopped once more, the soft sound of footsteps thumped on the wet ground outside the camp, directly toward him. Zayn squinted his eyes nearly shut, pretending to be asleep.

Wilso entered his line of sight, creeping on his tip-toes. Zayn's heart pounded through his eardrums as he waited for Levithe to follow. But no one came. Wilso laid back down and seemingly went to sleep. As more time passed, Zayn's heart began to settle. No ambush.

The snoring sounds of the old Healer filled the campsite. Once again, Zayn couldn't sleep. *I have to find a way to tell them. Wilso has betrayed us all. Levithe and his Guard could kill us any moment,* his thoughts wouldn't stop.

Chapter 9

The Barren Plains

AS NIGHT APPROACHED, Ganya continued forward, his massive hunter's net dredging through the thick mud. The heavy rain had swept through just as the sun set.

Approaching the Southeastern Gate, his mind continued to race, constantly worrying about Ryn's children. Ganya had always considered Zayn, Tanyel, and Lyu to be children of his own. He still didn't understand why Ryn would include them. The massive gates towered over him, allowing temporary relief from the pelting raindrops. Before he continued into the city, he detected two guards huddled underneath the gate's overhang.

"Ganya!" One of the guards yelled, jumping to her feet. "Did you see Levithe?"

"Deshome," Ganya said, bowing. "Yes. On my way back from the plains. What happened to Ryn and his children?"

Deshome frowned and responded, "Levithe is after them. Ryn actually went through with his plan." Ganya scratched his thick black beard as he listened, then noticed the other guard approaching. Ryn hadn't told him of his exact plan, but Ganya's shame slowly surfaced. He should have known. All of Ryn's confusing talk the other night now made perfect sense. *I could have stopped him,* he thought, bowing his head.

"Did you see Typher and the siblings on the road?" Naye said with blushed cheeks. "Before you encountered Levithe?"

"Thankfully, no," Ganya answered. "I plan on leaving first thing in the morning to search for them." Naye's eyes squinted.

"If what you say is true, they aren't the ones who need help," Naye responded. "A group of *our own* created a distraction so Ryn could enter the ruins. The Guard captured them all. They are in the Tower's prison awaiting execution as we speak!"

The conversation paused as a few Drudge hurried through the gates with their carts. Ganya stepped closer to Naye and Deshome. Meeting them eye to eye, he whispered, "Are you saying *we* are to help these prisoners escape?"

"Yes," Deshome interjected. "If Ryn's plan made them willing enough to be captured and face death, then it is certainly worth helping them. Especially now that Levithe is out of the city."

He nodded, thinking of Ryn and the siblings, and said, "Lead the way."

Naye removed some rope from her pocket and smirked. "We need a prisoner to take with us."

Ganya placed his hands behind his back, tapping his foot repeatedly, as Naye tied the rope around his wrists, leaving some slack. The creaking sounds of a wooden cart rushed by as the rain dripped down his beard. His heart slumped when he spotted three children pushing the cart, all of whom looked younger than the age of innocence. Grime and dirt poured down their discouraged faces from the showering rain. Their cart was empty.

"You three," Ganya said, catching their attention. "Take this hunter's net to the main market. Whatever they pay you is yours." The children's eyes swelled with both excitement and shock. From this moment on, wages wouldn't matter.

"Thank you, sir," they said at once, then heaved the heavy net filled with meat, horns, and pelts into the cart. Ganya smiled as the three children stood upright, pushing the cart away at a steady skip.

"Look at that," Deshome said, nodding towards two guards approaching. "Perfect time for a shift change. Now wipe the smile off your face, Ganya, and act like a real prisoner." Ganya's eyes descended, and Deshome grinned at him. Two guards replaced Naye and

THE SEARING STONE

Deshome's position at the gate, allowing them to move Ganya toward the city's center. Their next move would be more dangerous than any hunting trip he had ever taken. Even with the slow pace from the heavy rainfall, they would make it to the prison before the sun rose. Ganya's nerves heightened as they marched, wondering if Ryn's children would be safe. *We are coming*, he thought.

Ŏ

Zayn, wide-eyed, sitting on his blanket, rocked back and forth, holding his knees, trying to stay warm. Because of the evening's rain, the air was cooler than the day before. The dark blue tint of dawn brightened as the sun broke through the trees. The area where they camped remained decently dry despite the heavy rainfall. Zayn was still the only one awake, eyes bouncing back and forth between his family and Wilso. *How do I get rid of him?* Zayn thought, wiping his reddened nose with his forearm.

The sounds of morning settled as Lyu stretched awake. She noticed Zayn and gave him a nod as she yawned and checked the surrounding area, surprised she was still dry. Lyu picked up a small stick and tossed it at Tanyel, hitting him right in the forehead. He didn't budge. Lyu smiled as they rose to their feet. Just before he attempted to tell her about Wilso, Typher's voice boomed, startling them both.

"Time to move! We said we would have an early start, and the plains are not too far ahead." Tanyel and Wilso grunted and stumbled to their feet. Zayn's heart raced as he tried not to make eye contact with Wilso.

Tanyel smacked his dry lips together as he touched his forehead with a confused look and said, "Well, a decent night's sleep for once."

"I would agree," Wilso said as he gathered his belongings. "And Typher is correct. We need to get moving. We must make it to the caves before sunset. I don't want to take any chances of getting caught in the plains at night. Awful creatures in these parts... and they love the dark."

Zayn's blood boiled as Wilso spoke. No creature, except Levithe, was worse than the bald man standing before him. Zayn glanced around the camp to make sure no one was hiding in the distance.

Typher interjected with sarcasm, "Well then, Wilso. *Guide* us through the plains."

Zayn's thoughts swirled as he watched Wilso look back toward where he had his conversation with Levithe. Slowly turning his stiff body, the old Healer began the march. The others hoisted their packs onto their shoulders and followed. Zayn remained in front to keep space between Wilso and Lyu as the crisp air flooded their nostrils and tightened their muscles as they walked. Rays of light bursting through the trees thawed their bodies as the morning continued. The empty sky hovered above the plains just ahead, where the forest became thicker. It closed in on itself into a mound of brush, thicket, and trees, forming a natural border wall to the plains as far as the eye could see.

"Do you hear that?" said Tanyel with excitement, cupping his hand around his ear. "Do you feel the breeze!? We are close to the southern coast!" Zayn had not realized how far south they had gone since traveling along the river, but Wilso was correct. The route would be much faster than the one they used to take as kids. *We are exactly where he wants us,* Zayn thought as the knot in his stomach tightened.

They all stopped to listen. Sure enough, the faintest rumble of waves hitting the shore flooded their ears as the southern breeze chilled their faces. Lyu and Typher smiled at Tanyel and shared his excitement.

Lyu walked up to the tangled barrier of branches and thicket and drew her mother's sword. She held it up and stared as she signaled to the others for help. Tanyel let out a whistle as he clutched his hammer. "Finally, some excitement," he said with a grin.

"The *nacash* attack wasn't enough for you?" smirked Typher. Wilso maintained a stoic expression as Typher and Tanyel chuckled under their breath.

Zayn, still cautious, kept a masked smile for his siblings as he kept his eyes on Wilso. Tanyel came through with the hammer, smashing the larger branches to tiny shards of bark. Lyu swung the sword with precision, creating a perfect path for them to continue forward. Zayn and Typher used their bare hands to remove and loosen the limbs and branches that remained. Wilso stood at a distance with his arms crossed on his stomach and observed. Once more, Tanyel swung the iron hammer towards an enormous rotting stump, and immediately, light burst through the opening as the stump shattered. They all stepped through the barrier of brush and placed their hands over their eyes to allow time to adjust to the brightness. Their feet stood on soft white sand, and as they looked up, the sight before them took their breath away.

A vast stretch of white sand laid before them, glistening in the spring sunlight. The desert-like prairie extended from the southern shore to the north shore, taking the appearance of a gigantic white blanket strung across the eastern portion of the island. The massive cliffs containing numerous caves were still many leagues ahead. It would take them a day's journey to cross the Barren Plains if they hastened.

The sand below made it difficult to keep a steady speed. Wilso led, followed by Zayn and the rest. They trudged forward, constantly adjusting their packs as their feet sunk into the sand. A cool breeze from the southern shore kept them from getting too warm as they hiked. There was nothing to block their path other than the occasional dried-out patch of tall grass... and the betrayer, Wilso.

How do I get rid of this traitor? Zayn kept repeating to himself as he wiped a bead of sweat from his forehead, looking back to the tree line to make sure they weren't being followed.

"I have a question about the war," Tanyel broke the silence. "What is all this talk about Levithe being the only known survivor? I mean, are we all his descendants?" Zayn and Lyu stared at Tanyel with a curious look. They had listened to their father tell that story many times. Yet, they never thought to ask those types of questions.

Wilso let out an innocent chuckle with a modest, condescending look and said, "It's quite a silly question, son of Erym. Levithe *was* the only survivor. Of the war." He paused.

Tanyel cocked his head as his eyes squinted, saying, "That's why I'm asking..."

"The only survivor of the *war*, I said. There were many on the island at the time who hadn't participated in the war. For you don't think infants or children were all a part of the battle too?" Wilso said, maintaining his calm demeanor. Every time Wilso spoke, Zayn's muscles tightened. As they got further away from the tree line, Zayn wanted to stop and scream what he had seen, but he needed to wait. Levithe had to be watching them. They wouldn't be able to outrun the Guard, and they still weren't sure how they would navigate the labyrinth of caves once they arrived.

Tanyel's face turned red in embarrassment as the simplicity and truth of Wilso's answer set in. Lyu put her hand on his shoulder. "I thought it was a smart question." She winked. Zayn nodded to them, and they kept moving. Typher remained silent in the back, staring ahead absentmindedly.

They continued dredging through the white sand as the midday heat brought them even more discomfort. Lyu was spinning her mother's sword, showing a hint of boredom as Tanyel whistled, swaying his head back and forth, staring at the sand beneath him. Zayn kept his focus on Wilso in front of him while occasionally looking back at the tree line. As he took a sip from his waterskin, he saw something a few hundred paces in front of them. He nearly spewed water as he shouted, "What is that?!"

Everyone except Wilso leaped in the air at the shock of Zayn's yell. They looked up at where he was pointing. Tanyel squinted and jutted his head forward. "I've never seen anything like it before. It looks like a massive hole in the sand."

"It has to be in our heads," Lyu said with poise. "We have traveled to the caves many times and never seen…"

Zayn cut her off, saying, "We always take the southern shore, Lyu. We wouldn't be able to see this from there."

"This *hole* you speak of is nothing special," said Wilso in his typical tone with his hands resting on his stomach. "It's been here for centuries. Only guesses as to what it is or where it came from. Many have searched this crater to discover its mystery. It seems to me it is simply a pit of emptiness." His eyes twitched.

The sun beat against their necks as they approached the giant crater. Sprouts of dry grass huddled around the pit in much denser patches than the landscape surrounding them. The wind from the shore caused the grass to look like still water struck by a stone, rippling in all directions. Wilso stopped before entering the dried brush and said, "This is a fine place to eat. It is just past midday now, and we are making *decent* time."

Zayn's stomach had been at the base of his throat all morning, leaving no room for any food. He couldn't shake the gut-wrenching notion of Wilso's betrayal.

"What's bothering you?" Lyu said in a soft voice. "You keep looking back. I know I said I saw Levithe on the road, but that is a half day's journey north of us. We are safe now, Zayn." Zayn's face blushed in agony. *I have to tell her,* he thought, looking over at Wilso.

Zayn leaned closer to Lyu and whispered, "Lyu, Wilso..."

"Secrets safe with Lyu, but not with me?!" Tanyel shouted, stuffing his face with some bread. Zayn froze and glared at Tanyel. Tanyel's eyes widened, realizing Zayn's seriousness. Typher and Wilso both glanced at the siblings with a hint of curiosity.

"So, seriously," Tanyel said, trying to deter the conversation. "What is this pit? I mean, it's enormous, even bigger than the Stone itself!"

"It's probably something from before the war," said Lyu as she adjusted her cloak.

Tanyel stood on his toes to get a closer look. "Maybe people made it. If people built the grand city of Levitheton, this would have been easy."

"As I said," Wilso spat with a mouth full. "There are only guesses and legends." Zayn wasn't sure, but he thought he noticed a hint of fear in Wilso's eyes that he hadn't seen before.

"Maybe," Typher said. "A few hundred years of legend can make anything seem true. It's probably from the war, though. Sometimes, I wish I had been there to fight and see the real reason the great city was destroyed. Too much mystery can give a man a headache." He looked at Zayn with a smile.

Zayn took a drink and stood, lifting his pack. It always seemed heaviest right after a meal. "Let's keep moving. The caves are getting closer," he said.

"I want one last look before we go," said Tanyel, jumping to his feet. He removed his hammer from his belt to clear some brush to get a closer view of the mysterious pit. Zayn ran after Typher and Lyu as they followed Tanyel. Wilso remained where he was, staring curiously.

After a few steps through the brush, the sand beneath their feet became even softer, causing their toes to sink deeper as they walked to the crater's rim. "Not any closer," Zayn said, holding his arms up, stopping them from continuing. "Tanyel, are you pleased?" Tanyel smiled and motioned toward the pit. Zayn had been so concerned about his feet sinking he hadn't even laid eyes on the crater. *No man dug this,* he thought as he stared at the gaping hole with immeasurable depth. Most of the deep cavity of white sand was glimmering in the sunlight, but a black shade cast over the portion of the crater below their feet because of the time of day. Their eyes gazed deeper into the blackness below.

They all froze as Tanyel took his remaining piece of bread and tossed it off the edge into the darkness. He leaned over, pushing Zayn's arm out of the way. The soft thud of the dried bread hitting the hardened sand below echoed off the crater's walls. Tanyel smiled and patted Zayn on the back, turning away. "Wilso was right again. Just an empty pit."

Zayn continued to stare at the darkness below. His ears pulled back as a distressing pattering noise came from the pit. As he peered closer, the hair on his arms stood as he saw the darkened portion at the crater's deepest point begin to move. Lyu perceived Zayn's fear and placed her hands on the ground before her, laying her body flat to lean over the edge for a closer look. "I can't quite make out what it is, but I think it is a thick patch of grass being tossed by the wind."

Zayn froze as Typher's hand gripped his shoulder. He stared at his horrified uncle, gazing past him, motioning him to look. As he raised his eyes, Zayn knew exactly what his uncle was referring to. The grass surrounding them was at a complete standstill.

Lyu let out a blood-curdling scream as she jumped to her feet. "Run!" she cried. Tanyel and Typher turned to flee, not understanding why she was yelling. Zayn glanced down once more before dread consumed him. A horde of *baraqras,* almost a hundred of them, was viciously clawing up the side of the pit, straight for him. Lyu grabbed his arm and yanked him to move. They both bolted towards the camp, screaming, "Keep running! Don't stop!" Wilso had a massive head start. Zayn imagined tripping the man and leaving his decrepit body to the horde.

"You said we only had to worry about these nasty beasts at night!" Tanyel yelled ahead to Wilso.

Wilso gasped a response, "Darkness. *Baraqras* love the darkness!" He stumbled as he ran, lifting his cloak with both hands to avoid tripping. "And they are not in the least admirers of being disturbed."

Zayn glanced over his shoulder as the horde of *baraqras* flooded over the crater's edge on dozens of tiny legs that bent backward at the joint. Each one of them was the size of a rolled blanket, but together, they formed a unit with the ability to slaughter a dozen men. Their bodies blended with the white sand and glided through it with incredible speed, just as dried leaves rushed down a violent stream. An exoskeletal shell fully encased their soft underside, and their backs contained an uncountable number of tiny axe-shaped protrusions that jutted out in all directions. Not venomous, but sharper than the finest blades. Each creature had two appendages dragging in the sand to their sides as they sprinted, only used for propelling themselves toward their prey once close enough. Zayn knew the most fearsome aspect of the *baraqras* was their silence. No screeches, hisses, or warning cries. Only the soft padded touches of thousands of feet sailing through the sand below.

"We are faster than they are," said Lyu, looking back. "But we won't be able to keep this speed the rest of the way to the caves. We need a plan."

"The only way to stop a horde is to kill the queen!" said Typher, glancing over at Tanyel. Zayn remembered the creature at Typher's house and saw Tanyel nod back at their uncle.

"It has never been understood," Typher said between each deep inhale. "Every single creature in that horde is completely blind... Except for the queen who guides the horde. Every move she makes, they follow. A war general's dream." He panted as he continued, "Lyu is right. We won't be able to keep this up much longer. Zayn, can you get a clear shot with your bow? The queen is somewhere amongst the swarm. Look for the eye."

Zayn head darted back again to search for the queen, then detected something terrible. The horde was spreading out with each step. The outer ranks sped up, and Zayn realized the horde was expanding its rank to form a giant half-circle that would have them surrounded any moment. Jaws of a thousand tiny axes were closing in on them. Zayn signaled his siblings to look.

Typher, Lyu, and Tanyel gasped as they turned to witness the horde gaining ground. Wilso kept trudging through the sand without looking back, only managing to grunt and gasp for air. None of them had any luck spotting the queen.

"I couldn't even hit a *shenrosh* while on the run, Uncle. There is not a chance I can hit one of these," Zayn said, holding onto his bow as he ran.

"You have to try!" yelled Lyu.

"I already told you! I can't do it!"

"Zayn, remove your bow and at least be ready for a shot," said Typher.

Zayn gave up the protest, and just as he lifted his bow over his shoulder, his eyes shot open. He saw the queen's eye directly in the middle of the horde. As he drew his bow and slowed his breath, Zayn had a perfect shot at the queen. Just before he released the shot, his head began to spin. *No, not now,* he thought as nausea struck. His knees buckled underneath as he crashed to the sand, blindly releasing an arrow way off target. Everything blurred as his stew pressed upward towards his throat. He was useless. The horde would have them surrounding any moment.

Then suddenly, Tanyel let out a war cry. As Zayn's head

spun, he attempted to raise his head and saw Tanyel with Ryn's hammer held high, charging towards the horde. Typher stopped and bent down to help Zayn while Lyu tried to catch Tanyel. Lyu kept yelling for Tanyel to stop, but she was too late. The horde came to a halt as the queen noticed her prey charging. The half-circled horde seemed to shift their ranks into a smile of victory, surrounding Tanyel as he approached the wall of creatures. One by one, the *baraqras* used their dragging arms to propel themselves into the air towards Tanyel. He screamed in agony as the ax-like bones sliced through his skin, and the creatures collided with him from all sides. Zayn watched through blurred vision as Tanyel's blood painted the white sand surrounding him. The last thing he heard was a final yell from Tanyel that seemed to shake the earth. *Not again,* Zayn thought, lowering his head, gasping for breath.

Before any tears fell, Typher's strong hand gripped his shoulder. "Look," he said, pointing.

The spinning finally settled. Zayn brushed the sand from his cloak as he lifted his eyes toward Tanyel. He wasn't surrounded any longer. All the *baraqras* were frantic, sprinting away in different directions. As they drew close, they found Tanyel lying face down, covered in blood, no longer holding his hammer. The cuts on his body were too many to count, with fresh blood still seeping out onto the white sand. Lyu had already begun ripping shreds of cloth from her cloak to stop the bleeding. Zayn's face reddened as another wave of bitterness overwhelmed him. *If only I were a Healer, Tanyel would be fine. Or an Incinerator, Wilso would be ash,* he thought as his veins throbbed from the anger. His mind came to a crashing halt at Typher's startling shout.

"The queen!" Typher yelled. "Tanyel got the queen!"

All the blood had distracted him from what was lying only a few paces away from his brother. The unrecognizable body of one of the creatures. Its entire shell had numerous gaping holes, and both of its appendages were smashed flat, spewing yellowish pus. Tanyel's hammer stuck spike-side down, straight through a massive hole in the center of the creature's face. The queen's eye. Tanyel defeated the horde.

Lyu let out a gasp as Tanyel's body started to move. They rolled him over to check the severity of his wounds.

"I had to," Tanyel whispered as he coughed with a smile. "If we had waited for Zayn to take a shot, we would all look like me. Or worse."

"Tanyel, how did..."

"When Zayn hit the sand, I spotted the eye, and I went for it. I figured a few cuts wouldn't be that bad," Tanyel said.

Lyu and Zayn shook their heads. "You are going to get us all killed one day, brother," Zayn said.

"Your *shenrosh* spells might kill us sooner, brother," Tanyel replied with a grin. Typher and Lyu couldn't hold in their laughter as

Zayn's shoulders relaxed.

Wilso approached and spoke with a curious voice, "Well, with all the blood on the sand, I thought you might be dead. *Baraqras* sure do make a mess of things, but they take a long time to kill. You fared well today, youngest son of Erym." He turned and walked back toward the caves.

The adrenaline wore off immediately after Wilso spoke. The pit in Zayn's stomach returned as he stared at the back of the man's glaring head. *I could release an arrow right through his skull,* he thought, looking back toward the tree line. *Once I have the chance, I will.*

"Help me up, Lyu. It's really not that bad. I can walk," Tanyel said with a genuine smile, struggling to his feet. "I'm sorry for causing the scare. But I did just save the day." Covered in blood, he grunted as he lifted his pack and marched ahead towards Wilso.

"At least clean yourself up a bit," Zayn said, handing Tanyel a waterskin. "Nothing says suspicious like a blood-soaked cloak."

"Thanks, Zayn," Tanyel said.

Zayn gripped Tanyel's shoulder and looked right into his eyes. "No, brother. Thank you. You really did save us today."

Tanyel nodded, then looked down at his father's blood-stained hammer. His shoulders relaxed as he stood tall, smiling as he began wiping the blood from his skin, wincing at every cut he passed.

Chapter 10

The Tuskoth Caves

ZAYN STARED FORWARD as the sunset's reflection from the west painted the mountainous caves a glowing pink. His heel continued to bother him as he walked through the sand with a subtle limp, not noticeable to the others. The ground below was no longer pure white sand and became much easier to walk through the closer they got to the caves. The ground was littered with large, smooth stones and patches of dirt and damp grass. Wilso still led a few paces ahead as Zayn remained back with his siblings and Typher.

Tanyel's wounds didn't seem to hinder him in the slightest as he marched forward. Zayn was so proud of him as he raised his shoulders back and stood upright. He breathed in the coastal air as

THE SEARING STONE

they continued to march in silence.

The cliffs towered above them as they drew closer, casting a blanket of shade across half of the sandy plains. A mixture of both jagged and smooth mountains stretched from where they stood, all the way to the northern shore. Groves of lush grass and colorful flowering trees covered the cliffs' base. The mountainous cliffs held numerous entrances and caverns so deep that only a portion had been explored. Zayn looked back once they reached the base and lost his breath. The sun set over the city to the west, and the island seemed to glow red hot like iron forged in the flame. Still no sign of Levithe.

"It seems we have made it before dark," Wilso said, taking a seat on one of the large smooth stones. "It would be wise to rest a bit before entering the caves. Which entrance were you looking for?" He stared at Zayn with brows slightly descended.

He wasn't able to decipher if Wilso was stalling or being truthful. Nothing about the old Healer made sense. He guided but didn't heal them. He offered friendly advice, yet always accompanied by his odd condescending tone. Zayn wished he would have gone with his gut from the beginning. They had no reason to invite this man along. Before responding, Zayn froze as an idea flooded his brain.

"Lyu, Tanyel, Uncle. Wilso is right. We should rest and eat before we enter," Zayn said. "I will show Wilso the entrance. Save me some food, Tanyel."

"You got it," Tanyel said. "Don't take too long."

"Let's go, Wilso," Zayn said as his heart raced.

Wilso stumbled to his feet after scarfing down his rations. "Lead the way, eldest son of Erym," he said with a full mouth.

Three visible entrances were near their location. Zayn knew the one furthest south was the correct entrance but led Wilso to the one just north of it. A pile of large stones created a border blocking the human-sized hole in the mountain. Wilso approached the entrance and attempted to kick some rocks, blocking the way. They didn't budge.

"You are certain this is the entrance?" Wilso said, eyeing Zayn, continuing to kick the stones.

"If we can move enough of these stones, we should be able to see three tree branches laying across one another, just inside the cave. A marker to remember," Zayn lied, keeping a straight face.

"Well, would you mind assisting me? The stones are quite heavy," Wilso said.

Zayn kicked the rocks at the same time as Wilso. One of the larger boulders slipped off the barrier, creating a hole of darkness just big enough for a head to fit through. Without warning, Wilso bent down and peered inside. *This is it,* Zayn thought, bending down to grab a large boulder.

"It appears there are no sticks in sight," Wilso said, grunting.

"They are pretty far in," Zayn said, freezing as his hands clutched the boulder. "Press your head in further and let me know what you see." Zayn's hands grew numb as he thought, *I won't give you the chance to harm her, or us, anymore.*

As Wilso leaned his head further into the darkness, Zayn lifted the small boulder above his head. He eyed the spot at the base of Wilso's neck where his spine met his skull. Screaming, Zayn slammed the rock down with incredible force, crushing Wilso's spine. Dust from the other boulders soared into the air as the sound of cracking bones seemed to deafen Zayn's ears. Wilso's body went limp as his Healer cloak blanketed the stones beneath him. Zayn breathed at a rapid pace, seeing small flashes of light at the borders of his vision. He couldn't allow himself to faint, so he sat on the ground, lowering his head to focus on his breathing. The rush of fury and panic was something he had never experienced before. Killing beasts with his bow was the only murder he had ever committed. The others shouted in the distance, sprinting towards him, staring at Wilso lying on the stack of stones with his head still inside the cave. Typher bent down to inspect Wilso's broken body.

"What did you do?!" said Lyu, looking at Zayn with a pale face.

"Lyu," Zayn said, recovering his breath. "Wilso. He... he is working for Levithe."

"How could you possibly make that assumption?" she replied, her face switching from shock to confusion.

"Last night, I woke and heard Wilso in the distance talking."

Zayn paused. "With Levithe."

"You could have been dreaming!" she said, with her head tilted. "Wilso saved us from Stawb. I mean, he stabbed them."

"Lyu, I wouldn't do something like this if I was dreaming," Zayn said. "I saw him with my own eyes, and Levithe's voice is unmistakable."

Tanyel took a step back, saying, "Lyu, Wilso didn't kill them. What if he wounded them intentionally. A *perfect* way to keep them alive and build our trust."

Lyu shook her head as her face flushed. She could no longer make eye contact with him. Zayn was suddenly worried she may never look at him the same again.

"Either way, I took care of it, Lyu. And Tanyel, you're right. Levithe somehow knew about Father. He sent Labarth to our house. But he must have sent others ahead just in case Father had left the city."

"But why would Wilso help us? Why wouldn't he simply turn us in?" Tanyel said.

Zayn saw something in Tanyel's mind click. *Father's symbol. Levithe doesn't want us dead. He wants to know where we are going,* he thought. He was certain Tanyel had come to the same conclusion as him. Levithe was after the other Stone, and Wilso was leading him right to it.

"I'm not sure, brother," Zayn replied falsely, hoping Typher wouldn't notice. Still pale-faced, Lyu gazed out toward the plains.

Typher stood after inspecting Wilso's body and said, "We need to enter the caves now. Wilso is unconscious but still breathing. If he wakes up, he will heal himself." He looked up at Zayn and spoke, "And no, we will not kill him. The weight of taking a life is too heavy, Zayn."

"Typher," Zayn said as the tension in his jaw caused his cheeks to burn. "We have to kill him! He sold us out to Levithe! He was going to kill *us*!"

Zayn noticed Lyu look away at his words. *Of all people, she should understand. She hates Seared,* he thought.

"I won't let you kill him, Zayn," Typher replied, stepping closer to Zayn. "He may never wake up with that wound, anyway. Even if he does, it won't be until at least tomorrow. We will be deep in the caves by then, and he will have no idea which entrance we took."

Zayn began to fight back again, but Tanyel interrupted.

"Enough! Typher is right, Zayn. You don't need blood on your hands. We can tie him up if you are really that worried. But we need to get going."

"Fine," Zayn said, raising his hands, avoiding eye contact with Typher and Lyu. "We will tie him up. Help me cut some cloth."

Typher removed his dagger from his belt and sliced four strips of cloth from his blanket. He grabbed both ends and pulled tight, testing their strength.

"He won't be able to move with these around his hands and legs," Typher said, with an odd smile.

Zayn helped tug the knots tight then stood, wiping the dirt off his legs. He felt much better, at least knowing Wilso wouldn't be able to follow.

The sun had almost set as Zayn looked out to the plains once more. Levitheton's border wall glowed far off in the distance as sounds of waves battered against the cliffs behind him. Every moment spent with Wilso that day had been torture. He was finally free of the old man. Zayn turned toward the correct entrance and said, "The southernmost entrance is there."

Tanyel spoke proudly, *"The mist you feel will stir your heart, looking back to see the start, always move towards what is known, there you'll find the missing stone."* He smiled at his siblings and winked.

Zayn stared at the familiar entrance only a few paces away. The cave's hole was much taller than the opening where Wilso laid. As they approached the entrance, Typher began assembling torches with some branches and cloth from his pack. As he lit the torches with his flint, Zayn's heart sank, reminding him of his father only a few evenings prior. Zayn fought back tears as he grabbed the first torch and walked away from the entrance. "Wait here. I have an idea."

He sprinted north, past Wilso's body to the third opening in the cliffs. A small tree butted up against the cliffs next to the entrance. Zayn ripped some cloth from his blanket and stabbed one of the small limbs through the piece of fabric. As he released the branch, the cloth dangled and moved like a flag as the wind blew. A subtle diversion for Wilso or anyone else who followed.

Zayn turned to run back towards his family, and as he looked toward the tree line once more, his body rattled. The dreadful sight of Levithe's Guard at the opposite end of the plains seemed to cause time to stand still. Zayn ducked and crept towards his family. The Guard wouldn't be able to see them from that distance as their clothing blended in with the cliffs. It felt like an eternity, but when he finally reached his family, he shoved them into the caves.

The torchlight illuminated the massive chamber, exposing human-sized dagger-like stones jutting out of the ground and the ceiling. Wafting sounds of flames struck by the breeze from the entrance mixed with the faint dripping of water echoed through the chamber. Zayn found a spot to jam his torch between two rocks, then threw his pack to the ground, rushing to pull out the scroll.

"I remember this place from childhood," he said, scrambling through his pack. "But, we didn't quite make it past this cavern."

"*Too many paths,*" Tanyel said in a voice mimicking his father's. "*You will get lost if you wander too far.*" His worried face glowed in the torchlight.

"Correct," Zayn nodded. "There has to be something in here."

"Zayn," Tanyel said. "We have looked over the scroll a few times already, and there is no map of the caves. Besides, they didn't see us... and because of your distraction, they won't find us." Zayn noticed a slight tremble in Tanyel's words. Levithe was following them. No matter how good of a chance they had not to be discovered, Zayn knew the worry lingered over each one of them.

Zayn unrolled the scroll across his pack as Typher raised his torch to provide light. His eyes fixated on the writings and drawings, looking for any hint that would help them move forward. *Tanyel is right. There is nothing here,* Zayn thought, glancing at the others. He stood to his feet and removed the torch from the stones, rushing to observe the different pathways surrounding them.

Four paths were before him, and Zayn observed each one with intense care. The first three had wider openings, and Zayn found nothing but damp, jagged rock. As he approached the fourth pathway closest to the entrance, he noticed a portion of the rock that didn't quite match the smoothness of others at the top of the opening. He raised his torchlight and let out a discouraged sigh as he realized it was only a small patch of dried mud. Before he turned back to his family, an idea surfaced in his mind. *There is no way it's this simple*, he thought, facing the entrance once more. Zayn spat on his sleeve and began wiping at the dried mud. The dirt crumbled off and turned to a smooth layer as he wiped. Zayn's heart leaped as one corner of the patch of dirt exposed something underneath. *I can't believe it,* he thought, nearly losing his breath from excitement.

"It's here!" Zayn shouted. "The same red scratch mark as the ones in the scroll!"

Lyu and the others dashed towards Zayn. Zayn smiled, pointing at the scratch mark above the opening, and Tanyel's eyes bounced back and forth between the scroll and the mark.

"They match!" Tanyel yelled, and his laugh echoed through the chamber.

Lyu held a straight face, raising her finger to her mouth, reminding them to stay quiet. Zayn couldn't stand the thought of her seeing him as a killer.

"Your father would be proud," Typher said. Zayn took a deep breath and nodded. He wished his father could have been here to share this moment.

Typher patted their backs and signaled them to keep moving. Lyu bent down and grabbed some mud, and covered up the red scratch marking. They gripped their torches tight and moved through the pathway together as Zayn shoved the scroll back into his pack.

The caves' corridors winded in an endless labyrinth of twists and turns. Zayn's legs were tiring because of the slight incline of the caves, taking them higher into the cliffs. His breaths became heavy with each step he took. A few of the rooms opened up so tall, the light from their torches didn't even reach the ceiling. Other paths were so narrow, only one person fit through at a time. Each time they came to a split or fork in the caves, a red scratch modestly covered by dried mud marked the correct path. Zayn's eagerness and torch flame warmed his blood despite the damp, cool air as they traveled. *We're actually going to find the Stone. I'm going to be Seared,* he thought as he walked, shoulders back and head held high. He had waited for this most of his life. Zayn's imagination ran wild at the possibilities of what Gift he could possess and how he would use it. Then he looked down at his arm and ran his hand over the smooth flesh. Never in a hundred years would he have guessed that a small part of him would miss being Drudge. After all, he and his siblings had made it this far without a single gifting.

His mind flashed to Ryn's face standing on the ridges. His father really did have their best in mind, and his plan had been perfect thus far. Finally, they were about to accomplish exactly what their father had trusted them with. "I miss you both, more than you could know," Zayn whispered to himself as he looked towards the flickering torch flame.

Sometime later, they entered a chamber unlike the others. Not a single jagged rock was jutting out from the ground or the low ceiling. The rounded room was so long their torch lights didn't expose the opposite end. Something about the hallway-shaped chamber seemed unnatural.

"Typher and Lyu, you two take the right side," Zayn said. "Tanyel and I will take the left. Shout if you find the next pathway."

THE SEARING STONE

The others agreed and moved along opposite ends of the hall.

Once they reached the middle of the room, the torches exposed the entire chamber, but there were no signs of any pathways. Zayn's heart sank as he grabbed Tanyel and ran to the chamber's opposite end, recklessly waving his torch in all directions to find some hint of escape. He only found damp walls of stone with hairline cracks scattered throughout. His knees hit the ground as he shouted, "It can't be a dead end. We followed everything perfectly!"

Lyu was running in the other direction, double-checking if she missed anything. She returned with a defeated look. "There is no way forward. Where did we go wrong?" she asked, discouraged, sitting next to Zayn, still avoiding eye contact.

His heart pulsed with bitterness as he stared in utter confusion. It didn't make sense. Every red scratch mark was a perfect match. Had they misinterpreted Andyr's clue? Was there even a second Stone? The silence lingered so long that Zayn's anger simmered to the point of tears welling behind his eyes. Just as the drops began to form, a subtle noise came from above their heads. At first, he assumed it was his imagination until he noticed the others lift their eyes to the ceiling. Zayn jumped to his feet and stood on his toes to get closer to listen. The noise stopped.

"Did you hear that?" Tanyel said.

"Yeah," Zayn said, eyeing his siblings. "It sounded like rushing water or some type of airflow."

Tanyel raised his torchlight to the ceiling, revealing a sight that caused them all to gasp. A smooth section of dried mud in the shape of a circle, just like the ones covering the red marks. Except this section wasn't tiny like the ones above the pathways. Zayn's hope rose as he examined the dried mud circle, containing a circumference wider than even the largest man on O'Varth. Zayn was certain the noise had come from behind the mud barrier.

"Only one way to find out," Tanyel said, smiling as he reached up to the smooth dirt barrier. He began clawing away at the dirt spot, and sure enough, his fingers dug in, ripping down clumps of dirt, sticks, and grass. *Some sort of patch*, Zayn thought as the debris crashed to his feet, echoing off the chamber walls. They stared up as Tanyel tore at the hole until finally, he exposed a pathway just big enough for a person to climb through. A tunnel of darkness. Zayn sighed with relief. *We found it,* he thought.

"Lift me," said Zayn impulsively. "I will go first."

Lyu opened her mouth to object.

"Trust me," Zayn responded. "I have to do this. I'll be okay." A surge of relief flooded his body as she glanced at his face and nodded.

Typher and Tanyel lowered their packs and cupped their hands together, giving Zayn a stepping platform. They raised him into the dark tunnel, and Zayn lifted his torch into the cavern to get a better look. He immediately realized the tunnel took a sharp turn at

THE SEARING STONE

its entrance, allowing him to grab a hold. Zayn handed the torch back down to Lyu. "I will have to go at this blind. Can't risk bringing fire into a coffin." He saw Lyu tense, gripping the torch.

Zayn held onto the ledge as they lifted him, giving him the ability to pull himself into the tunnel's curve. He breathed heavily, his heart increasing as the smooth walls closed in around him. As he looked up to begin the crawl, he saw nothing but blackness. *This has to be the way*, he thought, creeping his way forward.

Tanyel shouted up to him, "You got this, Zayn!"

Using his hand to guide him through the blackness before him, he shifted his body deeper into the tunnel. A palm's distance laid between his body and the surrounding walls. Every time he would raise his legs to crawl, his back would hit the stone above, causing his mind to remember the tight space that seemed to close in on him. He had to pause for regular breaks to slow his breath and talk himself through the panic that rose. Sweat dripped from the tip of his nose as he moved, and the sound of his heart echoed through his eardrums. Suddenly, his face shuddered as a terrifying noise from ahead caused every hair on his neck to stand. It sounded like breath mixed with a spring thunderstorm echoing through the tunnel, coming straight for him. Zayn closed his eyes and ducked his head as the warm gust slammed into his face. Before he had time to scream, the gust halted, and the black tunnel fell silent.

"Are you okay?!" Lyu shouted from below.

"Yeah! It was just wind." *If there is wind, there is an exit,* Zayn thought, moving his body forward with intensity.

The sweat from his forehead continued to bead as he pressed ahead, no longer using his hand as a guide. Zayn didn't let up, and the fear and panic had vanished because of the adrenalin. Before he could stop himself, his head slammed into smooth stone. He looked to his left and saw a glimmer of light. He maneuvered his body through the turn in the tunnel and scrambled towards the light. The closer he got, the tighter the tunnel became. No longer able to crawl on his knees, he had to use his toes to push himself forward while his hands grasped for even the smallest crevice. His breathing increased, and his heart pounded in terror. Zayn realized the light was coming from above the tunnel's end. *The exit,* he thought.

Even the tiniest movements of his body caused the stone to press in tighter on his shoulders. He tried to press back against the stone, but it didn't budge, causing more panic. His toes curled, reaching to grip the stone and push his body forward, but they slipped. His fingernails cracked as he aggressively attempted to find a grip. Then, to his horror, he realized his shoulders were stuck. He panicked and tried to push himself backward with his hand. His body didn't budge. Zayn screamed, causing the fibers in his throat to shred. Panic consumed him as his eyesight blurred. The veins in his neck felt like they were going to explode as every muscle in his body tensed with a visceral terror. The faint sounds of his siblings' yelling echoed

THE SEARING STONE

through the tunnel behind him. *I'm going to die,* Zayn thought as fuzzy darkness consumed his eyesight.

Just before he passed out, he saw a hand reach down from the lit exit in front of him. With his final ounce of energy, he grabbed hold of it, exhaling all of his breath to make his chest as small as possible. The arm pulled him one bit at a time through the opening. His body was lifted into the room above, and he laid on the smooth stone floor with his eyes closed. Slowly, his breathing returned, and his heart slowed. Zayn blinked multiple times to allow his eyes to adjust to the torch-lit chamber. He saw a blurred figure standing before him, trying to communicate with him, but he couldn't make out what they were saying. As his vision and senses returned, the person approached and stood directly over him. As the woman bent down, the torchlight revealed her face.

"Zayn?" the soft voice said.

Zayn froze in shock as chills ran through his body and tears flooded his eyes.

"Mother?!"

Chapter 11

The Remnant

WILSO REGAINED CONSCIOUSNESS, breathing in clouds of dust from the fallen stones surrounding his body. His head throbbed in excruciating pain as he listened to his surroundings. *How long will this paralysis last?* He thought as the panic devoured his insides. A slight confusion surfaced as to how he had regained consciousness so quickly. The sun still hadn't set, and the spine-crushing blow from Zayn happened just before dusk.

Before Wilso attempted to move, the subtle sound of tearing cloth, followed by soft footsteps to his left, riddled his mind. As he recognized panicked breaths coming from someone passing behind him toward the south, a smile distended in his heart. *So they are using the southernmost entrance,* Wilso thought, remaining hopeful and still. He knew that if he lost them, it would be worse than treason. He quieted his breath, eager to hear anything else. His hope faded as their voices diminished, most likely having entered the cave.

Small tears dripped down his wrinkled cheeks as he focused all of his mind's strength toward healing the bones between his neck and spine. The grinding and cracking of the bones shifting into place reverberated through his eardrums, almost causing him to faint. The pain's severity caused him to pause for a moment, taking a few deep breaths as he gazed into the darkness of the cave before him. His fists clenched together as his toes flexed inward. Finally, he attempted to push himself out of the entrance, realizing his arms and legs wouldn't budge. Reaching his fingers towards his wrists, Wilso felt the soft texture of cloth binding his hands together. He cursed in agony as he continued to heal himself.

"I have failed," Wilso whispered as spit flung through his teeth. His exhaustion from the healing had made him useless once more, and the cloth bindings made it even worse. He wished the boy had simply put him out of his misery. He had no hope or reason to live any longer. Except for her. As he fought to stay awake, a familiar shout echoed out of the southern entrance, causing his eyes to shoot open.

"*The same red scratch marks from the scroll!*" Zayn's voice yelled.

The scroll by the stream, Wilso thought as his entire body relaxed. The one Tanyel had snatched away after it had unraveled before his eyes, giving him one split moment to examine. *The map was covered with red scratch marks,* he thought as his hope returned, clearly remembering the scroll. Leaning forward on the boulders, he rested his chin against the cold rock until his weariness consumed him.

Wilso's eyes bolted open as the awful sounds of footsteps and clanging armor approached. Momentarily, he had forgotten where he was and attempted to leap to his feet, slamming the back of his head on the rock above. His chest wall rose and fell a few times before his typical energy returned to him. The glow of looming torchlights consumed and exposed his surroundings, reminding him of his fate. Wilso felt the blood in his cheeks disappearing as the cloth straps binding his legs and wrists were cut.

Pushing himself out of the entrance, Wilso slowly turned to face his executioner. "Lord Levithe, I can explain."

"Wilso," Levithe said with a smooth voice as his brilliant armor reflected the flames surrounding them. Wilso shuddered as a few of the guards marched towards the three entrances behind him.

"I had them on course," Wilso begged. "I can still help…"

Levithe raised his right hand and snapped his fingers, causing the brigade behind him to stir. At first, Wilso was distracted by his decision to preserve his life. But as he looked closer, his eyes widened, and horror flooded every fiber of his body. A female Incinerator in the back was being bound by the others and forced forward towards him.

Levithe lifted his right arm again to snap, and his voice boomed a single command. "Hands!" he shouted. The sound echoed through Wilso's ears as time slowed.

The Incinerator standing next to his shackled daughter wore an overly confident grin. Dust clouded the air as two guards threw her to the ground and forced her wrists onto a smooth flat stone. The short man's hands gripped his massive axe as he raised it above his head, grimacing. Wilso screamed as the axe fell toward her wrists, cleanly detaching her hands from her body. Behk's skin-crawling howls echoed off the cliff walls as fountains of blood coated the ground. The short man's face, now dripping with blood, turned cold. His chest glowed as he aimed for the wounds. The violent flames cauterized her wrists, leaving blackened, charred stumps. As the guards released her, she crashed onto the blood-covered stone. Wilso stared, frozen in horror, as his precious daughter fainted from the torture.

Levithe walked towards him, towering above the rest.

"I have already given you enough chances, you pathetic waste of space. Your goal was simple, and you failed. What didn't you understand about my instructions last evening? I will have them burn every last limb off your miserable daughter's carcass and hold open your eyelids with my own bare hands as you watch."

"Wait! I know where they went!" He said, kneeling and hoping Levithe would buy it. "I overheard them discuss their path. I can lead you!" If he told Levithe everything, he would most likely be disposed of. "Please, let me serve you by guiding you the rest of the way. These caves are an endless maze. You will never find them without me." His eyes fixed on the patch of blood-soaked dirt beneath his daughter's body.

Levithe turned his head in multiple directions, observing the caves' entrances. He looked at Wilso with a ferocious scowl and piercing eyes and said, "Lead. Now. But any hint of failure moving forward, and the punishment remains." Levithe turned and marched back towards the center of his troop.

"Lord!" One of the female Healers yelled from the northern entrance. "We found a tear of cloth on the rocks leading to this cave." She held it up to the torchlight.

Wilso responded with masked confidence, "That cloth is a false trail. I loathed every moment spent with those four traitors. Certainly, they are selfish, insolent, and treasonous. But one thing they are not is foolish. I am quite certain they used the southern entrance." He prayed they would listen as he turned and rushed towards the southern entrance.

Once he entered the caves, he would only have a few

moments to find the clue before the others arrived. He desperately searched the four pathways for any sign of a red scratch mark. His panic rose as the stomping sounds of the Guard and Levithe neared the entrance.

Panic increased with every eye movement, not noticing anything helpful or out of the ordinary. Then, as he looked at the top of the path closest to the entrance, he froze. *There,* he thought, raising his hand to a dried spot of mud. As he wiped a tiny portion away, he spotted a peculiar red marking. *This is it,* he thought, sighing deeply. Wilso wiped some mud back over the marking. He had to keep the red scratch clue to himself. Just as he finished replacing the mud, the Guard entered the dark caves. As Wilso turned to Levithe, the god-like face stared back and nodded with a grimace, then glanced over at Behk. She was being carried by two of the Healers, still unconscious, but the bleeding had stopped.

"It's this way," Wilso said, pointing toward the correct path. "I promise not to fail you again, Lord."

"Your daughter is counting on it," Levithe sneered.

Wilso turned back to the pathway and walked through as Levithe and his Guard followed. As Wilso paced forward, four words consumed his mind, *She will not die.*

Ŏ

Zayn leaped to his feet and backed up against the wall behind him, staring at his mother with tear-filled eyes. His feet almost buckled beneath him as the dull pain from being ripped through the tunnel below radiated through his body. However, the woman standing before him distracted him from the pain. She was just as beautiful as he remembered, and despite a few white streaks scattered through her shining dark brown hair, she looked as if she hadn't aged a year. Her dark brown eyes held a slight angle at their edge, and the dimples in her jawline caved as she smiled. She wore what appeared to be a modified Healer's cloak cut off at the bottom with slits cut into the sides. The torchlight radiated off her olive skin as she stood upright, firm and confident, which both intimidated and comforted him. *It can't be her,* he thought, terrified. *Possibly a Shifter?* His heart continued to race, and his eyes remained wide, with no sign of blinking.

"It's okay, Zayn," she said as the words forced their way past tears. "Are any of your siblings or your father with you?" She seemed just as shocked as he was.

"Wait! Don't come any closer," Zayn said, raising his hand. "My mother died ten years ago! Who are you?!" His body was trembling as it pressed against the wall behind him.

The words caught her off guard, and she froze in place, squinting her eyes as she tilted her head. "Son, it's me," she choked on her words.

"Prove it then!" he said, tears welling. "I've already seen you once in the past few days, and it wasn't you!"

She nodded, putting both hands in the air as she moved towards him, presenting herself unarmed.

"I will," Erym said, placing her right hand onto Zayn's shoulder. All at once, the throbbing in his shoulders and knees both intensified and dissipated. The cracks in his fingernails sealed as he regained an immense amount of energy through her healing.

"You see. I am not a Shifter, Zayn." Erym pulled her sleeve up, exposing the four-petaled branded symbol. Without hesitation, she recalled every close memory imaginable from Zayn's childhood without missing a detail. Even reciting more events than he could remember. Zayn's rigid shell shattered as chills radiated through his entire body, and tears streamed down his face. *How is this possible?* He thought.

Zayn looked down at his mother and said, "It's really you."

She threw her arms around him, laying her head on his chest, weeping with joy. He joined her and kissed her on the forehead as they embraced, the sounds of their tears mixed with laughter resounding through the cavern. His father's words from three days ago, just before they entered the ruins, echoed through his mind. *"We have to do this... as a family... for your Mother."* Zayn continued to weep. His Father's perfect plan had once again shattered his expectations. As they released their embrace, Erym stared up at him, grabbing his face with both hands, examining him with an unstoppable grin.

"You have grown into an amazing young man," she said. "Brave, handsome, and strong. I wasn't sure if I would ever see you or your siblings again. I have so much to tell you."

Zayn's eyes shot open at her words. "Mother! Tanyel, Lyu, and Typher are in the cavern below this tunnel!"

"Typher?" she said with a confused look.

"Yes," Zayn replied, not ready to share the news about Ryn. "And there is something else." Erym's eyes squinted as she nodded, signaling him to continue.

"Levithe and a band of twelve Incinerators and twelve Healers have been following us," Zayn said. "But they are at least a half-day behind, and they don't know which entrance we used or how to navigate the caves."

"You're certain?" Erym asked with raised eyes, displaying a hint of panic.

"Yes," he replied. "I set the false trail myself, and they were on the opposite end of the plains when we entered the caves."

"Come with me, Zayn. We have hidden this place from the Levithe for three hundred years. We will lose every ounce of the progress we have worked for if he discovers us." She kicked a large boulder into the tunnel's narrow opening below, making it impossible for anyone else to enter. Then she turned and ran, signaling him to

THE SEARING STONE

follow.

The first room they entered was filled with dozens of men, women, and children sitting at large wooden tables, conversing and eating together. *The Remnant. It's really them,* he thought, smiling.

A vast cavern that contained several large pockets carved out of its border, creating individual rooms filled with cots, traveling packs, and clothing. Before entering the narrow path ahead, Zayn examined a child off to the side, sitting on a cot holding a waterskin. The child held up the container and let go. Zayn nearly tripped over his own feet because of what he saw. The container was floating right in front of the child's face. It remained suspended in midair for a few moments and then fell into the child's lap. Zayn's mouth hung wide open as he stared in disbelief. Looking back towards his mother, with no time to process, they entered the narrow path ahead.

The corridor before them split in two separate directions. Zayn's ears pulled back as he detected strange clicking, hissing, and shouting from the path to his left. *What is this place?* He thought, trying to keep up with Erym as she headed through the pathway to his right.

They approached a stairway that led them down into a large room filled with numerous washbowls and cleaning supplies. A tall man with dark golden skin, wearing light armor over a hooded cloak, stood confidently. Leaning against the smooth stone wall on the far side of the room, his green eyes stared back as he wore a relaxed grin.

Erym stopped and caught her breath.

"Kayel!" she said in a hurry. "I need you to open the chamber." Zayn stared around the solid stone room in confusion.

"On it," he responded, walking towards Erym and facing the smooth wall behind him.

Kayel raised his hands towards the massive wall, causing the entire cavern to quake. The grinding stone's piercing shriek caused Zayn to raise his palms to his ears as he stared in disbelief. The stone wall split perfectly down the center, creating two colossal doors opening towards him. Dust from the ground and ceiling clouded the opening as the surrounding walls trembled. Kayel released the wall, and as he looked back towards Erym with a smile, he said, "I'm *too* good at this."

As the dust settled, Zayn stood in awe as he saw the outlines of three people in the next room, frozen in place, staring back at him.

"Tanyel, Lyu, Typher!" Zayn shouted. "Come through the doorway!"

Erym looked at Zayn and winked as the footsteps and torchlights approached through the clouded opening.

Tanyel and Lyu sprinted through the opening as Typher followed closely behind. Silence fell over the room, and the three stared wide-eyed at Erym. She looked at them with overwhelming joy and spoke, "Tanyel, Lyu, my..."

"Mother!" Lyu shouted as she rushed forward, flinging her

arms around Erym. The muffled sounds of weeping and laughing echoed throughout the room. Zayn's head tilted as he noticed Tanyel and Typher remaining still. Typher looked like he had seen a ghost. But Tanyel's face had turned stone cold.

"It's really her," Zayn whispered to them, attempting to break their stares.

Typher snapped out of it, stepping forward, but Tanyel remained.

Erym released Lyu, placing one more kiss on her forehead. Her smile reached from ear to ear as she gazed at Lyu, carefully wiping her tears, saying, "You are a much stronger woman than I was at your age. I am so proud of you."

"Thank you, Mother," Lyu responded, shaking her head in awe. "I've missed you so much."

"I've missed you too," Erym replied, looking down. "More than you could possibly imagine." Zayn's heart swelled as he listened to his mother's warm voice. If their father had led them here, then he must have known all along she was alive. He wished more than anything his father were here to see this moment. *We made it,* he thought, as a deep smile caved across his face.

Lyu wiped the tears from her eyes and, turning to Zayn, said, "We thought you died! What happened?"

"I thought so too," Zayn replied, remembering the mind-crushing claustrophobia. "Mother pulled me out just in time."

Lyu stepped toward Zayn and grabbed his hand. "I'm sorry for avoiding you, brother. You did what you had to do. I believe you."

His shame washed away as he stared back at her. "Thank you... I would kill to protect you, Lyu. I love you.

"I love you too," she said, hugging him tightly.

Then Zayn saw Typher walking toward them, eyes wide, with a face as white as Levithe's robe. Erym looked up at him and reached for Typher's shoulder.

"Thank you," she said with tear-filled eyes.

He stared back in silence.

"I know," Erym continued. "Ten years is a long time."

Typher sighed and finally responded with descended brows, "Erym... how? The Guard... ten years ago. They said Levithe incinerated you."

She ignored the comment and spoke quieter, looking into his eyes, "Thank you for bringing them safely, Typher."

Before Typher had a chance to respond, Tanyel's bitter voice echoed through the cavern, "Ten years... you've been gone for ten years. Doing what? Hiding in the mountains. Leaving your *children* alone." Zayn was taken back by the strong words as a few tears ran down Tanyel's reddened face.

"Tanyel!" Lyu fought back. "She is..."

"No," Erym interrupted with a soft voice. "Tanyel has every right to feel this way. If I'm honest, I was expecting all of you to feel the same." She paused and stepped towards Tanyel, eyeing his blood-stained cloak. The golden torchlight reflected beautifully off her tear-filled eyes as she held his gaze.

Without saying a word, she placed her hands onto Tanyel's skin, and the scabbed cuts on his body sealed at once. He recoiled, stepping back immediately, glaring back and forth between his skin and Erym. Zayn had never seen Tanyel act like this. He tried to understand but couldn't grasp feeling anger towards her. The moment he saw her, all the grief and pain he had to bear over the past ten years washed away.

"You don't have to say anything, son," Erym said, stepping back. "Just come with me. I have a few things I want to show you."

"But Mother," Lyu responded. "We have to…"

Erym gently raised her hand. "We all have a lot to share, Lyu. You still have to share about your father, and I certainly owe it to you to fill you in on the Remnant. But if what Zayn says is true about Levithe trailing you, we need to hurry. Come with me, and we can talk along the way."

Before leaving, she looked back towards Kayel. "I don't think there is any chance of Levithe finding us. But if you hear or sense any danger coming, seal off the living quarters' entrance. Do not attempt to fight. Levithe has an army of twenty-four."

"You have my word," Kayel nodded. "But if it were an army of twenty, they wouldn't stand a chance against me." He specifically looked at Tanyel and winked. Oddly enough, it seemed to cause Tanyel's demeanor to soften.

Before they turned to leave, Kayel raised his hands toward the clumps of dirt and grass scattered along the floor from the patch. Maintaining a steady smirk, the debris began to float in mid-air, fusing into a perfect circular plug for the hole above. With one wave of the hand upward, the dirt plug jammed itself into the tunnel's entrance that Zayn had climbed through. *Another gifting,* Zayn thought, filled with anticipation. Then Kayel closed the door behind them, stirring up more dust, causing everyone to brace themselves as the ground shook.

Erym led them all back up the stairway to the room with multiple pathways. Torchlights clung to the walls surrounding them as Erym entered the path where the foreign noises were coming from earlier, now silent. Zayn couldn't contain his broad smile as his eyes flashed as they walked. He kept grabbing hold of his left wrist, imagining his father's symbol branded onto his unblemished skin. *She is taking us to the Stone,* he thought, as his heart beat with excitement.

"Tell us, Erym, how are you alive?" Typher spoke. "And what is this place?"

"You first," she responded, glancing back at Tanyel to check on him. "I need to know why Ryn is not with you."

Zayn's memory flashed to his father falling with the stairwell. His chest tightened as a lump formed in his throat, knowing he had to be the one to tell her. Gathering the courage, he forced the words, "He died, Mother. In the ruins. He saved us from sharing the same fate. Levithe's Incinerator Guard killed him." As the words left his mouth, his face burned red with rage. Glancing at his siblings, they clearly felt the same. It had been less than three days since his death. The haunting part was that it had seemed like both an eternity and only as if seconds had passed all at once. Grief was the only feeling that could tamper with time.

Erym stopped and turned to look Zayn in the eyes. Her face held a confident stare with a hint of sadness. She looked up and to the right as she seemed to ponder something.

"And you're absolutely certain he died?" she responded.

Zayn's eyes descended at the question.

"Well, I guess we shouldn't be," Tanyel interjected. "We were *absolutely* certain you died. Now you torture us again with the suggestion that our father could be alive. Even though we saw him turn to ash right before our eyes." Tanyel looked at his feet, shaking his head. Zayn placed his hand on Tanyel's shoulder to help calm the trembling. Zayn knew Tanyel's anger was a mask, hiding a deep sadness and hurt. He pulled him in close as the tears crashed to the cold stone floor.

"I got you, brother," Zayn whispered, looking back toward Erym. "No matter how confusing and painful this all is, we made it, and we are here with you." Tanyel didn't respond, and Lyu approached.

"Zayn's right, Tanyel," she said. "Remember just after the blast from the Incinerator on the ridges? Just before we entered the ruins. Zayn and I were both panicked, and what did you say to us?" Tanyel raised his eyes, looking at them both.

"He said to trust him," Tanyel whispered.

"That's right," Lyu said, with tears forming. "I know this is all terribly confusing. But just like you've reminded us this entire time. We have to trust that he had our best interest in mind."

Tanyel's eyes glanced over at Erym. But before he said a word, Erym stepped toward them.

"I'm so sorry," she said as she hugged them. "He would be deeply proud of all of you. I hate to admit this, but I have been preparing for this news ever since I discovered your father's plan years ago." She paused as tears welled. "I would have done the same thing for you kids."

Tanyel kept silent, but by the look in his eyes, his walled heart had begun to crumble. Trust was extremely hard, especially when the person had caused so much confusion and hurt. Zayn was familiar with the feeling.

Erym turned to keep walking, allowing the tensions to settle. After passing a few of the torches, she spoke, "The past ten years have been the most difficult in my life. Being apart from you and your father nearly brought me to the point of death many times.

THE SEARING STONE

I owe it to all of you to share why I left… and why it was kept from you. You deserve to know how I escaped Levithe, how I came to this place, and everything since. My story began similarly to how your story began a few days ago. Someone I loved gave up their life for mine, just like your father did for you." She paused, breathing through her nose, before uttering her next words, "The story begins with Sara."

"Our sister?" Lyu said with a confused stare. "But Typher said *you* were the one trying to save her?"

"I was, Lyu," Erym responded. "I had told Sara of my plan almost a year before that night. Every time she came home bruised and broken, I told her I would kill him. Sara fought me every time I tried to plan his assassination. She always told me she was okay and it wouldn't be worth it. But one night, she came home with both hands and feet blackened and charred. She could barely move or breathe, and I had enough. After I healed her, the next day, I told Sara nothing she could say would stop me, and she could either help me or step aside." Erym looked down at her feet as she hesitated to continue. "So she decided to help me. The next time she was scheduled to see Levithe, we would attempt to kill Levithe together. Sara had the idea of wearing the same clothes in case we needed to escape. Once we arrived in Levithe's quarters, I realized Sara had changed the plan. As I sat in the dark chest, waiting for the cue, I cracked open the chest and saw Sara blindfold Levithe. Then, as I swung open the chest to go in for the kill, I stared in horror as my own voice spilled from Sara's mouth. She had shifted into me and stripped her colored cloak, revealing a Healer's cloak beneath. Before I could stop her, Sara sliced the dagger through Levithe's neck, and flames burst from his chest, decimating her body. As the guards entered, I grabbed the colored cloak Sara had tossed aside and jumped out the window. I found my way out of the city and fled to this place. A place Ryn and I agreed we would go if we ever faced the charge of treason." Erym paused and gazed at all three of her children. "Sara knew what I was blinded by at the time. She knew that I would have died if I tried to kill Levithe, leaving you three and your father alone. Sara knew the only way she could escape Levithe's constant torture was death. So she chose to give her life for me." Erym stopped to wipe her tears as the others kept silent.

"You see, what we possess in this cave is the island's only hope of escape from Levithe's tyranny. For myself and the countless others involved, we are confident our lives are worth giving away for this to succeed. Your father knew it, Sara knew it, I know it, and many after this day will know it."

Zayn and his siblings were speechless. Death in any context had a severe sting. But death as sacrifice stung less because it was accompanied by hope. Lyu held a look of disbelief. Tanyel was wiping a few tears from his eyes. But Zayn's mind fixated on his mother's last words. *"What we possess in this cave." The Stone,* he thought excitedly.

"So, Father knew?" Tanyel said, choking on his words. "That you were alive?"

"Yes," Erym responded, making eye contact. "And I have to be honest with you, Tanyel. All those trips to the caves you took when you were younger. Your father came because he was visiting me. And those visits were the only times that allowed me to see you three from a distance. Well, after the sun would set, we would watch you all sleep and weep together. We couldn't risk you knowing or Levithe finding out. You have to understand that you couldn't know. If any of you knew I was alive and the Guard caught wind, you and anyone we were close to would have been tortured for life." Erym broke down as she spoke the final words, lowering her chin to her chest. Zayn was certain every ounce of her words were genuine. A deep empathy washed over him as he envisioned being separated from his family for that long without ever being able to tell them.

Unexpectedly, Tanyel stepped toward Erym and placed his hand on her shoulder. "I'm sorry, Mother. I still don't fully understand. But I'm sorry."

"You didn't do anything wrong, son," she said, placing her hand on his. "You can be bitter at me for the rest of your life, and it wouldn't change how I feel about you. Better to have you near and angry than to have no chance at all." Tanyel seemed to clench his jaw. Undoubtedly, he still wasn't ready to fully trust her.

They continued down the long corridor, breathing in the

damp, cool air. Zayn's ears twinged as the strange sounds filled the hallway from far-off ahead of them. Before he asked, Erym said, "I have so much more to explain, and I promise I will. But first, tell me about your journey."

Zayn shared the events of the past few days with Erym as they passed several smaller rooms filled with supplies, weapons, and materials alike. Erym stopped at one of the rooms, grabbing a blanket wrapped around some unknown items, just like the one in the storage room beneath the floorboards in their home. Every few steps, Zayn would pause as he felt his skin rise from a soft, warm breeze coming from ahead. As his story came to a close, the pathway forward took a sharp turn to their right. Turning the corner, Zayn's eyes widened as he detected two large wooden doorways twenty paces in front of them. The sounds and gusts of wind were clear as day and coming from the room on the right. The room on the left seemed silent, and surrounding the doorpost were dozens of small symbols carved into the stone.

Erym stopped before the two entrances. She turned and looked at her children with a genuine smile. "I don't know how you made it here in one piece... but I am so glad you did." She paused, breathing deeply. "What I'm about to show you is the whole reason you came. It is the reason your father died. It will give us a chance at overthrowing Levithe." Zayn's heart raced as he eyed his siblings. Tanyel remained calm, probably still recovering from his bitterness,

THE SEARING STONE

while Lyu's brows descended slightly.

Just as Erym lifted her hand to press the barracks door open, a loud crash came from the room behind the door on their left. Erym tensed and signaled the others to stay and wait while she reached for the door. As Erym entered, Zayn's jaw loosened as he examined the elegance of the room before him. He attempted to follow, but Erym patted his chest, signaling him to stay.

The vaulted cavern resembled the bedded rooms cut out of the walls Zayn had seen previously. It reminded Zayn of the exquisite houses closest to Levitheton's city center, meant only for the Seared. Furniture built from metal laid perfectly organized across the room. Colorful drapery clung to the stone walls, making it nearly impossible to tell the room was a stone cavern. Dozens of scrolls were stacked in perfect order on a wooden shelf in the corner. As Zayn's eyes reached the middle of the room, they squinted as he noticed a woman in a sand-colored cloak sitting in a wood-carved chair rocking back and forth. Instead of the typical matching headband, a shimmering metal band with intricate details wrapped around the woman's head. He couldn't quite make out the details on her face, but the woman seemed distinctly ancient. Even older than Wilso.

"Mother Aven," Erym said with a slight bow once she detected the broken stoneware scattered across the floor next to her. "Is everything okay?" *Aven?* Zayn thought, recalling the name at the top of the genealogy. The woman who started the Remnant. The founder of the rebellion. He looked over, realizing that Typher, Tanyel, and Lyu had reached the same conclusion.

The old woman's face lit up as Erym drew closer. Dark pits swelled underneath her black eyes as she looked across the room. Dense wrinkles covered her arms, and the base of her wrist contained an unrecognized branded symbol, faded and barely visible. The lines on her cheeks creased as she smiled, and the dark color of her skin glistened in the torchlight.

"Yes, dear," she replied, smiling as her beautiful, crackling voice echoed through the chamber. "I simply dropped my drinkware again. Old age comes with a price." She coughed as she chuckled, looking past Erym towards Zayn. Tears filled her swollen eyes. "So they actually made it. After all these years, we finally have a chance."

Erym nodded and filled another set of stoneware with water, carefully handing it to Aven. "Drink and rest," Erym said. The old woman smiled and lifted the cup to her mouth to drink. Her shoulders relaxed as if the weight of the world fell from them in an instant. She laughed through her nose with her lips closed. The grin she wore was one of contentment.

Zayn almost burst from excitement and said, "Mother Aven... you were there during the war... between the Seared and the Drudge?"

Aven smiled as her eyes glistened. "Oh, my dear boy. There wasn't a war. In fact, before the devastation, there wasn't any such

THE SEARING STONE

thing as Drudge. Everyone had a gift without any need for those brutal brandings. You see, before Levithe's plot unfolded, all people of O'Varth were born with a gifting of their own, and the abilities themselves were much stronger than those you see today."

Zayn's jaw hit the floor, Lyu's face turned red, and Tanyel's brows lowered in confusion. *Everyone had a gift,* Zayn thought as he gazed at the old woman.

"Ah yes, Levithe would have everyone on this island pitted against each other, creating some false story such as this one. It's a terrible lie, my children. The island was in perfect harmony, and Levithe was the one who caused its devastation. His lies buried deep within a third of our people, and at just the right time, they attacked and destroyed both the Stone and our beloved city." Her brows descended as her lips formed a cunning grimace, instantly shifting her tone of voice. "That's why we are here. The Remnant. The great irony of the past three hundred years. A new rebellion formed just as Levithe's reign began. Now, we finally have a chance to cause devastation of our own. The utter destruction of Levithe, his Guard, and his city!" Zayn's body seemed to tremble at her words. Everything his father had said before entering the ruins was true. Levithe's history was a terrible falsehood, and Aven's words confirmed his lies.

Zayn opened his mouth to ask more questions, but Erym interrupted, "We can hear from Mother Aven later, son." Erym turned towards Zayn, motioning him towards the door. She reached for the other door and looked at the others, and said, "It's time."

Zayn looked at his siblings and uncle, perceiving their minds were racing as much as his. Erym shoved open the door, and a blinding light from the other side burst through, causing them to shield their eyes. *Daylight?* Zayn thought, not realizing how long they had taken to hike through the caves.

"I know this will come as a shock," Erym said. "But do not be alarmed by what you see and hear in this room."

The muffled noises from earlier now flooded their ears as the door burst open — growls, hisses, and clicking mixed with the shouts and laughter of both men and women. As his eyes adjusted, Zayn's eyes flashed as he stared into the chamber. Its massive scale reminded him of the Forging Room in the ruins. The morning daylight pierced through dozens of head-sized holes carved into the stone wall at the opposite end of the room. The faint sounds of waves from the eastern shore crashed into the cliffs outside the stone windows. From sword to spear, every type of weapon was scattered along the giant chamber's walls. His heart leaped as he looked to his left, noticing a pack of *shenrosh*. He froze as he realized a slew of other creatures accompanied the pack. A *baraqra queen, muwrs, tallephs, nachash,* many different island birds, and varmint all seemed to be communicating with each other. Standing beside them were a few men and women who wore a belt around their waist with different pouches strung together. One of the men reached into a small pouch, grabbed what seemed like a

THE SEARING STONE

clump of fur, and then his body shimmered. Instantly, the form of a *muwr* took his place covered by the man's clothing. The elegant fawn casually stepped toward the other creatures.

As Zayn's eyes moved away from the creatures, a warm gust of wind slammed into his face. However, the powerful gale hadn't come from the windows. A group of women dressed in cloaks like his mother were breathing giant gusts of wind from their lungs, causing them to fly into the air. The group of men standing by wore gloves and seemed to be tossing stones at the flying women. Zayn realized the men weren't touching the stones at all. Somehow, they were lifting and throwing them with a simple hand signal, just like Kayel had done with the debris. Zayn gasped as the women in the air dodged the levitating stones with ease. *A training barracks for new giftings,* he thought, barely able to contain himself.

All the commotion distracted Zayn and the others from what stood at the far end of the room. He looked at his siblings and uncle, noticing they shared the same wide-eyed gaze. Erym marched ahead through the training grounds, signaling them to follow. Zayn and the others' eyes grew wider as they approached the structure. Excitement and terror filled Zayn's heart as he dropped his travel packs to the floor, causing a small cloud of dust to form.

Towering above them stood a colossal boulder with four giant, unfamiliar symbols carved into its side. As they stared in awe, they noticed the stone held a familiar glow of soft blue flame. Leaning against the boulder's base were three metal rods with forged symbols fixed to their ends. Zayn's eyes filled with tears as he saw the smile on Lyu and Tanyel's faces. Ryn was right all along. They had finally made it to the new Searing Stone.

Chapter 12

The Weapon

THE SHOUTS AND SOUNDS from the men and women training behind them continued as Erym turned and spoke, "Three hundred years ago, the woman we call Mother Aven, along with a few others, found this fragment of the Stone in the Barren Plains." She paused to clear her throat. *The giant crater,* Zayn thought, picturing the dark *baraqra* filled pit.

Erym continued, "Using their giftings, they brought this fragment to the caves. She is the only one we know of besides Levithe, who has been alive since before the Devastation. For three centuries, she has been secretly procreating a people of her own as well as recruiting people from the city, both Seared and Drudge. Our numbers are small, so we alone cannot overthrow Levithe, but if your father accomplished what I think he did, you hold the key to our victory." She smiled as Zayn tensed in excitement, glancing towards his pack.

The sound of a metal bell rang in the distance. The training in the barracks came to a halt as the men and women grabbed their belongings and headed towards the exit.

"Breakfast bell," Erym said, watching the others leave. "Typher, will you follow them and fetch us some food? We can eat together, and you can get some rest once you return."

Typher hesitated, curiosity still alive in him. He had been mostly silent since he had laid eyes on Erym. It made sense to Zayn, considering Typher's response to their father's death. He didn't seem to fare well with his emotions.

"Don't worry, Typher," she said softly. "You and I can talk later, and I will be sure to share with you everything I know. The more people we have on our side with the full knowledge of this island's history, the better our chance against Levithe."

Typher's shoulders relaxed, and he smiled with a faint scowl, saying, "I look forward to it, Erym." He turned and followed the men and women out of the room.

Through the windows, the soft sounds of water crashing against stone became more discernible as the room quieted. As Zayn examined the massive glowing Stone, he realized it held two major differences from the Stone in the city. First, maybe the most obvious were the four symbols. It held the same width as the one in the city, but the height was different, which revealed the other distinguishable difference. The Stone before him was not flat across the top. Instead, it rose into the shape of a mountain peak and within the extra portion of Stone was the fourth symbol. As he looked closer, his heart leaped as he realized the symbol's shape. *This is it,* Zayn thought. *Four new symbols, just as father planned.*

"You may have noticed by now," Erym said. "This Stone grants the ability for three new gifts. So far as we've discovered, the ones on the bottom work the same as those in the city. However, as for the fourth symbol, the one at this Stone's peak, we are still unsure." She paused and breathed in through her nose, leaning in to whisper. "Now that we are alone, please tell me you have the symbols. Your father forged them and gave them to you, right? Tell me he found the Forging Stone," her voice rose.

Tanyel and Lyu reached for their packs, digging through them as Zayn stood, eyes fixed on the symbol carved into the Stone's peak. The others unrolled the cloth they had wrapped their symbols in, revealing them to their mother. Tanyel appeared to be holding back his excitement as he handed his to Erym. The moment Lyu touched her symbol, her brows bent, most likely realizing what was about to happen. Erym's shoulders fell as she released a sigh, grabbing the symbols and stepping towards Zayn, extending her open palm. His knees crashed to the floor in a hurry, shuffling through his pack to remove his symbol. As he lifted the shimmering metal to his mother, she let out a gasp of joy. Tanyel and Lyu were staring at Erym as she held Zayn's small metallic symbol up to the blue flame.

"Zayn," Erym said with a wide grin, tears welling. "If this symbol is what I think it is, we may finally have the ability to win this. We have planned and hoped for this day since before you were born." She paused, clearing her eyes of tears with her fingers. "It's time for your Searing... are you ready?"

Zayn gazed back and forth from the Stone to his Mother as his mouth hung open. All the resentment, all the anger, seemed to disappear at his mother's words. He had been waiting for this moment his entire life and never believed it would come. No more Netting Docks. No more feeling embarrassed. No more hating who he was. He would finally become who he was meant to be. Zayn, son of Erym. *Seared.*

Looking back towards the Stone, Zayn thought of his father. He would never doubt his plans again. Without the last ten years of pain and confusion, the extreme joy of this moment would not have been the same. He only wished his father was here to experience it with him. *I will finally be able to protect them,* he thought, smiling wide as tears welled.

He looked into his mother's eyes and said, "If I'm honest...

THE SEARING STONE

I've been ready for this since you left, Mother. I don't want to wait a moment longer."

She handed Lyu and Tanyel their symbols back and reached down to grab one of the rods leaning against the Stone. Tanyel and Lyu stood in silence as Erym removed the existing symbol from its end, replacing it with Zayn's. His heart sped up as he saw his mother press the symbol to the fourth carving on the burning Stone. The sound of metal against stone seemed to echo through his ears as time slowed. Erym put out her left wrist, signaling Zayn to do the same. Without hesitation, she pressed the scolding symbol to Zayn's wrist, not giving him a chance to react. The hissing screech of burning flesh churned his insides as he screamed through his teeth, causing the most gratifying pain he had ever experienced. Erym immediately placed her palm over the burning flesh, soothing the pain with her Healing.

As the pain dissipated, an unimaginable sensation flowed through Zayn's entire body. Immediate awareness of immense power pulsed through his veins. His lungs swelled as an extraordinary tingling sensation rippled through his hands. The hair on his neck stood straight up, and all of his senses seemed to amplify tenfold. His eyes flashed at his mother as his breathing slowed. She wore a face of awe and excitement. Staring at his siblings with a wide grin, he spoke with bold confidence, "Levithe is no longer the only Seared on this island with three giftings." Tanyel and Lyu gasped, staring at Zayn.

"It worked!" Erym yelled, throwing her arms around her son. "Tanyel, go grab a large rock from over there. Lyu, there are some small leather pouches on the floor just past the rocks. Bring one of them to me!" Lyu sprinted to the pouches as Tanyel began looking around the cavern for a rock. Erym released her hold on Zayn as she backed up a few paces, readying her stance.

"Zayn, I need you to focus on your breath," she said, widening her stance as she glanced over at his pack. "Imagine the air around you as a bowstring. As you inhale, focus on drawing the air towards you, just as you would your bow. Hold for a few moments and then release your breath as you release an arrow, controlled and focused on your target."

His brother and sister returned with the stone and pouches as Zayn tried to follow Erym's instructions. He breathed deeply in through his nose and released his breath. Nothing happened.

"I forgot one thing," she said with a smile. "You must breathe in through your mouth... like this." Zayn watched in awe as Erym took a massive breath, causing the surrounding air to shift in her direction. Her glistening, dark hair tossed behind her shoulders before she released her breath. As she did, an incredible whirlwind burst from her pursed lips down towards her feet, lifting her into the air. The slits in her cloak danced as the caved dimples in her jawline flexed. As her breath emptied, the room stilled, and the wind halted to a perfect calm.

"Mother, that was incredible!" Tanyel shouted, nearly dropping the rock he held. For the first time since seeing Erym, Tanyel had sounded like himself. He caught himself and calmed his voice. "How did you... how many gifts do you have?"

Erym raised her hands to the back of her neck and lifted her hair above her head, tying a quick knot. Raised branded flesh appeared at the base of her neck, revealing a symbol that matched one of the three along the new Stone fragment's bottom portion. "I have two, Tanyel. But before I explain, Zayn, try again."

Zayn focused on his breath and imagined the invisible bowstring. He grabbed hold of it as he inhaled, pausing at the full draw. As he released the air from his lungs, a tempest of air shot from his mouth, and he directed it towards his feet, lifting himself higher into the air. He let out a laugh, realizing the gift was much easier to control than he expected. As he neared the ceiling, he ran out of exhaled breath, realizing a fall from this high could be deadly. "Just repeat the process, son!" Erym shouted as Zayn fell. In a panic, he breathed deep and released, providing another gust that allowed him to lower himself safely to the ground. As his feet hit the ground, he laughed with wide eyes, shaking his head.

"We call it Guster. Its old name is *epha*," Erym said. "Now, Tanyel, I want you to back up a few paces and throw that rock as hard as you can at your brother."

Tanyel hesitated, then trotted backward with a faint scowl.

"When I say so, throw it right at Zayn's chest," she said, looking back at Zayn. "Zayn, I want you to stop it from hitting you."

Zayn glanced back at his mother with a confused look. But before he spoke, his mother shouted, "Now, Tanyel!"

The jagged rock propelled at bone-breaking speed directly towards Zayn's ribcage. The panic rose inside him as he tensed his entire body and raised his hands to block the stone from hitting him. As he braced himself for impact, eyes squinted, the sound of the stone crashing to the floor never came. He stared in awe with hands still raised and saw the rock floating mid-air a few paces in front of him.

"No way," Tanyel gasped, wide-eyed. Lyu continued to stare in silence with a slight bend in her brows.

Erym spoke, "Now send it back."

His calloused fingers gripped the rock even though it hovered out of reach as if he was holding it tight in his hands. When he moved his hand to the right, the rock followed. He looked towards Tanyel and smiled, tossing the rock back with a slow flick of the wrist. Tanyel caught it and held back a laugh, shaking his head.

"Lifter once called *nasa*," Erym said, smiling at Tanyel. "The main thing you ought to know about this gift is its limits. You will only be able to *lift* inanimate objects. For some reason, anything living won't work. The other thing worth noting is that you must maintain eye contact with the object you are lifting. If you lose sight of it or close your eyes for too long, you will lose your grip." Zayn nodded back, staring down at his open palms, feeling unstoppable.

"Lyu, the pouch. Give it to your brother," Erym said. "Zayn, take the debris inside between your fingers and close your eyes. Now, imagine connecting yourself to the debris and becoming one with it."

Lyu, with a bit of reluctance, handed the pouch to Zayn. He reached inside and plucked out a black, smooth, skin-like strip. As he closed his eyes and focused on the material, he felt a slight shimmer to his body as his chest hit the floor. When he opened his eyes, he realized he was lying on the ground, staring up at his family. Lyu and Tanyel jumped back as they stared back at him in terror. Zayn tried to raise his arms to lift himself to his feet but froze as he realized he didn't have any arms. His eyes dashed behind him to examine his body, and he tried to scream as he noticed a long black scaled tail with tiny humps strung across his spine. His scream poured out of his mouth in the form of a terrifying hiss.

"*Nachash*!" Lyu yelled, reaching for her sword. "Where did Zayn go?!"

Erym pointed toward the creature and responded. "Isn't it obvious, Lyu? The knife-spine serpent you see below is your brother. It works similar to Shifting, but with one major difference. A Shifter only needs to see a person to take their form. From what we have discovered, a person must contain an actual part of the creature they wish to shift into for this to work. Hence, the pouches." She bent down and patted the scaled serpent on its head and said, "Zayn, simply focus on returning to your form. It shouldn't be too difficult."

The hissing stopped as Zayn rose to his feet as his body shimmered. "That felt incredibly strange," he said, brushing the dust from his cloak.

"I don't think people ever get used to the feeling of Bruteshifting, son," she said, chuckling. "Formerly known as *chay*, It can prove to be exceptionally useful for hiding, casting fear in your enemies, scouting, and much more."

"And now the final test," she said. "Unlike my own two giftings, which are from separate Stone fragments, The *Tri-Symbol* should allow Zayn to use all three of his giftings simultaneously. Just like Levithe." Zayn wasn't expecting this. He already felt invincible with the three new giftings. If he could truly use them all at once, the opportunities would be endless.

Zayn didn't even allow his mother to speak before taking a slow deep breath and drawing the invisible bowstring. He released the whirlwind, causing him to soar upward, then reached his hands towards some weapons across the room, clutching them with his mind. Two long-spears glided across the room with immense speed, halting just before reaching Zayn's hands. Taking another quick breath to keep himself suspended in midair, he eyed some targets across the room. Focusing on the *nacash* skin that remained curled around his finger, he used *chay*, causing his cloak's weight to lay heavy

THE SEARING STONE

on his new serpent spine. Breathing once more as the *nachash,* he saw the spears falling out of reach. *I need my hands,* he thought, shifting back to himself. As he drew the spears back, he focused on aiming, then launched each of them directly into targets' centers. Taking a deep breath, his lips curled into a bright smile. He was invincible. Finally Seared. *Guster, Lifter, and Bruteshifter. I can win,* he thought.

Erym and the others stared back at him, utterly shocked, as his feet hit the cold stone. She stepped toward him, removing the symbol from the rod, handing it back to Zayn.

"You fared perfectly, son," she said with a smile. "Levithe doesn't stand a chance."

Tanyel stepped forward and spoke. "Mother, I believe it is our turn. The symbols Lyu and I brought you... which gifts do they represent?"

Erym sighed and looked at him, "I'm afraid I may be more of a disappointment to you in answering that question... Tanyel, neither of you will become Seared today. Your symbols don't match any of the ones on this stone." Tanyel's nose creased as his face blushed. Lyu let out a sigh of relief.

Tanyel spoke again as the bitterness began to show on his face. "What are they for then?"

Erym looked back towards the Stone and pointed as she responded, "Look at the shape of the fragment... what do you notice?" Tanyel's eyes glanced toward the Stone, but he remained silent.

"It looks like the one in Levitheton," Lyu replied. "Except, the one in the city doesn't have the..." Her words trailed off as she made the connection. "The fourth symbol..."

"You are exactly right, Lyu. The top portion of the Stone in Levitheton has been removed. Levithe has most likely hidden it somewhere or destroyed it to maintain his power of the three gifts," Erym said with a slight scowl.

"But that still doesn't tell us why our symbols don't match," Tanyel interjected, confused and still red.

Erym pointed again. "Look at the *shape,* son." The siblings squinted as they examined the Stone.

Zayn broke the silence. "It's a circle! At least, a fragment of a circle. If the one in the city held the same peak, they would make up two-thirds of a circle!" Tanyel and Lyu gasped as they realized the shape's significance.

"Yes, Zayn," Erym said, placing her hand on his shoulder. "From what we have learned from Mother Aven, this isn't the only other Stone. There is one remaining fragment. Mother Aven was there when Levithe fractured the completed Stone. The only clue we have for the third fragment's whereabouts comes from Aven's memory of the event. *One fell to Levithe. One soared to the east, and the other to the west.*"

"So this means our symbols are like Zayn's," Tanyel

questioned. "Symbols that will give us three giftings at once?!"

"Yes, Tanyel," Erym nodded. "And when the time comes, you and Lyu will become Seared, just like your brother. You will be the most powerful of the Remnant."

Lyu wore a faint scowl as she rescinded. "Mother... I mean no disrespect. But I don't think I will ever be able to commit to becoming Seared. I am coming to realize there is some good in the giftings, but I truly believe the island would be better without them." Erym cocked her head.

"I can see why you would say this, Lyu. But do you remember Mother Aven's words? Before the devastation, there were no Searings. All were born with a gift. It is how things are supposed to be. Besides that, when the time comes, you may not have a choice," Erym said.

"There is always a choice, Mother," Lyu responded, still squinting. "We can't go back to before. The giftings have caused so much destruction. It seems so contradictory to become the thing I despise. It's not the Seared I despise. It is the giftings." A slight bitterness crept towards Zayn's throat.

As he opened his mouth to respond, Erym said, "I can only ask of you, what we have always asked... that you trust me. That you trust the Remnant's plan. It is our only hope, Lyu."

Lyu softened and said, "I can promise that I will follow you. That I will trust you every step of the way. I will keep my symbol safe.

I will protect you and the Remnant in any way I can. But what I can't promise is that I will become Seared." Zayn didn't understand. Sure, the giftings had caused destruction, but as their power coursed through his body, he felt more alive than he ever had before.

"I understand, Lyu," Erym responded. "What's most important now is that you keep them safe and *hidden*. No one outside of these caves can know that you have them." Zayn flinched, hearing his father's words echo through his mind.

"Mother," Zayn said, chin bowed. "Typher and Wilso saw my symbol." Erym's face tensed.

"Wilso? The healer you nearly killed?" She paused, thinking to herself. "We can only hope he doesn't tell Levithe once he wakes. If he finds out we have the symbols, there will be no place that is safe on this island."

"There's something else," Zayn said with his head bowed. "Father had his symbol when he died. The Incinerators took it to Levithe. I think it's the main reason they are after us." Zayn spotted the terror in Erym's eyes as she gaped at him.

"It's okay, Zayn," Erym said, shaking her head as her eyes returned to normal. "First off, Typher is perhaps the only person besides your father I would have trusted with you three. Second, if Levithe knows, we can't do anything about it. Just because he's seen your father's, and will most likely be informed by Wilso, does not mean he assumes Tanyel and Lyu are carrying one." The words left

THE SEARING STONE

her mouth unsteadily, attempting to keep them from worrying.

"Mother, I still don't understand why can't we receive one of these individual giftings here, right now?" Tanyel said as his furrowed brow remained. "Having the ability to fly or shift into a beast could prove useful until we find the next Stone. Also, you said there are three fragments? That means either Lyu's symbol or mine is the same one as Levithe's. You said it yourself, his is either destroyed or impossible to find." Tanyel drew his finger across his nose as he took a quick breath.

"Your idea is one I have contemplated often, son. But our concern is that the *Tri-Symbols* will no longer work once you receive a single gift. We have found that combining individual gifts from the two known Stones works fine. Like me, for example, Healer from the fragment in the city, and Guster from the fragment here. However, we can't risk your *Tri-Symbols* not working once we find the other fragments… I'm sorry, Tanyel. Along with Mother Aven, your father has made it clear that you must only use the symbol given to you. Besides, we have a few Drudge among us we have kept for this very moment. By the end of the day, we will have multiple *Tri-Symbol* warriors on our side to protect us as we begin our search for the final fragment." Erym paused. "I only pray we find it before Levithe finds us." Zayn knew the look of Tanyel's disappointment. *Your turn will come soon. I will make sure of it,* Zayn thought.

"We will," Zayn said. "*He* won't have a chance at stopping

us."

Erym bent down and picked up the blanket of items she had brought along. She looked at each sibling before unraveling the blanket. "Tanyel, I may not be able to give you the gift of Searing today, but I do have a few items for each of you. I have been waiting for this moment for the past ten years. I hope you receive them well."

As the blanket unrolled, Zayn's eyes squinted as he leaned forward. Erym removed three metallic chest pieces made from the same material as Levithe's tower. Across the top of each were the engraved words *The Remnant,* and right in the center was a perfect circle, cut into thirds, representing the completed Stone. One-third was blank, representing the final fragment. Light coming through the cavern's windows brilliantly reflected off the armor as the soft chiming of metal reverberated through their ears. Erym smiled, handing one to each of them.

"These are for new recruits," she said as she pulled her cloak away from her neck, exposing the same armor underneath. "This metal is strong enough to momentarily repel Incinerator flames."

"What do you mean momentarily?" Lyu asked, removing her outer cloak, placing the chest piece over her shoulders.

"The metal can protect you from the initial blast, but remember, it's still metal. If exposed to fire for too long, the metal becomes scorching hot, eventually burning the person it protects."

"Then what is the point?" Tanyel asked, already having

THE SEARING STONE

fastened the armor to his chest.

"The point is, son, it is better to have a scarred chest than to turn to ash. You've seen what Incinerator flames can do to a body. This armor prevents that from happening." She lowered her head as she finished. Zayn knew the words had cut all of them deeply. Erym had seen Sara's body disintegrate ten years ago. Incineration was one of the worst ways to watch someone die. Zayn shuddered at the thoughts.

As the silence remained, Erym retrieved the second batch of items from the blanket to reveal hundreds of square-shaped individual parchments neatly tied together in three separate stacks. Tears flooded Erym's eyes as she gave one stack to each sibling. Zayn noticed the same curious look in each of his siblings' eyes. *What are they?* He thought, untying the string.

Erym didn't say a word. She just watched with tears flowing down her cheeks. As Zayn flipped over the first one, his heart shattered at what he read at the top. *Dear Zayn, It has been one day since leaving you...* Zayn's tears collided with the parchment as he read on, finishing one, then flipping to the next. Hundreds of letters, written to each of them, over the past ten years. He looked up at Tanyel and Lyu with blurred eyes and heard them sniffling as they shuffled through their letters. Wiping his eyes, he saw Tanyel staring at Erym with tears streaming down his face.

"This whole time," Tanyel choked. Erym nodded back,

maintaining eye contact.

"The most painful ten years of my life, son," she said. "Writing these letters was my only hope of eventually... one day... proving to you that not a day has gone by that I haven't loved you."

Instantly, Tanyel leaped towards their mother, wrapping his arms around her. Zayn and Lyu joined as an eruption of weeping filled the room.

"I've missed you so much, Mother," Tanyel said. "I love you."

"And I love you too," Erym's muffled voice responded. "I'm so sorry I left."

"I understand now," Tanyel responded. "Please promise not to leave us again."

"With everything in me, I promise. I will never leave any of you again."

They held each other as their sobbing slowed. Eventually, all of their expressions softened. Zayn stepped back, and just as he went to reach for the rest of his letter, the sounds of footsteps approached from the hallway behind them. Typher strolled through the entrance with five bowls of food and long strips of cleaning cloth. The aroma of fresh bread and cooked meats flooded their nostrils. The three siblings slid their symbols back into their pockets as they all set their stack of letters next to their packs.

"Thank you, Typher," Erym said. "You missed quite the show."

Typher stared at the Stone as the dust from Zayn's whirlwinds settled. He seemed to be putting all the pieces together in his mind at once. "So the symbol wasn't a toy," he said, staring at Zayn, then back at the Stone. "From what I remember, the only symbol that looks familiar is…"

"It's a *Tri-Symbol*," Zayn said, smiling at his uncle. "We now have a chance at defeating Levithe." Typher breathed through his nose, his eyes glowing pridefully.

"Well done, Zayn. You can show me your new talents after we eat," Typher said, handing each of them a bowl.

He hadn't had time to process how incredible it was that they were sharing a meal with their mother for the first time in ten years. He listened intently to his mother laugh as Lyu, Tanyel, and Typher retold some stories from their trip. Seeing Tanyel's smirk again, exposing the dimples beneath his blue eyes, brought Zayn immense joy. *We're all going to be okay,* he thought.

Once he finished eating, Zayn pulled his pack towards him, laying down to rest. The others did the same as the sounds of waves crashing against the cliffs below rumbled through the stone windows. Because they hadn't slept since before the Plains, exhaustion gained control.

Erym rose to her feet and headed towards the door to the hallway, saying, "You rest while you can. I am going to check in with Kayel and bring back those Drudge for branding so that we can be prepared in the off chance Levithe finds us." As his eyes became heavy, Zayn watched as her tiny figure disappeared through the doorway. He looked back at the others and perceived the same fatigue on their faces. While Lyu and Typher were nearly asleep, he saw Tanyel was still going through his letters. As Zayn adjusted his head on his pack, he closed his eyes and drifted off to sleep with one feeling flowing through his mind, *Peace.*

Ŏ

Kayel leaned against the stone wall, examining his fingers as a small knife with a hallowed handle floated in the air at eye level. He had his eyes fixed on a small wooden plank hanging above a washbowl across the room. With a quick flick of his leading finger, the knife flung towards the wall with immense speed. A thudded, clapping noise echoed across the room as the knife buried itself deep into the center of the board. Kayel smiled and let out a satisfied grunt as he reached under his chest armor to remove another knife. *I can't believe they actually came,* he thought to himself as he launched another knife into the wooden plank.

As Kayel went to retrieve the knives, his adrenaline pulsed more than ever. Today wasn't like the rest. He was one of the most powerful Lifters in the caves, so naturally, he oversaw protecting the entrance. However, he spent most of his days opening and closing the stone doors for others to leave and return. Some were sent out to scout and get word from the city. Others were in charge of finding food and supplies. Either way, that day, in particular, brought a new sense of excitement and purpose to Kayel's soul. He knew Erym had said the chances for Levithe finding this place were slim. But strangely enough, even the possibility of a breach made time pass quicker. Erym had always been one of his favorites because she treated him like a son. He smiled as he plucked the knives out of the wooden plank, placing them back into the strap underneath his armor. Erym's family had finally arrived.

Kayel's ears twitched as the sound of voices and laughter filled the hall above the stairway. A few of the trainees came down to wash up before breakfast, sending jokes his way. He clapped back with a few of his own, having a particular love for messing with the recruits.

Before long, the room was empty again and the sounds above faded. Sporadically, Kayel would place his ear up to the massive stone doors to check for any sign of enemies approaching on the other end. As he went to press his ear to the stone once more, he held his breath. His eyes squinted as faint footsteps resounded beyond the stone gate. *Levithe?! It can't be,* he thought, jumping to his feet to sprint towards the stairway. Before he moved, his shoulders relaxed, and he found that the sound was not coming from behind the stone but from above the stairway. The echoes of this chamber constantly played with his mind. Kayel took a breath as his heart settled and shouted, "Is that you, Erym?"

A man's voice shouted back from above, "It's Typher! Erym's brother."

"You scared the spit out of me," Kayel responded. "I could have sworn Levithe and his gang had arrived."

"Sorry to disappoint," Typher laughed. "Just grabbing breakfast for Erym and the kids. Do you want anything?"

Kayel smiled. "Thank you, but someone else already offered. You are much kinder than Levithe." The echo of Typher's chuckle rumbled as the footsteps faded.

Kayel walked back to the wall and sat against the cold stone, resting his head. As the blood in his veins slowed, his eyelids became heavy. *Now is not the time to be lazy,* he thought, leaping to his feet and slapping his cheeks. A washbowl filled with cool water stood upright to his left. He cupped some water in his hands and splashed it to his face, causing his fatigue to dissipate temporarily. The warmth from the nearest torchlight allowed his face to dry. Kayel paced in silence back and forth across the room, keeping an open ear towards the doorway.

A few moments later, more footsteps approached from above again, heading in the opposite direction. *Just Typher,* he thought as he adjusted his knife belt. Daydreams flooded his mind as he continued to pace. Faint sounds of laughter and clanging plateware came from

THE SEARING STONE

the meal hall above, signaling the end of breakfast. His stomach's growling snapped him out of his mindless pacing. Kayel wasn't sure how much time had passed, so he stopped to press his ear against the stone doors once more. He slowed his breath and placed his hand on his opposing ear to block out sounds coming from above.

After a few moments of holding his breath, Kayel's eyes darted open as his body froze. Muffled voices were coming from the other side of the stone doorway. The increased rate of his pounding heart pulsed through his eardrums, making it difficult to make out what the voices were saying. Only the sounds of deep guttural shouting and the subtle whimpering of an older man. Kayel stepped away from the wall in silence. *There is still a chance they won't discover the doorway,* he thought, creeping back towards the stairs.

The shouting stopped, along with the whimpering. For a moment, Kayel's shoulders relaxed, hoping they might be in the clear. He waited for any sign of disturbance, and then suddenly, something crashed into the stone wall in the room outside the entrance. Dust burst from the wall as the silence from the other room remained. Kayel stared in horror at the massive stone doorway. Somehow, the force from the impact on the other end had cracked the stone doors open, allowing the flickering torchlight to seep through. *No!* Kayel thought as the sounds of awful laughter poured through the tiny cracked opening.

Before he turned to run, a terrifying command burned his

ears, causing his bones to grind within.

"Fire, now!" The command froze time.

Violent red-hot flames pierced through the small crack in the doorway, causing the entire room to shake. Kayel fled up the stairway, avoiding the inferno below him. The tiny crack in the doors widened as more flames poured through, destroying everything in their path. The awful voice in the other room shouted louder, "Don't let up!" Kayel spit through his teeth, desperately trying to hold the stone doors closed with his *nasa*.

Kayel knew he had to fulfill Erym's command. As he released his hold on the stone, he looked back once more, and the colossal doorway burst open, fire filling the room. The flames released, and he saw an elderly male Healer lying in pain next to the opening. As Kayel sprinted up the stairs, Levithe's horrifying laughter seemed to cause the entire quarters to quake.

Sweat dripped from his forehead as he breathed heavily, running towards the hallway ahead. Before he turned, someone crashed into him, making him stumble. Erym.

"It's him!" Kayel shouted. "Levithe is here!"

Erym's face was pale as she nodded towards him, out of breath. "You must do as I asked Kayel, now!"

Kayel turned to the path leading towards the meal hall and examined the rocks above. He raised his hands, focusing on tearing the rocks from the wall with his mind. One by one, thick immovable boulders crumbled to the floor, stacking atop one another, creating a barricade. Cracks appeared above as he pulled, splintering the stone, causing chunks to release one at a time.

Erym grabbed Kayel's shoulder, looked him in the eyes, and said, "You need to be on the other side first. Then finish the barricade. I don't want him finding the rest of the Remnant."

Kayel protested but noticed Erym's breath as a gust of wind lifted him gracefully through the remaining opening. He shook his head, and tears welled as the gust caused the splintered stones above to release, closing the pathway. His last sight of Erym was a confident smile on her face, nodding to him.

"I need Levithe to come to the barracks," Erym whispered through a hairline crack in the stone barrier. "Zayn has the *Tri-Symbol*, Kayel. We can finally win! Hold everyone here until we come to get you."

Before Kayel responded, the corridor shook, and he heard Erym fleeing in the other direction. He pressed his ear to the barricade of crumbled stones as his heart pounded. A stampede of footsteps and angry voices charged toward the barracks' direction. *Erym, I hope you're right,* he thought, shaking his head as he turned to dash towards the meal hall. The surrounding stone hallway continued to rumble as fear consumed his entire body. *She has to be right.*

Chapter 13

The Searing

BRIGHT RAYS OF SUNLIGHT from the dawn reflected off Levithe's Tower as Ganya, Naye, and Deshome approached its entrance. The Tower's peak pierced the low-hanging clouds above as Ganya stared in awe. His nerves mimicked the times in the forests when he would stalk the most dangerous of prey. A sharp pain radiated through his back as Deshome jabbed him to keep going.

"We don't know how long Levithe will be gone," she whispered, with slight irritation. "Let's go."

Ganya's eyes snapped back into focus, and he turned and glared at her. Naye prodded him further by shoving him forward. Deshome and Naye laughed. As Ganya turned to shout, he noticed the Stone behind them. The awful wailing sounds of infants had suddenly become noticeable as he stared. For a moment, he was glad he didn't have to worry about putting children of his own through the torture of Searing. Naye snapped her fingers, signaling him to continue moving.

"We need to escort this Drudge to the tower's prison," said Deshome, exposing her branded wrist to two Incinerators guarding the entrance.

"We don't get many Drudge to the Tower," said the taller guard. "Usually, they are killed outright. What makes this one so important?"

Naye interjected, "He is connected to the ones who escaped. We need someplace to keep him so that Lord Levithe can deal with him later."

Ganya pretended to resist, and Deshome hit him with another jab to the back.

The other guard spoke up, "But... our Lord is..."

"Away at the moment," interrupted Deshome. "We know. Now would you please step aside and let us put this filth where he belongs." Ganya kept his head bowed as he fought back a smile at the brutal comments.

Naye and Deshome shoved him through the narrow entrance as the two guards handed them a key and stepped aside. As they entered the Tower's base floor, Ganya's eyes broadened to adjust to the low-lit chamber. Only a few torches clung to the walls, exposing a tremendous dark barracks filled with storage for both armor and weaponry, and in its center, a massive spiral stairway. As they made their way to the stairs, Ganya looked up, realizing the stairway was the Tower's main support beam. It spanned upwards out of sight, with every floor connecting to its center.

"It's only a few floors up," Naye said as they began their ascent. "We need to keep an eye out for Labarth. I'm certain he has been given the responsibility of the Tower while Levithe is gone."

"There is only one way out of this Tower," whispered Ganya. "How are we supposed to help these prisoners escape?"

"We will figure it out once we get there," said Deshome. "I'm sure the prisoners have information for us that will be helpful." Ganya nodded and kept walking.

His legs burned with each step up the steep stairwell until finally, they reached the prison floor. Ganya shielded his eyes as they entered the prison hallway. An uncountable number of torches lined the walls, revealing the most immaculate chamber he had ever seen. The colors and elegance caught him off guard as he began to feel an odd sense of harmony. As they moved further down the hall, the joy turned to a knot in his stomach as awful smells struck his nose. Ganya's insides churned as they came across the first cell. Prisoners were crammed together in the exquisite chamber, leaving barely enough room for any of them to move. Tortured groaning and weeping echoed off the beautiful walls surrounding them, reminding him of wounded prey left to die. Ganya almost gagged as he noticed a combination of blood, urine, and feces soaking the floor. The prisoners didn't even seem to notice them pass, as their glossed eyes stared blankly ahead.

Deshome tapped Ganya and pointed ahead to a cell further down the hall, whispering, "It's them."

They darted for the cell doors and realized multiple people they recognized were in the last few cells.

"There are more than I thought there would be," said Ganya through the side of his mouth. "What now?"

Naye ignored his question and unlocked the three cells at the hall's end. Ganya had a shiver run through his spine as he wondered whether the prisoners were asleep or dead.

Deshome pointed as she said, "I'll take the first cell. Naye, you get the second, and Ganya…"

"Yeah, yeah. I got it," he said as he slipped his hands out of the loose bindings.

Ganya crept toward the third cell as his heart rate steadily increased. The hinges screeched as he pulled the door open, causing the prisoners to stir. He noticed a prisoner in the back, lying covered in a blanket, trembling and murmuring to himself.

The prisoner closest to him grunted as she struggled to her feet, using his shoulder to maintain her balance. Her golden hair hung past her shoulders as her glossy brown eyes stared back at him. Ganya recognized her tan-skinned face beneath the sunken eyes and grime.

"Shayde," he said, helping her balance. "We're going to get you out of here."

Shayde's brows raised as she shook her head. "Ganya. You shouldn't be here..."

"It's okay. Deshome and Naye are in the other cells. They have a plan for our escape," he said, hoping he was right.

Shayde's face displayed a hint of relief as she signaled to the others. Every last one of the prisoners rose to their feet, brushed the dust from their armor and cloaks, and moved toward the door. All except the man lying in the back. Ganya moved his way towards the trembling man as Shayde spoke. "It's no use, Ganya. He won't eat. He won't move. We've tried."

Ganya glanced down at the man and said, "What happened to him?"

Before Shayde answered, the blanketed man's murmuring became louder, allowing Ganya to make out some of the words.

"My fault... he won... ruined... they don't know..." the man whimpered.

The voice sent a shiver down Ganya's spine, so he reached down to remove the blanket. As he gripped the cloth and pulled, the man's voice became more violent, repeating the same rambled words.

Ganya's heart raced as he went to uncover the man's head.

Suddenly, the cell doors behind him slammed shut, causing his ears to ring. His head darted toward the doors, and as he noticed the man on the other side, his veins filled with rage.

Stawb, accompanied by Feeld, stared through the cell door, grimacing back at Ganya and the other prisoners. Ganya froze as he realized Stawb was holding someone hostage with a knife to their throat.

"Naye!" Ganya screamed. "Take me instead! Let her go!"

Stawb sneered, "You think I would leave a Healer alive in these cells? Everyone knows the treasonous Healers die first." Ganya stared back with hatred as he dashed for the cell door, cursing at Stawb.

"No use fighting, Drudge," Stawb mocked. "As soon as Levithe and my father return, you and every traitor in these cells will be ash."

Suddenly, Ganya's eyes broadened as Naye lurched her head backward, crushing Stawb's nose, then turning toward him to shove herself off. Her strong fist lunged towards Feeld's face, squaring straight across his jaw. Both Feeld and Stawb stumbled backward, hands clinging to their faces, and ran behind the Guard, yelling one command. "Execute these traitors!"

As the familiar clanging of armored footsteps rushed up the stairway, Naye turned and stared Ganya straight in the eyes with a swift nod of the head. Deshome was begging her to move out of the way. Ganya noticed something shiny in her opposite hand. *She still has the key,* he thought as his excitement grew. As the footsteps grew closer, Naye quickly unlocked his cell, then did the same for Deshome's. As Ganya turned back to Shayde for help, Stawb's terrible voice shouted once more, "Fire, now!"

Ganya's eyes both widened and blinded as two beams of flames fired toward his cell. He squinted his eyes to brace himself for his imminent death. But it didn't come. As he looked toward the cell door, his heart sank to the floor. Naye was blocking the flames as her back melted before his eyes. She had jumped in front of the blasts, protecting him and the prisoners. Tears began to surface in Ganya's eyes as he realized what Naye was doing. The blasts of flames weren't turning her to ash because she was Healing herself to hold off the flames as long as possible. Her tormented shrieks caused Ganya to want to rip his eardrums out. Suddenly, out of the corner of his eye, he witnessed Deshome clench her fists and release a powerful beam of flame toward the exit. Her howl echoed through the chamber as the blast collided with the two incinerators, turning them to dust. As the flames subsided, Deshome dove towards Naye, breaking her fall.

Stawb and Feeld stood toward the back, frozen with faces of terror. Without hesitating, Ganya viscerally sprinted toward them, removing both his daggers from his belt. Before they turned to flee, he plunged each dagger through their stomachs, causing them to collapse to the floor. Ganya breathed heavily, leaping toward them, placing the daggers to each of their throats.

"Ganya, don't!" Shayde said, grabbing him from behind. "They are just children."

Panic consumed him as he imagined ending their lives. But no matter how vile these two were, Shayde was right. He removed the blades from their throats as he stood to his feet, remembering Naye. Deshome was kneeling beside Naye's body, which laid face down at the cell doors opening. Her blackened flesh barely clung to her back, causing Ganya's head to shake with fury as he fought back tears. Naye had saved them.

As he approached Naye and Deshome, a rush of hope flooded his veins as he saw Naye's hand move.

"Did you see that?"

"See, what?" Deshome said through tears.

Suddenly, another twitch from Naye's hand, but this time, the one Deshome was holding. Ganya watched as the visible pain on Deshome's face turned to a wide-eyed look of hope. She leaned in close to Naye, holding her breath to listen.

"She's breathing, Ganya. She's going to be okay!"

Ganya felt the tears well in his eyes as he knelt beside Naye to speak, "Naye, if you can hear us, I need you to focus on healing your back. I know you don't have much energy, but if you can heal yourself, we will carry you the rest of the way."

After what seemed like a day's worth of silence, which, in fact, was only a few moments, Ganya blinked as he noticed the flesh on Naye's back begin to change color slowly. Naye didn't move or say a word, but she was healed within only a few moments. As Deshome carefully rolled over Naye's body, Ganya smiled as he met her eyes. The twinkle in her eye met his as she wore a peaceful smile. Deshome placed her hand on Naye's forehead, saying, "Rest, Naye. We will get you out of her. Ganya, get her a blanket."

Before heading to the cell, he glanced back at Stawb and Feeld. His shoulders relaxed as he noticed they had passed out from the gut wounds. Ganya knew he and the others didn't have much time before more of the Guard came, so he sprinted past Deshome and commanded all the prisoners to exit the cells. As Shayde and the others entered the elegant hallway, the murmuring man in the back corner remained. Ganya rushed over to him, grabbing hold of the blanket attempting to help him up. As the blanket slipped off the man's face, Ganya stared in disbelief, recognizing at once who he was.

"If you're here... then who is with them?" he said, nearly choking on his words.

"Ganya," Deshome shouted. "The blanket! She is freezing!"

Still gazing at the man before him, a giant lump formed at the base of Ganya's throat as he attempted to yell back.

"The siblings aren't with Typher!"

THE SEARING STONE

Ŏ

The faint rattling of weaponry along the barracks walls caused Zayn's eyes to shoot open. Sunlight beamed through the windowed openings behind him, providing immense warmth and light to the massive chamber. The stone's subtle tremble beneath him caused his eyes to dash around the room, searching for his mother. To be sure, he glanced down at his wrist to make sure his Searing wasn't a dream.

"Lyu," he whispered. "Lyu, wake up."

Her eyes fluttered as she woke.

"What is it, brother?" Then leaped to her feet as she became aware of the rumbling.

"It could be nothing," Zayn said, raising his hands towards her, motioning her to calm.

Before Lyu yelled to wake Typher and Tanyel, the rumbling halted. She held her breath as both she and Zayn turned their ears toward the exit to listen.

"Must have been nothing," Lyu said as she turned to pace the chamber. Zayn's heart slowed as he watched his sister walk a straight path towards the weapons in the corner. She held her arm out, tapping each weapon she passed, and then stopped at the swords. As she bent down to reach for one, her cloak caught on the edge of the neighboring weapon, causing a chain reaction of crashing metal. The resounding clash of a dozen swords echoed through the barracks, causing both Typher and Tanyel to shoot up to their feet. Zayn smiled as Lyu looked back with a wide-eyed smirk.

"I had just fallen asleep!" Tanyel shouted, rolling his eyes at Lyu. He laid back down and threw his blanket over his head. Typher was still half asleep while he stood to stretch.

Zayn froze as the rumbling began again.

Tanyel flung his blanket off and said, "Did you feel that?"

"Lyu and I felt it once already," Zayn said, looking back towards the exit. "It was so subtle, and it stopped so quickly, we figured it was normal for the caves."

Before anyone else got a word out, the terrifying distant sound of their mother's scream poured into the barracks. It filled Zayn's ears, and he stared at the others as they realized what their mother was shouting as she approached.

"Levithe! He's here!" Erym burst through the barracks' entrance with terror on her face, shouting orders to the others, "Tanyel, Lyu! Grab your weapons and hide behind the Stone. Do not make a sound."

Her eyes bolted toward Typher, and she pointed across the room. "Typher, you need to stay with them." Typher nodded without question and grabbed Tanyel and Lyu by the shoulders to hide.

Zayn stood in shock as his mother approached, placing her hand on his shoulder.

"Zayn, you can do this," she said, giving his shoulder a slight

THE SEARING STONE

squeeze. "Whether or not you believe it, you are the most powerful person on this island. Levithe doesn't understand the giftings you possess, which gives you an immense advantage." She paused as the distanced sound of clanging armor marched towards them. "Your powers can be used to both defend and attack. Levithe can only Incinerate and Heal; His Shifting will be useless in battle."

"You're right, Mother," Zayn said, as his face changed to a confident glare. "It is time to end this once and for all."

Erym slowed her voice and said confidently, "You must always remember that your father and I love you. It is for this exact moment we chose to forgo the Stone at your birth."

Zayn's eyes filled with tears as her words struck his core. He had spent his entire life desperately wishing he was Seared. Now finally, he had a chance to come face to face with Levithe. Finally, a chance to fight not with sword or bow, but with true giftings. He stood upright and stared down at her, smiling. "Thank you, Mother. I'm sorry for not trusting you. All that to say it has been worth the wait." He nodded, turning towards the doorway in a ready stance.

Suddenly, an explosion of flames filled the entrance with awful black clouds of smoke. Zayn saw Erym's face pale as vile laughter resounded through the chamber.

"Mother Aven," Erym gasped as she started to dash forward. "The blast was toward her door, just outside the entrance!" Immediately, she froze in place and stared as two guards at a time entered the barracks. Erym backed up towards Zayn and grabbed his arm, and whispered, "Wait for my signal."

The gigantic chamber around them seemed to dim as the last pair of guards entered. Until finally, Levithe stepped through, dragging Mother Aven by the hair across the dust-covered floor. His perfect armor and flowing golden hair glistened in the torchlight. Thick blood poured out of Aven's body as he dredged her towards the center of the barracks. His hand wrapped tight around her white hair, and he wore a cunning smile as he looked up to meet eyes with Erym. Levithe released his grip, and Aven's head crashed onto the stone floor, sending the sounds of cracking bone throughout the chamber.

"Erym," Levithe said with a violent glare. "Surprising to see you again. Is this one of your pathetic sons?" She stared back in silence. "We can make this simple. If you help me bring the Stone back to the city, I won't kill you or your children. I will give you the privilege of serving me for the rest of your life." His brows descended as he smiled through his teeth. "However, if you resist, I will murder every last one of the treasonous filths living in this cave while you watch, starting with your children. Then I will force you to serve me just like I did with *Sara*."

Zayn stood firm as he perceived Erym's breaths becoming heavier with each moment.

"So, what will it be?" Levithe prodded.

Zayn shouted back, interrupting his mother, "Neither,

THE SEARING STONE

Levithe. You're the one who needs us. You failed this island, and it's time for your reign to end."

The band of guards burst into laughter, and Levithe joined in.

"Well, Erym," Levithe said, stepping forward. "Maybe, I ought to start with your son." Levithe raised his hand, and all at once, the Incinerator Guards' chests glowed red hot.

Zayn stared Levithe straight in the eyes and said, "Go ahead. Fire away."

The words caused the slightest discomfort to show on Levithe's face. As he lowered his hand, he shouted, "Fire!"

Scolding hot beams of flame released from all twelve Incinerators' chests at once. Erym and Zayn both inhaled deeply, pulling the invisible bowstring tight. As they exhaled, a massive wall of air crashed into the oncoming flames. The air twisted into a tornado of fire, and Erym and Zayn pushed it right for Levithe. Each Incinerator released their flame and stared in shock at the massive whirlwind of fire heading towards them. Zayn gritted his teeth as he watched Levithe's face turn to horror as he retreated backward and leaped out of the way. Zayn looked back to his mother, and they released the tornado, causing the flames to extinguish. Levithe rose to his feet, staring back in awe with hatred. A giant cloud of dust filled most of the room.

Zayn noticed the Healer Guards dashing towards the

weapons, so he reached his hands towards the spears across the room and focused. Using *nasa*, he grabbed hold of ten spears at once and maneuvered them in the air to point directly toward the Healer Guards' throats. They froze, stepping backward as Zayn forced them away from the stash of weapons. Levithe's voice screamed once more, "Fire again!" Zayn breathed deep and held the spears simultaneously, creating a vast whirlwind once again, blocking the flames. Erym stared at him proudly as her hair tossed in the wind.

The thick dust and smoke filled the entire barracks, nearly making it impossible to see. The sound of spears crashing to the ground echoed throughout the chamber. Zayn shook his head, remembering the ability only worked if the object was within sight. Zayn squinted his eyes to try to see through the dust, and without warning, to his right, a spear flew right for his chest. He stopped it in midair with ease, flipping it around and tossing it back with ten times the force. The whimpering sound of a man's scream filled his ears. The scream intensified and resounded across the chamber. *Healing,* he thought as anger fluttered in his chest. He wanted them all dead. Typher was wrong about killing another human. If it came to saving his family, Zayn would kill as many as it took.

Again, another weapon launched towards Zayn through the smoke and dust. He found himself overwhelmed with multiple swords, axes, and spears coming at once. He tried to use his breath to clear the smoke, but the cloud was too thick. Every weapon thrown, he caught and threw back, sometimes striking an enemy, but mostly striking the wall or ground. Eventually, the weapons stopped coming as Zayn heard the Guards' footsteps, attempting to file back into formation.

Zayn tried to settle the dust with another whirlwind, but it only made it worse. Then suddenly, out of nowhere, dread struck as his head began to spin. Extreme nausea consumed him as the effects from the *shenrosh* venom returned in full force. *Not now*, he cursed in his mind as he fell to his knees to balance himself. But nothing was helping. His vision was blurring as if he would pass out from the dizziness at any moment. The room filled with the muffled voices of Guard's shouting mixed with his mother's voice yelling for him. A whirlwind gusted right past him as more weapons clashed to the ground. His mother was yet again keeping him safe. Protecting him at his lowest, just as she had always done.

Then suddenly, Zayn sighed as the wave of nausea settled. But as he rose to help his mother, his bones shuddered, and the room grew silent. Before he turned back towards Erym, his eardrums nearly shattered as he recognized Levithe's voice behind him.

"You may have new giftings, boy. But you must always remember, the hand kills just as easily."

Tears streamed down Zayn's face as the smoke cleared. Levithe was clutching Erym by her throat, high into the air, as she frantically kicked her legs, with no sound exiting her mouth.

Levithe's strength and excruciating grip were crushing her throat as Zayn stood still, helpless.

Spit flung from Levithe's mouth as he shouted at Zayn, "Give me the symbol, or I'll crush her throat in front of you!" It was clear now that Wilso had informed Levithe of the symbol. Erym's eyes rolled into the back of her head as her kicking slowed.

Zayn's head darted back towards the Stone as Lyu's deafening scream seemed to pierce his skull. Tanyel and Typher were trying to hold her back, but her fury wouldn't allow it. She escaped their grip, allowing her to sprint to Zayn. Tanyel and Typher followed, and as they arrived, they all stared blankly at Erym's nearly lifeless body in Levithe's grip.

"Perfect!" Levithe spat. "The whole family gets to watch!"

Zayn didn't have a choice. He reached into his pocket and held the symbol high, muting the desperate whispers of his siblings not to give in.

"Here!" he shouted through hateful tears. "It's yours. Just let her go!" Lyu and Tanyel grabbed him by the shoulders, trying to stop them, but Zayn tossed the symbol towards Levithe. Zayn stared, frozen in place, as Levithe's armor-covered hand snatched it out of the air while the other still clutched Erym's throat.

"You are such a fool, boy," he said, as his awful grin widened. "Unfortunately for you, I will not be holding up my end of the bargain! I am Levithe, god of this cursed island. The founder of lies and deceit. You ought to have known better."

Levithe lifted Erym higher into the air as he tightened his grip. Erym's legs went limp as Zayn and his siblings' screams seemed to cause the cavern to tremble. He only had one more chance at saving her, and he knew he had to act now. Reaching his hand toward the symbol in Levithe's opposing hand, he triggered *nasa* with as much force as possible. As he felt the symbol's cold texture release from Levithe's grip, he flung the symbol to the floor, causing just enough of a distraction for Levithe to loosen his grip on Erym's throat. *It has to be now,* he thought, recklessly sprinting towards Levithe to attempt to save his mother. *I will not let Levithe kill her,* he thought, propelling himself forward. Time slowed as he met eyes with Levithe, and just before he made contact, a shower of blood splattered across his face.

"No!" Zayn screamed, blinded by the blood and tears in his eyes. As he viciously wiped the blood from his eyes, he stared up at Levithe. *It isn't Mother's blood,* he thought, recognizing the sharp blade of a spear pierced through Levithe's neck from behind. Zayn and the others stood in shock as they saw a bald man wearing a sand-colored cloak holding the spear.

Wilso released his grip on the spear and caught Erym as Levithe's body crumbled to the floor. Wilso carried her toward the others and placed her gently on the stone floor. Zayn, Lyu, and Tanyel bent down to their mother. Their tears struck Erym's cloak, soaking it as if it were the beginning of a mild rainstorm. Typher leaped up with his dagger in hand, sprinting towards Levithe. "I will make sure he never heals himself again!" Typher yelled.

As the dust settled, the other Incinerator and Healer guards stood by with a look of relief on their faces. Their *baraqra* queen had died, and they were no longer blind.

Zayn, still utterly confused, held back tears as Wilso placed his palms on Erym's throat and closed his eyes to focus. Steadily, the red and purple bruising faded, and her skin returned to normal. The sound of her crushed wind-pipe cracked as it opened, causing Zayn to clench his jaw and wince. Erym remained motionless, eyes glazed over. As the last bit of redness disappeared, Wilso removed his hands. He looked at Zayn and the others with tears and said, "I'm so sorry, children. Levithe promised to kill my daughter if I didn't help him. He sent me ahead to make sure I traced your every move. She means everything to me." He paused, tears streaming down his red face. "I have done all I can to help your mother. I hope you can forgive me."

As Wilso stood, Erym's eyes shot open, and she held her throat, coughing violently and gasping for air. Zayn's heart jumped as he patted Erym's back, trying to get her to take deep breaths. Lyu and Tanyel smiled wide through tears as they hugged their mother. Erym looked at each one of them with a smile as her cheekbones caved. Somehow, against all odds, she had kept her promise never to leave them again.

"Thank you," Zayn said, looking back towards Wilso. "You saved us all." Lyu and Tanyel looked up at the old man and nodded with gratitude as tears continued down their faces.

Wilso nodded and walked back towards a woman wearing Incinerator armor. Her arms ended at her wrists, forming into bandaged stumps. *His daughter,* Zayn thought as he smiled.

"We are finally free," Erym said with a rasp in her voice. "Zayn, you did it."

"Mother," Zayn responded, placing his hand on her shoulder, "We did it. I told you he didn't stand a chance against us."

"I wish your father was here to share this moment," Erym said. "The plan worked. After three hundred years, it finally worked!" She reached over for Tanyel and Lyu and pulled them in close. Zayn didn't think it possible for any feeling in the world to compete with being Seared. But holding tightly to his family after Levithe's defeat was the only feeling he ever truly needed.

Zayn looked back at his mother, and just before he responded, the hair on his neck rose to the shape of a thousand blades. Unbearable darkness seemed to fill the damp air as if Levithe's horn had blasted just paces away. Except the room was silent.

His eyes and ears twitched in confusion as the dreadful sound of familiar laughter blared from behind him. Zayn and the others turned their heads to find their uncle Typher standing at the Stone, holding a rod with a Symbol attached. The blue flame reflected off his face as he glared at them, pressing the scolding metal to the back of his neck.

"Typher, what are you doing?!" Zayn shouted as his bones rattled.

Typher removed the other three symbols from their rods, placed them in his pocket and pointed to Levithe's body in the room's center.

Zayn's heart nearly stopped as he recognized the face underneath Levithe's armor. The scowl-eyed, bloodied face with a perfectly shaven goatee laid lifeless on the floor. Wilso hadn't killed Levithe, but Labarth in disguise. As Zayn's mind raced, the terrible laugh continued to rattle his eardrums.

All at once, Typher used his new abilities to lift multiple cloth straps into the air. He launched them towards Erym and Zayn. Before they had a chance to react, one strap bound their arms behind their back while synchronously looping around their ankles, forcing them to their knees. Another strap twisted tight around Zayn and Erym's mouths. Lyu tried removing her sword to cut the straps, but Typher ripped it from her hands with ease, using *nasa*. The sword stood suspended in midair and turned at a sharp downward angle, aimed right at her throat. Both Lyu and Tanyel raised their hands in surrender as another set of straps tied off their hands, feet, and mouths.

Wilso and his daughter fled toward the exit as an Incinerator, carrying an axe, attempted to follow. Wilso turned displaying a face of rage, lowering his shoulder and knocking the short man on his back. Scrambling to his feet, Wilso dashed for the exit. Zayn's eyes shot open as Typher hurled the floating sword directly towards Wilso. Blood sprayed across the chamber floor. However, to Zayn's relief, the sword hadn't struck Wilso but the axe-wielding Incinerator. Wilso and his daughter slipped through the exit as the man screamed in agony, crashing to the floor.

Filled with both power and rage, Typher breathed a heavy gust of wind towards the exit, creating a violent tempest that caught the rest of the guards as they tried to escape. Before he released his breath, Typher jerked his head toward the windowed wall behind him. Zayn watched in horror as boulders, weapons, and human bodies crashed into the wall, smashing it to pieces. Blood painted the room as every body part imaginable scattered across the floor. The sunlight burst through the opening, causing Zayn's eyes to squint. He hadn't realized how high up the chamber actually was. Sounds of the waves crashed below, exposing an open view to nothing but water and sunlight.

Zayn attempted to escape the straps. The harder he strained, the tighter the straps became. Because his mouth was covered, *epha* was impossible, and with his hands bound, all the pouches were out of reach for *chay*. Every fiber in his being believed they had won. But the supposed victory had turned into a nightmare.

"I didn't assume it would be so effortless," Typher said, walking towards Labarth's body. "When I discovered your father had infiltrated the ruins with three *others,* I almost took pity on him, realizing he had led his own *Drudge* children to their eventual death sentence. But *children* have always been my favorite." He smirked, bending down to remove the armor from Labarth's body and place it on his own. "I'm sure your father forewarned you about a distraction before you entered the ruins." He placed the shimmering helmet littered with spikes over his head. "But did he mention his *own* brother was one of the few chosen to be a part of that divisive *explosive* distraction?" He hissed as he smiled. "You see, my Guard seized and imprisoned everyone involved with the explosion. And when the tattered handle of your father's hammer unraveled before my eyes, I knew exactly which prisoner I would *become.* Don't you remember? *I'm the best actor Levitheton has ever known.*"

Zayn's mind flashed back to Typher's words during their encounter with Labarth. He shook violently, trying to escape the ties, but they wouldn't budge.

"If you haven't figured it out yet. I am not your father's brother." Typher's body and grimacing face shimmered until it transformed into that of Levithe's. "And now, thanks to you, I have even more power than before." His roar seemed to shake the chamber.

No! Zayn's mind wailed as he clenched his jaw, nearly

shattering his teeth. *I have to protect them!*

Levithe walked up to Erym and grabbed her by the chin.

"So here's the new *plan*," Levithe said as he stared into her eyes. "A much more appetizing one than your pathetic *Remnant's*. First, I am going to kill each of your children. One by one. Oldest to youngest. Then, I will head back through that entrance and decimate every living person in these forsaken caves. Everything you have built in secret will disappear. No shred of memory will remain. Just like the *war*." He paused. "And lastly, I will take this Stone back to the city. It will be another gift I grant to the people of this wretched island, and I will be one step closer to freedom."

Levithe released Erym's chin as her teardrops shattered against the ground beneath her. Zayn paled as Levithe turned and stared him in the eyes as he approached, grabbing him by the throat and pulling him back towards the Stone. Bone-chilling muffled screams poured out of his mother and siblings' mouths, causing his chest to almost explode. Levithe looked at him with a terrible gaze and removed a dagger from his armored belt.

"Let's begin with the eldest. The *protector*," Levithe scoffed. "The ironic part of this whole adventure is that we would never have made it here if it weren't for me." Zayn's eyes widened. "Don't you remember, Zayn?" Levithe continued, "I am the one who convinced the group to include Wilso. Even *he* didn't know who I truly was. A perfect way to keep an eye on him." Without hesitation, Levithe plunged the dagger into Zayn's side.

Time slowed, and Zayn gasped as the cold metal pierced through his right lung. His breathing convulsed as pain radiated through his entire chest as blood and air sprayed from the gaping wound.

Levithe whispered into Zayn's ear, "I'm sure you're curious as to how the Guard found this place? Well, after you shattered Wilso's spine... when I was examining him, little did you know, I healed him just enough to regain consciousness, hoping he would hear the direction of our path. Sure enough, it worked." Levithe's breath pounded against his face as the excruciating pain crippled his chest wall.

Levithe removed the blade and shoved it deep into Zayn's opposing side, piercing the other lung. Zayn's head fell as his breath rattled under the muffled cloth. The screams from his family flooded his ears as he fought desperately to hold on to his life. Several events from the past few days flashed through his mind, one after another.

Typher's face after they told him about Ryn's death. No tears, just a stone-cold stare.

Typher briefly shifting into Levithe to scare Stawb away before entering his home.

Typher not recognizing Naye and Deshome at the gate.

Typher snapping at Tanyel when he asked about their mother.

Typher's desperate face when he saw Zayn's symbol crossing the river.

It was all so obvious as Zayn reflected. *Levithe has won,* he thought.

Suddenly, Levithe grabbed ahold of Zayn's hair, yanking his head up, exposing his neck. The ice-cold blade touched his throat as he choked on his breath. He was moments from passing out as the corners of his vision darkened. He opened his eyes to Levithe, and a subtle breeze from the coast cooled his face. The light from the sunset reminded him of the night at the ruins with his father. He had failed each of his father's instructions miserably. Now he had failed the entire island. Zayn couldn't bear the pain any longer. At that moment, every fiber in him wanted to be Incinerated. *Get it over with,* he begged in his mind.

"And the *shenrosh* bite," Levithe said. "It wasn't the herbs that healed you. It was *me.*"

Levithe glared at Zayn with a twisted smile and pressed the knife into Zayn's throat. Just before the blade punctured Zayn's skin, a single flicker of hope fueled his body. *The shenrosh venom,* he thought as a faint smirk developed on his face. *My third gift.*

Without hesitation, Zayn triggered *chay,* shifting himself into the form of a *shenrosh.* The change of shape caused the straps of cloth to fall from Zayn's new body. Before Levithe had a chance to react, Zayn lunged for his throat and sunk his fangs deep into Levithe's neck. The venom poured into Levithe's veins as Zayn clenched his jaw tight. Releasing his bite, he inhaled as deep as possible through his pierced lungs while simultaneously changing back to his original form. Zayn exhaled as blood shot from his lungs, and he sprinted forward, slamming Levithe into the Stone. Levithe's body seared as it crashed into the blue flame while Zayn placed one hand over Levithe's mouth and the other toward the Stone. Levithe gripped the rod containing Zayn's symbol in his opposite hand, holding it high out of reach. Zayn used his breath to blow them towards the cliff and *nasa* to pull the Stone towards himself, keeping Levithe pinned. Suddenly, flames erupted from Levithe's chest, colliding into the metal chest piece given to him by his mother. The pain in Zayn's chest amplified tenfold as the flames began to heat the metal. He fought to maintain consciousness as the skin on his chest boiled.

Levithe tried to fight back, but the *shenrosh* venom was setting in, paralyzing him. Zayn kept pressing forward until they reached the edge. Looking back once more at his family, Zayn nodded to them with a smile. *I will protect you,* Zayn thought. As he stared at Tanyel in the eyes, he forced his final words, "I'll be okay. Take care of them. Trust each other. It is our only hope of escape."

With one last push, Zayn screamed through his teeth as he pressed the Stone, Levithe, and himself off the cliff. His whole life, he was certain that becoming Seared was his ultimate purpose. But at that moment, he realized he had it all backwards. The great irony made him smile. To save his family, he had to give up being Seared, which ended up being the easiest decision he had ever made. Because his ultimate purpose... his true gifting... was his family.

As he and Levithe fell with the stone, Zayn looked up towards the cliff's opening and grabbed hold of the overhang, using his mind. With one last force of effort, he wielded *nasa* with immense force, causing the cliff's overhang to collapse, sealing off the barracks. The last thing Zayn remembered as he fell was seeing the glowing Stone shatter into hundreds of pieces as Levithe's paralyzed body smashed full force into the jagged rocks below. Zayn smiled and felt complete peace as he breathed his final breath.

Ŏ

The chamber darkened as the overhanging cliff collapsed into the room. Thick clouds of dust filled the room as it trembled. Tanyel, Lyu, and Erym screamed so fiercely that the blood vessels in their necks were close to bursting. Tanyel knew deep down that even if Zayn had somehow survived the fall, he would never survive the deep wounds left in his chest by Levithe's dagger. His insides bubbled in torment as he screamed, picturing Zayn's eyes staring back at him as he fell out of sight. He lost his balance and fell to his side, still bound by the ties around his arms and legs.

Zayn's final words echoed through his mind. How could anything be okay again? Would it even be possible to defeat Levithe now that he had two *Tri-Symbols?* It was foolish to think that Levithe had died from the fall. If he hadn't already, Levithe would heal himself when he regained consciousness.

As the sweat from his lip continued to dampen the black cloth, Tanyel also knew Zayn's sacrifice wasn't in vain. Zayn had given his family and the Remnant a final chance at survival. Without Zayn's bravery, the entire Remnant would have been slaughtered, erased from history. But a deep, agonizing part of Tanyel would have preferred the latter to losing his brother. He laid on the cold floor with his eyes closed, continuing to weep.

Moments that seemed like days passed before Tanyel heard footsteps rushing toward him from the barracks' entrance. Suddenly, his arms and legs released as the person behind him cut the strips of fabric free. Tanyel reached up and untied the remaining cloth from around his mouth, inhaling deeply as he looked back to see Wilso cutting free Erym and Lyu. Wilso's daughter, still wearing her Incinerator armor, stood beside him. Tanyel was still surprised by Wilso's bravery. It turned out Wilso was just another victim, forced to serve Levithe or face the execution of a loved one. He nodded to Wilso as the old Healer and his daughter held tears in their eyes.

Tanyel and Lyu collapsed into Erym, wrapping her tight, finally able to hold each other. Their gasping coughs, muffled by each other's cloaks, rang terribly through Tanyel's ears. Their pain piled an immense burden onto his own grieving heart, too much for any of them to bear. Everything in him was more shattered than the thousands of crumbled stones before him. The tears and pain felt as if they would never cease, and all he could do was weep.

It seemed as if they had clung to each other for an entire day before his mother loosened her grip. She sniffed through her nose as she wiped the tears from her cheeks with both hands. Then, with her forefingers and thumbs, she grasped Tanyel and Lyu by the chin, pulling them close. Tanyel couldn't imagine how she was feeling. After ten years of waiting... for this to happen now.

Erym's throat crackled as she attempted to speak, "Tanyel, Lyu." She paused, taking a deep breath. "Give me your hands." Tanyel maintained eye contact as he and Lyu placed their hands in hers. Her skin's warmth sent the slightest feeling of relief through his body. She continued, forcing the words through tears. "I have healed some of the most violent wounds imaginable throughout my lifetime. But every single one of them, no matter how terrible, pale in comparison to the wound that is left by losing someone you love." She paused, choking down her tears. "And the worst part is that no amount of Healing will ever fix this type of wound. You two have had to experience it twice in the span of only a few days." Her grip tightened as her eyes widened. "Tanyel and Lyu. No one at your age deserves this kind of pain. I need you to know that I will carry it for you and with you every step of the way. As we all carry the wound together, we will see Zayn in each other." She gave them a moment to take in her words.

Tanyel glanced at Lyu and immediately knew Erym was right. "Like in Lyu's eyes," he said through tears.

"Or Tanyel's laugh," Lyu responded.

"Yes," Erym said with a pale smile. "Death is a terrible paradox. Zayn *is* gone, but in one sense, he is *still* here, in each of us." Tanyel and Lyu lowered their heads as the words struck.

Erym gripped their hands once more and said, "We will remember Zayn amongst our greatest heroes. Just like Sara, your father, Mother Aven, and countless..."

Erym was suddenly interrupted by a subtle sound of shuffling coming from behind. As Tanyel looked up, his eyes grew wide as he detected what was causing the sound. *How?* Tanyel thought, letting out a gasp as a sliver of hope filled his heart. The elder woman, covered in blood, was sitting up, staring back at them.

"I wouldn't count me as one of those heroes just yet," she said with a crepitated voice and a broad smile.

"Mother Aven!" Erym said as she approached. "You are alive!"

"I've lived through much worse than this, my dear," she responded and shifted her gaze to Lyu and Tanyel, tears welling behind her wrinkled eyes.

"Lyu, Tanyel. Your brother is much more than a hero. He is a *savior*," Aven said. "If it weren't for Zayn, every single one of us would have been horrendously tortured until we breathed our last.

Don't think for a moment his death was meaningless. No demonstration of love surpasses that of one dying, so the ones they love the most can live. Zayn did this because he loved you."

Her words were more than true. The weight of Zayn's love was felt, but it didn't fix the crippling pain. He saw the same paralyzed look in Erym and Lyu as they nodded to Mother Aven.

"Thank you, Mother Aven," Erym responded. "Are you okay to walk?"

"Ahh, yes," Aven responded, standing to her feet, placing a gentle kiss on each of their foreheads. "I will go and inform the others. Stay here and continue to give Zayn the grief he deserves."

Tanyel nodded and watched as Aven limped her way out of the barracks. He gripped his mother and Lyu tight as the mixture of both grief and rage flowed through his veins. The dust in the chamber had settled, and his chest warmed as the slightest sliver of hope inundated him. Carefully reaching into his pocket, Tanyel gripped the cold metal symbol between his thumb and forefingers. A faint smile drew across his face as he continued to hold Lyu and Erym.

We still have two symbols.

Epilogue

LEVITHE'S EYES BLINKED OPEN as excruciating pain radiated through every muscle and bone in his body. The world spun around him as his gut pounded against his throat. He couldn't move, and his forced breath barely exited his mouth. His disoriented mind made producing even a single movement extremely challenging. Rage filled his mind as the cool mist from the battering waves showered his face, causing the blood from his forehead to seep into his mouth. Levithe clenched his teeth and released a tortured scream as he focused on healing his shattered bones. Red mucus sprayed from his teeth as the sounds of bones and tendons clicking back into place resounded through his eardrums. As he regained control of his movement, he cupped some water from a small crevice beside him and washed the blood from his face and arms. He remained seated with his eyes closed, focusing on every cut and gash on his body, moving from his toes to his head, sealing them back to health. When he placed his cold palm on his neck, the cavernous holes left from the *shenrosh* bite were still seeping copious amounts of blood and pus. The veins in his forehead pulsed as he remembered Wilso's words in the forest. *A full dose will severely hinder one's physical and gifting abilities for the rest of their life.* His throat continued to throb as he removed his hand from the wound, choosing to allow it to heal on its own.

After a while, some relief surfaced as the effects of the venom retreated. Levithe stood to his feet, not knowing how much time he would have before the next wave. His eyes shot towards his surroundings, and his stone-layered heart crumbled to pieces as he realized what he was seeing. Hundreds of shards of stone surrounding him were encased in a faint blue flame. From large boulders to insignificant pebbles, the recovered Stone fragment had shattered. Levithe's mind raced with fury as he reached down with his armored gloves to gather a few of the pieces near him. *I will kill them all ten times over,* he thought, staring at the broken pieces. Suddenly, his hatred settled as the glowing shards of Stone in his palms moved towards each other as if trying to repair themselves. A roar of victory exploded from his lungs as he witnessed the tiny fragments fuse.

Without hesitation, Levithe heaved a giant gust of wind,

tossing the glowing stones into the air. One by one, he used *nasa* to bring the shards together, restoring the Stone to its full form. He released the newly forged Stone to the ground as he stared wide-eyed. *I am one step closer,* he thought.

The sky grew darker as the shade from the cliffs stretched further out into the sea. As Levithe decided his next move, he noticed something in his peripheral. The body of the boy, Zayn, laid on the rocks just to his left. Levithe approached him and grabbed his arm, pressing his finger to the boy's wrist to check for blood flow. Levithe sighed, dropping Zayn's wrist to the ground. As he stood, his brows descended as he observed the boy's face. Beneath the blood-soaked skin and bruising, Zayn's face wore the widest grin Levithe had ever seen. The smile rattled his bones, causing his face to burn red.

Remembering the survivors above, Levithe took a deep breath and expelled it from his lungs, causing him to soar up into the sky towards the sealed chamber. He stared at the crumbled cliff from which he fell as hot fury filled his mind. *I will incinerate every one of you,* he thought as his chest smoldered. Before the beam of flame released from his chest, he gasped as a pit in his stomach smashed upward towards his throat. The whirlwind suspending him in the air had dissipated, causing him to plummet back towards the rocks below. His mind raced as his glowing chest returned to normal. He breathed a violent breath once more, giving him just enough of a tempest to cushion his fall. The flame from the Stone beside him reflected off his armor as the sky turned to a darkened blue. He let out a howl, realizing what this failure meant. His new giftings wouldn't work simultaneously with his old ones.

Levithe lifted himself into the air with another deep breath while reaching toward the gigantic Stone and grabbing hold of it with his mind. Memories flooded his mind as he and the Stone levitated. *The dining hall,* he thought. *Hundreds of people, women, and children, most of them Seared with one or two gifts.* His eyes descended to a hateful glare, realizing he couldn't risk trying to defeat them. He would have to deal with them later. He breathed deeply and blew another deep gust, lifting himself and the Stone above the cliffs. As he spotted the tiny flames from Levitheton's torchlights glimmering far off in the distance, a memory filled his mind, causing him to grimace. Reaching under his armor into his pocket, he grabbed hold of the smooth parchment. Unraveling the scroll, he gazed at the dozens of red scratch marks scattered across the detailed map of his glorious city. *The Remnant will be decimated. Just like when my reign began… gathered and slaughtered, only to be forgotten forever,* he thought.

He placed the scroll back into his pocket, then propelled himself toward Levitheton with a massive vortex of breath. A single thought raced through his mind as he flew back towards the city, *Only one left.*

Soaring above the Barren Plains, he glanced back once more at the southernmost entrance to the caves. He nearly lost his breath at what he saw below. A man carrying a torch, dressed in a Healer's cloak, was staring up towards him. As Levithe released his breath to lower himself, his eyes widened as he caught a glimpse of the man's face. *It can't be,* he thought, shaking his head. Before Levithe was able to get any closer, both the man and torch vanished. A strange feeling consumed him as he used *epha* to gust himself back toward the city. The foreign feeling was his favorite to stir up in those he controlled, but something he never expected to feel himself. Not worry, or panic, or even fear. But for the first time in over three hundred years, Levithe felt deep within his body a slight sense of terror.

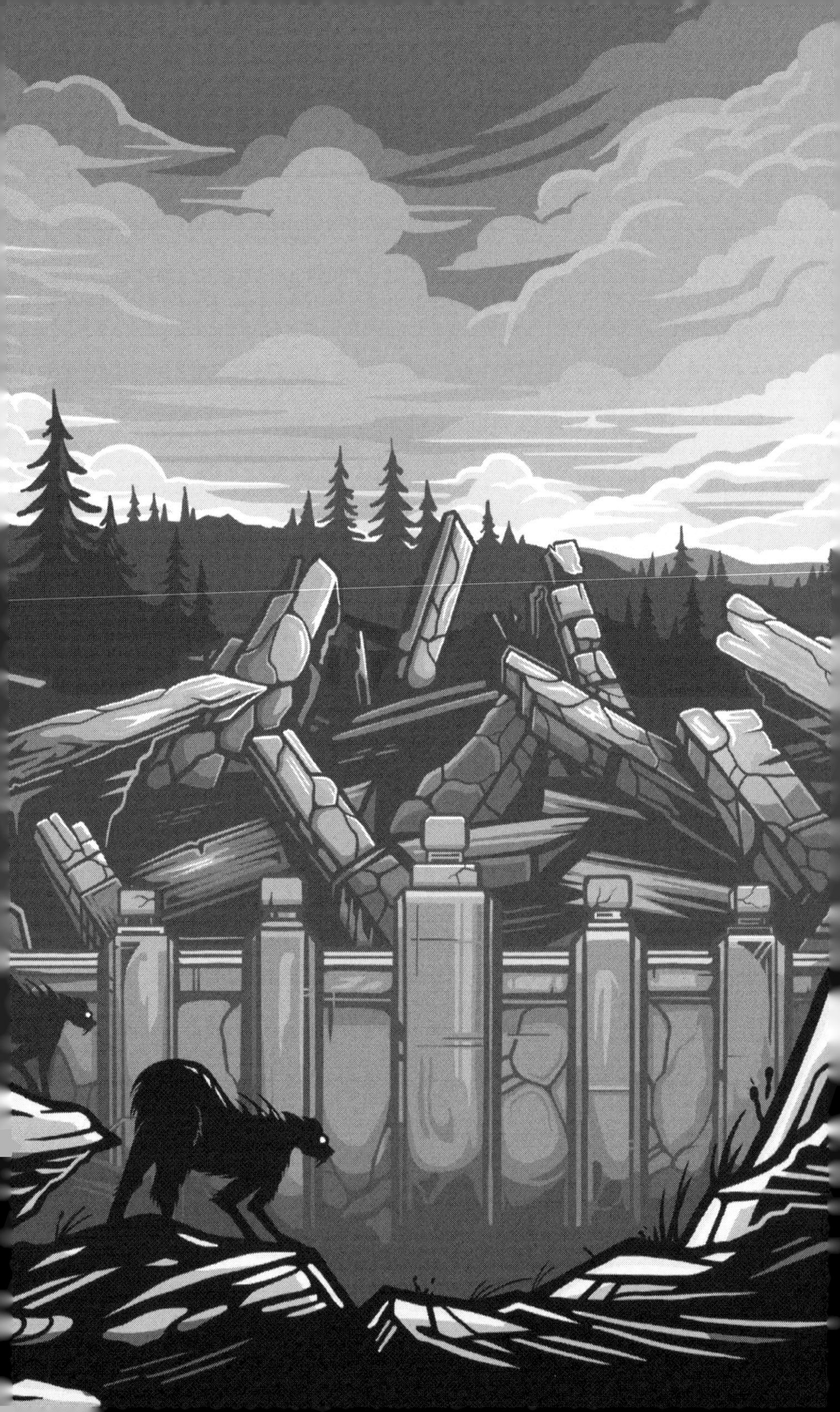

About the Author

Thank you for taking the time to read The Searing Stone. I hope it was as fun for you to read as it was for me to write. I have always loved the art of story, especially as it's portrayed in the fantasy genre. Reading fantasy has become one of my favorite hobbies, and my desire is that this book gives people a launching point into a genre that can feel intimidating.

August 15th, 2020, I was sitting on my couch, battling some newly discovered depression, mostly brought on by grief and the isolation from the pandemic, when suddenly, an idea popped into my head that I couldn't shake. "What if your parents were the ones who chose your magical ability?" A few days later, I typed outlines for three novels and just like that, The Children of Erym Saga was born. The problem was, I had always been great at telling stories, but I had never written anything in my life.

September 1st, 2020, I just went for it and started typing Chapter One. Five months and thirteen chapters later, I finished my first draft. All while working two jobs and wrangling two toddlers. Now, after beta-reading feedback and nearly 10 revisions, The Searing Stone has been released. Thank you for giving me, a brand new author, a chance.

Did you like the book? If so, please consider buying a copy to give to a friend or leaving a review on whichever avenue you purchased from. Being a self-published author, I rely mostly on reviews, and word of mouth, so anything is greatly appreciated.

If you would like to get in contact with me, please visit my website www.rdneal.com

R.D. Neal grew up in Indiana and has had a knack for storytelling his whole life. He currently lives in Arizona with his wife and kids. His first novel, The Searing Stone, explores the important topics of family, grief, the advantages and dangers of magic, and nature vs. nurture. He is passionate about his faith and mentoring others, loves spending time with his family and friends, and always has a book or two close by.

Acknowledgments

To my wonderful Beta Readers - Haley Mircheff, Ben Ihms, Patrick Emmons, Josh Perez, Austin Adams, Kory Miller, Casey Borden, Veronica Morrison, Matt Magaña, and my dearest grandmother, Beverly Olinger. Your detailed, chapter-by-chapter feedback took this book from good bones to a full-body with muscles and all.

In regards to editing, many thanks to Susan Caldwell for reading through and editing my first draft. Though you were ruthless in your edits (in the most gentle and loving ways), you encouraged me to keep writing and rewriting. Additionally, to Kate Popa, for your detailed editing skills, both after my first draft and my last.

The breathtaking cover art was designed by Kory Miller with Park St. Studios. Not only does this cover change the game for fantasy art, Kory brought my story to life in a way I could have never imagined. And to my brother and best friend, Chris Neal, for teaching me so much about the art of story, and for building me a gorgeous website. If you want to see his handiwork, visit www.rdneal.com

Lastly, to my wife, Erica. You have been an amazing cheerleader throughout this entire process, and I'm so thankful you were my final feedback filter before release. Your encouragement, critique, and honesty molded the final draft into something even more special.

Printed in Poland
by Amazon Fulfillment
Poland Sp. z o.o., Wrocław
05 January 2022

ca73147e-9aea-4223-a04e-60d2b9b13885R01